Short Stories from the Heart

H. C. Heartland

for

Write On Press

ISBN: 1494496283
ISBN-13: 978-1494496289

DEDICATION

I would like to dedicate this collection of my short stories to my many muses:
To Mom and Dad Kambach who fell in love at age 13,
Beth-birie who keeps me humble, and to my Grandpa Lowe who keeps me proud,
To my two grandmothers who have always been a source of inspiration to me,
To Mom and Rikie who thanks to their love of sci-fi while growing up, helped me to laugh at strange shadows in the dark,
To my Uncle Mike who taught me to never judge a book by its cover,
To Jan, president of my fan club,
To Bron and Chet, the hardest workers I know and to Rik's friend, the unknown farmer, who taught him how to meander in the prairie fields of the Midwest,
To my dad, the hopeless romantic,
And, to Joel and Kellie who have added a new level of beauty to our family structure, making it a family stronger than ever before.

CONTENTS

ACKNOWLEDGMENTS

Thanks to Marshon Bentley and to everyone else at Write-on Press who helped make this book possible.
Thanks to my readers, who are helping me develop and grow into the author I hope to become with all their great feedback.
Last, but not least, especially regarding my two island stories, thanks to the native people of the island of Madagascar. Because of their willingness to share their lives and culture with others, I have great fuel for what I personally find my most enjoyable writing.

COURAGE IN A COFFEE CUP

Recently, while on a business trip Linus Nettle noticed something peculiar in his general appearance and stature. It is of note, that Linus had suffered with this particular human insufficiency his entire life but it wasn't until one day in May, that he came to the revelation of its existence. You see, Linus Nettle had never had the courage to kiss a girl or ask her out on a date.

"May I take your order Sir?" the girl behind the counter asked while looking completely bored and complacent.

Linus searched the menu list over the girls head, wondering if she might notice that he had forgotten to shave. Why a checkout girl would care that he had not shaven is beyond the average readers care, but for Linus, such nervous thoughts were always lingering in his mind like the rustling of fall leaves in ones backyard. Trapped between the fences of reasonable thought, these single worries caused him to lose focus altogether on what was important in life.

"Sir, may I please take your order, there are other people in line, if you can't decide then feel free to step aside and rejoin the line when you know."

The girl was now watching Linus as he scrapped his chin. She began to wonder if he had some sort of rash and unconsciously stepping back while crinkling her nose at the thought of catching something.

“I will have one black, medium coffee, thank you.”

Linus didn’t realize how incredibly boring his order was and smiled satisfied with having made what he felt was a good decision. The counter girl rolled her eyes, and punched in the order not wasting a moment before asking the person behind him what they wanted.

Linus’ life revelation didn’t come at this point but rather at the point when he walked over to the counter where all the customers went to pick up their order. A different counter girl with long black hair, thick eye make-up and a silver nose ring gently put his coffee down on the counter and looked Linus straight in the eyes.

With a sultry voice that Linus had only heard on infomercials for late evening callers she said, “May I compliment you on making the wisest of choices in your coffee selection.”

Little did Linus know the girl was lacing her words with sarcasm.

Linus not only was not used to receiving such compliments, or any compliments for that matter, he was not used to strange looking women, or women of any genre talking to him. This unexpected interaction caused him to gulp his coffee hard, thus scalding his throat. He choked and coffee spilt out of his mouth and onto his blue striped tie.

The girl took her tea towel off her belt and handed it to Linus. He took it gratefully and began patting off the coffee while still smiling meekly at her as she began filling her next order. Several customers later, Linus was still patting, and the girl was still pouring only now Linus was feeling a bit awkward.

Trying to decide whether or not to walk away with the towel, interrupt her work, or set it back on the counter, he kept patting.

“I think you got it.”

The girl was now looking at Linus again with her hand extended. With his extended hand wrapped around the damp towel, he smiled and said, "I really can't thank you for all that you've done."

The girl grabbed the towel and slapped him rapidly in the chest with it two times, causing her thickly cut black bangs to swing back and forth.

"You are a trip! If you are that thankful for me handing you a towel to clean up your mess, I can't imagine how thankful you'd be if I did something really worthwhile. Where are you from anyways?"

"I'm from Wichita, Kansas. But I'm here on business."

"Really? What's your business, Mister...?"

"My name is Linus Nettle, pleased to meet you."

They shook hands firmly causing the girl to laugh again at his formalities. Linus looked to be in his late 20's as was she, but his dress and manner of speaking was that of a 50 year old man from a film set sometime in 1940. He was tall, wore a tightly fitting gray suit, and wore a hat with a navy blue ribbon that matched his tie.

"I am a window salesman. There is an expo being held here this weekend and I have come to set up a booth."

Linus suddenly began to think about all that was left to do before the expo began. If he didn't hurry he would be late for the sign up desk.

"Wow! Sounds like a pretty wild time Linus Nettle. So is that how you always spend your weekends."

"Well, yes."

Linus cleared his throat and struck up the nerve to ask, "And may I ask what your name is?"

"My name is Starling. And I get off in an hour."

Starling winked and shut the cash register drawer causing Linus to jump.

Linus picked up his drink, took two steps back, and bumped into someone behind him who mumbled the word *idiot* as he walked over to the seats that were empty against the wall.

He had not expected such a stirring change of events. Here before him stood one of the most delightful creatures he had ever set eyes on. From what he could tell, she gave him a perfect window of opportunity to ask her out on a date. She got off in an hour. Now, Linus had one hour to work up the courage to do what he had never yet done; ask a girl out.

Sitting nearby two tables away from Linus was an old woman sipping on a cup of Earl Gray tea. Linus could see that it was Earl Gray because her tea bag was still in the cup and the label was big and purple. Linus felt a bit distracted from thought as the old woman kept staring at him and sipping on her tea.

Linus had intended to go to his hotel but all he could think of to do was watch Miss Starling finish making her coffee orders for the rest of the hour.

Linus marveled at the way this counter girl interacted with people. Some people were very business-like, not taking time to make much chit chat. Starling was the type that liked the talkers. Although she didn't flirt with anyone like she had flirted with Linus.

He had never had the gift of gab, but now he was increasingly aware of the fact that he did not know how to talk with a girl, or rather a woman. Linus was 26 years old and had spent the better part of his young manhood learning the ins and outs of the window selling business. Even in high school, he never had been inclined to ask a girl out. His parents, who were older and lived on a farm, never were concerned over his lack of a social life. They were proud of their son who always took his responsibilities seriously and got good grades.

He had travelled several national bus systems as far east as Boston and as far West as California. The pride he took in such a stereotypically boring job was unprecedented. His work compensated him for his loyalty by giving him good pay, and good insurance. These were the things a good life was made of; so he had been told since the time he had been small. However, as of late, his loneliness began setting in stronger than it had in the past. Moreover, what did he have to offer a girl like Starling? She obviously had the world at her fingertips. She worked that counter like it was amusing to her and not like it was the job she desperately needed.

Her hair was raven black and she had the tiniest beauty mark just below her left eye. Her wrists were arrayed with a variety of strange costume jewelry. To Linus Miss Starling had all the courage to do and wear things he would never dream of. How he wondered what it must be like to live in a world where you weren't afraid to be someone different.

"So are you going to get the nerve up to ask her out?"

Startled by this abrupt interruption of his daydreaming, Linus turned to see the old woman was no longer sitting two tables away but right up next to him even though there was no room at his single person table for her. She scooted as close as possible and tried to get up close to his ear even though he was much taller than she was. The elf-like woman caused Linus to shutter and reply, "I hadn't really thought about it."

The old woman was tiny with huge round blue eyes. She had obviously had her hair curled that very day and they were practically standing on end with a barrette clipped to the top of her head. It was very easy for Linus to picture what she must have looked like as a little girl. Now with aged lines around her mouth and eyes, she stared up at Linus with all the courage of a woman in her 80's that clearly had nothing to lose.

"Well, that's obviously not true," she remarked still looking up at him with several blinks of her eye lids making her look somewhat like a butterfly.

"You've spent the last 20 minutes staring at her, practically drooling over the sight of the girl. I think she likes you too."

The old woman nudged him with her elbow.

Linus rubbing his arm and looking down said, "What makes you say that?"

"No need to be afraid my boy, you like her after all, that should be an encouragement. I have ordered one cup of hot water to soak my tea bag in every Monday for the last 3 months in this coffee shop and I have never heard her tell anyone the time she gets off work.

Linus, having calmed down a bit from this attack on his personal space, looked at the old woman and then looked at Starling. He looked down at his cup of coffee, which had one cold sip left in it and then looked back up at the counter again. This latest piece of information gave him a dose of courage, which he sorely needed. He didn't know exactly what he had the courage to do, but he suddenly felt a surge of adrenaline running through his veins.

"You're out of coffee. Why don't you go back to the counter and order another one. I see people do that sort of thing all the time. There's nothing out of the ordinary about that."

The old woman then gave him another nudge with her elbow, decidedly harder than before.

Wanting to get away from the old woman, Linus stood up and exited the dining area, heading straight for the cashier's counter.

The small coffee shop suddenly felt very big. It took forever for him to walk up to the counter where a new person who hadn't taken the previous order was. Starling was watching him out of the corner of her eye but Linus didn't notice.

Normally, after making their order, everyone walks over to the little station near where Starling pours. However, hoping to not look like the stalker that he felt like, Linus decided to wait in front of the cash register. The young man working the register tapped Linus on the shoulder and asked him to please move over to the waiting area. Linus could feel the beads of sweat forming on his head. He approached the counter but said nothing for several seconds that felt like hours. Music was playing over the speaker system to a rather funky beat causing Linus to tap his foot and attempt to gain some impetus to conversation.

"Great tunes!" Linus said in a loud voice hoping his voice could travel over the sound of the frothing machine. Starling stopped the frothing machine and said just as loudly as Linus had projected, "What was that?"

Linus now felt self-conscious that others including that nosey old woman who was probably watching his every move, might be listening. He leaned closely and said, "I said, there are some great tunes playing over the speakers. Do you have a hand in picking out some of the song choices?"

Linus gave a gentle smile feeling very pleased at how smoothly his first few words came out.

Starling turned her frothing machine back on and yelled, "No, they are all on pre-recorded CD's. We have certain ones for certain days and they always play. I am sick of listening to them to tell you the truth, but we only get new ones quarterly so we're stuck listening to it over and over again."

As she said this, she was swirling caramel on top of someone's frothy latte.

"Yes, I could see how this would be tiresome."

Linus now felt the need to take his handkerchief and wipe his sweaty forehead with it. He looked back towards where the old woman had been sitting to see if she approved of how it was going so far but she was nowhere to be seen. Feeling better now that he didn't have the old lady watching him, he began to open his mouth to speak again but was interrupted by the man standing behind him.

"Excuse me pal, but my coffee is getting cold."

The man pushed him to the side and grabbed the frothy drink from off the counter, throwing some change in the jar sitting there for tips.

Starling was now finished with Linus' drink. It was the same black coffee he had ordered before.

"Here ya go. Another exciting order of black coffee. You need to get out more, did you know we have 24 different ways to make coffee here. And they are all twice as expensive as the local diner down the street. But you come here just to drink an everyday cup of Joe? Doesn't that strike you as strange?"

Feeling a bit defensive Linus barked, "Well, don't you think it a bit strange that out of 24 varieties of coffee, and several varieties of music, you still have no satisfaction with your work. Whereas I have found the thing which brings me contentment and it literally can be found anywhere I travel."

Starling looked at him and retorted, "Coffee contentment is important, but there are other things in life which make one happy you know. Variety is the spice of life. Don't you ever long to do something spontaneously that you've never done before?"

Linus had not often felt the need to be spontaneous. In those rare moments where it would have been appropriate, his lack of spontaneity always stopped him from embarrassing himself past the very thought of doing something. He looked down at his coffee cup and noticed it was only filled ¾ of the way full. This happened to be one of his pet peeves. Distracted by the annoyance of what he considered a disregard for competence, he pushed the cup back towards Starling with his fingers and said, "Sorry Miss Starling, I'm a to the rim kind of guy, could you please fill it up to the top."

Starling looked at him for a moment thinking he was joking and then squeezing her eyes and forming a frown with her mouth grabbed the carafe and dumped it into his cup.

"Hey! Don't pour it like that, you'll scald my hand!"

Linus pulled his hand away which made some of it spill.

Starling took her towel and began wiping it, not making eye contact she said, "Well what do you expect to happen when you're greedy like that and want it filled to the rim, there's barely room for those big lips of yours to sip it."

Linus had always been self-conscious about his big lips. Having an eastern European ancestry he never understood why he inherited the lips of Howdy Doody. Being thankful not to have inherited the freckles and thick red hair he contented himself with just the lips. But now he felt even more self-conscious than before. He had wanted to ask starling on a date, but when you ask one on a date there is the thought behind it that it might lead to a good night kiss and who would want to give a good night kiss to Howdy Doody or in this case, Linus. His self-confidence being shattered he didn't say another word and walked away. Sitting down at the same table from where he came, he noticed the old woman had returned and moved over to her table again. Looking up at him she sighed shaking her head slightly.

Trying to decide what to do next and looking down at his watch as it was getting late, Linus began to think this was a silly moment in time that needed to be erased forever. Just as he was about to get up and walk out the door he noticed two multi-colored striped tights standing before him. They stood in a pair of loosely tied army boots. An outfit like this could only belong to one worker in the coffee shop. He looked up to see Miss Starling holding a coffee cup in her hand.

"Sorry about spilling your coffee. Here, this is on the house."

She set down before him a stainless steel travelers mug.

"This way you can always have it filled to the brim and it won't burn your hand. And the first Monday of every month, you get one free refill if you bring it in. I don't know if you'll be back here anytime soon, but I got this free for being a good employee, and I don't really drink coffee."

Overcome with such a generous gift Linus was left speechless. He watched her walk away and return behind the counter much like one might watch the sunset. Linus had never met a woman like Starling before. He had received bonuses in the past but had never had anyone to share them with. He looked over at the old woman who gave him an affirmative nod as if she knew what he was thinking. Linus stood up, straightened his suit jacket, picked up his new travel mug in one hand and coffee cup in the other, he walked over to the counter where Starling was now restacking napkins into the tray.

He stood directly in front of her. Starling stared at him waiting for him to speak. But Linus didn't speak. He put his coffee cups to the left of the counter and then took his hands and swept it across the countertop that was standing between them, knocking over several empty coffee cups and lids along the way. The noise of the plastic hitting the ground caused several customers to look up and see the man who was clearly out of his league use both his forearms to lift his body up onto the counter top and jump over the counter into the area for making coffee. The jump in itself was a little awkward; when he landed his hat fell off his head.

The store manager upon seeing this yelled out, "Hey! Get out of there!"

This made Starling laugh out loud and yet she couldn't take her eyes off of Linus' determined stare. That laugh, those lips, smiling at him was all Linus needed to take the last step.

That and the sound of the 5 foot, 3 inch old woman who had now wondered right up to the counter for a front row view and whispered, "You can do it! Just kiss her!"

It gave him the last dose of courage needed. Linus looked over and nodded to the old woman who was holding one fist up like she just won a victory.

Starling was leaning over to pick up Linus' hat but he intercepted her before she reached it. He grabbed Starling squarely with both hands on her shoulders forcing her to stand up right again. Then placing his hands softly around her neck with his thumbs landing on her blushing cheeks, he kissed her hard on the lips. Starling reacted as one only does when being kissed with spontaneity - she felt her left foot go up on her tip toes and her right one bend slightly at the knee. The old woman began to cheer, the other clients were laughing, and the manager was yelling some sort of obscenities at the two of them.

Seeing as Starlings shift had been over for the last 10 minutes, she ripped her apron off from around her waist and threw it in the bin behind her where all the used aprons were kept. Right before Linus' eyes he saw her leap over the counter, knocking over several napkins sending them flying like doves being released on someone's wedding day. Linus in his own clumsy fashion, attempted to leap over the counter again only this time he landed on the ground next to starling. She leapt to her feet like an acrobatic performer and put out her hand to help him up. Both of them laughing as if they were the only two people left in that coffee shop.

"Well, Linus, are we ready to go have some fun?" Starling asked with her hand still in Linus' even though both of them were now standing and facing one another.

Linus nodded and said, "I was wondering if you'd like to help me set up a window expo?"

Starling said, "That sounds like a blast!"

Linus wasn't sure if her laugh meant she was serious or making fun, but regardless he would need to make some good sales that day if he was going to keep a woman like Starling happy for the rest of his life. He bent over and picked up his hat, wiping it off and placing it backwards on Starlings head. He grabbed Starlings hand and led her out the coffee house doors. She called a cab by whistling loudly like he had seen in the movies. And the two drove off. Starling never did return to that coffee shop. She ended up being a sales rep for windows and the two of them spent the next 25 years selling windows and traveling the Midwest, never passing a coffee shop without giving one another a kiss in remembrance of the day Linus ordered courage in a coffee cup.

CHICKEN POX REVENGE

Eileen's head was beating at such a rapid pace she felt her ear drums would burst. Tossing and turning she must have fallen asleep around midnight, and the following morning, the sheets were soaked.

Before opening her eyes she heard her husband Terrence say, "What the…"

This pause caused her to open her eyes and see him staring at her, but he wasn't really looking at her eyes he seemed to be scanning her face like he had lost something in the grass.

"What are you doing?" she asked groggily.

"You have things all over your face" he said aghast as he continued to scan.

"What does that mean?"

Eileen jumped out of bed feeling her white cotton sleeping-gown sticking to her body from the sweat that drenched her. She ran to the tiny mirror that was hanging on the wall next to the closet. As if not seeing her own reflection but rather a monster on the other end she gasped, "What is it? What's wrong with me?"

"I think you may have the chicken pox. Didn't you ever have them as a child?" Terrence asked still staring with his mouth slightly open in shock.

"No! I never had them, and I had been exposed several times! I thought I must have built up some sort of immunity! Are you sure? I mean, look at the size of these blisters; they're huge, is that normal? It's 1934; I didn't think adults could get chicken pox anymore!"

"I heard adult cases can be the worst, my mom made sure to have me play with the other kids so that I'd get it over with because they said it was too painful to have when you got older. I had better call the Doctor and you better go wash up," said Terrence in an empathetic tone.

Terrence got up and got dressed quickly. Eileen stood for a few minutes staring at the bumps all over her face and felt sudden shakes come all over her. Expecting another fever to come on she grabbed a clean set of clothes and went in to take a bath so she could spend the rest of the day in bed.

The Doctor came by that afternoon; more spots had erupted on her back, arms, and torso. Dr. Hammond was only in his sixties but had turned prematurely gray by age 30. He knew everyone in the town since they were born except ones like Eileen who had moved in later on in life, so he had lots of questions about her past. None of these questions, Eileen felt, had anything to do with her present situation, but she was too weak to fight the nosiness which had probably been killing the old man since she first moved to town.

"So, you never had the chicken pox where you lived as child? Where was that again by the way? Oh, you say it was a bigger town, 'bigger the town bigger the epidemic,' usually. Odd, you weren't exposed in school, what grade did you say you ended up finishing?" He kept inquiring without giving Eileen much time to answer. She could barely whisper a groan since her fever had peeked and she felt faint.

"You had better try to stay as cool as possible, so that more spots don't come on, but, unfortunately more probably will. You had better stay out of sight until those spots dry up, and don't scratch them or your husband won't be too pleased at your appearance anymore," said the Doctor while putting his tools back into his black medicine bag.

He picked up his black medicine bag and went off leaving her alone in her dark room to groan from the pain of her headache and toss and turn from the pain of the blisters on every corner of her body. The next day the blisters looked more like clusters of grapes.

"Honey, I hate to leave you like this but I've got to go to work." Terrence looked down at her with pity and yet enough personal revulsion to stay a few steps away from the bed any time he was in the room.

Eileen attempted to ease his conscience. "It's okay; there is nothing you can do for me. Please just make sure I have enough water by my bed stand with the aspirin the Doctor left me."

"Don't you want anything to eat?" he asked concerned as she had only had liquids and a few bites of food since the outbreak of the first bumps the night before.

"No, I think they have gone into my throat, I don't think I could bare a bite."

"Alright then, I hope you feel better soon."

He left, happy to get out of the dismal room.

~*~

The last thing Eileen felt inclined to do was to receive visitors. Of course, who of all people would come by but the most obnoxious of all the town's residents? Not to mention the very individual who happened to give Eileen the chicken pox at that! Mrs. Leighton's daughter in law, Mary, who had recently come from Ireland, had also never had the chicken pox. She reportedly got them from her nephew on her husband's side and didn't feel the need to stay indoors after a weeks' time.

"This town is full of weaklings," she was heard saying, "I'm not going to stay cooped up in the house for 2 weeks or more just because I look ugly!"

She went to town and everyone rolled their eyes, but it wasn't until she transmitted the virus to Eileen that she now realized she may have actually been the cause of loathing for the very sight of the innocent woman.

Feeling some remorse over what happened, Mary decided to pay Eileen a visit; Eileen didn't see how she could possibly refuse her so she let her in.

"Well, just look at you! You look like a walking polka dot!" spurted Mary trying to sound humorous.

"Yes, I suppose you would know something about it, Mary. I can see you still have a few marks left on you. How are you feeling?" asked Eileen.

"Oh it only took me a few days to be feeling ready to get back to work again. Some people just have a weaker constitution I guess."

She said this looking at Eileen with her mouth turned upside down making the sort of sad face you make when children bump their knee.

Within minutes, Eileen felt the evil crawl up inside of her. She wanted to avenge herself of the agony that she felt. And the only person she could think of who deserved to feel her wrath was sitting right in front of her, mocking Eileen for suffering the very affliction she had given her.

Under the guise of hospitality, she forced herself out of her chair and offered Mary some tea. She had read once that certain medicines put in tea were not traceable by taste but gave the person the worst case of diarrhea within a matter of minutes. She ran to the medicine cabinet scanning for something to sweeten Mary's tea with. She found just the bottle, something her husband hadn't used in a year or so. Hoping it would still be effective she slowly stirred in the drops, smelling it to see if there were any signs of its existence. Eileen said a short prayer, hoping it wouldn't do more harm then she intended, and then handed Mary the tea swiftly before she could change her mind. Mary drank the tea down so quickly Eileen wondered if she had scalded her throat.

Mary sat the cup down and said, "I wouldn't mind another cup of that lovely concoction. I must say the tea you have here in America tastes quite different from what I'm used to in Ireland but I like it so much I must beg for another."

Not wanting to disappoint her guest and also not wanting to spoil the surprise, Eileen again added the same amount of medicine to the second cup of tea. This time, Mary attempted to sip it like the lady she was trying to be. Within the half hour, Eileen could hear Mary's stomach begin to gurgle; she could see her visitor squirm in discomfort not really knowing what to do in the presence of company when needing to release certain unpleasant gastric movements in her intestinal wall.

Eileen thought all of this would force Mary to run home but instead she heard her say, "Just need to use your water closet for a moment if you don't mind my dear, it seems that tea has gone right through me!"

Much to Eileen's dismay, what ensued was the loudest concert of bodily noises she had heard since her Uncle Wally had gotten worms from the cow's milk he bought on the roadside. Eileen's guilt turned into panic at the thought of having to clean up the mess after Mary left.

It was some time before Mary came out. Once the concert had ended, everything had become very quiet. Eileen became worried that Mary may have passed out on the floor so she knocked on the door and asked, "Mary is everything alright in there?"

Mary slowly opened the door, her face drained of all color, and said, "Oh Ms. Eileen, it seems I've caught a bit of stomach flu. But don't you worry, I've taken it upon myself to clean up everything and made sure to light some matches so as not to offend you too much with the remnants of my visit."

Eileen tried to smile and lead Mary slowly to the door, assuming she would be taking her leave. She was very quickly taken aback by the ease in which Mary sat right back down in the parlor chair making no attempts to leave. Still holding onto her arm, Eileen said, "Are you sure you are up for the rest of the visit? I would understand if you deemed it necessary to return home, Mary."

"Oh. No!" Mary said rather jovially, "I feel much better now, I wouldn't think of leaving you here all by yourself."

The day carried on in such a fashion, Mary talked and talked and Eileen listened wondering when her dreaded company would leave. At this point she would have thanked Mary for giving her the chicken pox if only it meant her leaving sooner.

When it did come time for Mary to leave she put both hands on Eileen's shoulders and said with all sincerity, "I just want to tell you this is the loveliest time I've had with anyone since coming to your country. Thank you for being so kind. Since we both have shared the same ailment, it has brought us closer together and I hope we can share many more a moment such as this. When you are better, you must come over to my place for a turn and try some of the tea from Ireland."

And with that, Mary left Eileen standing there mouth gaping at the door.

All Eileen could do was smile, wave...and scratch.

FALLING ASLEEP AT MIDNIGHT

Awake

It was another sleepless night for Eileen. No matter how hard she tried, her eyes would not close. She had not yet allowed herself to take a prescribed sleeping pill, fearing that the addictive power of its substance might cling to her for the rest of her life.

Eileen had enough weighing heavy upon her mind without the unnecessary addition of drugs. Each night she would watch the news, filled with horror at the real calamities plaguing mankind. If she were to confess what kept her up, she would meet with laughter from even the most empathetic of listeners. But then again, she often bartered with herself that it would mean someone would have been listening. Here within lied the thing that kept Eileen from sleeping at night; her husband never listened when she spoke.

To some this might seem a cliché of sorts. Most wives doubt that their husbands listen to them. However, Eileen was certain that hers was a situation of a higher level of being ignored than any other. It had been 10 years of observation. And 10 years had shown her that it didn't matter how upset she got over a subject or what had happened. Without a shadow of a doubt, in fact, the worse the thing that happened, or rather, the more upsetting it was, the deeper her husband would furrow into his renowned depths of opinionated silence.

Eileen being 31 years old and childless had resigned herself to this life for some time. And yet, recent events had stirred in her the desire to make a change. But how does one make a change in one's life after so long?

A woman in the year 1931 wasn't often at her leisure to make such changes. Her insomnia led her to reminisce about how they had met.

Terrance and Eileen met in a little coffee shop on the corner of Donner Street and Lily in a small mid-western town. She was the one of two waitresses who happened to wipe down the table where he always sat. Having sat too soon one day, Eileen accidently wiped a bunch of old toast crumbs right onto his lap.

"Oh pardon me, Sir!"

She muttered as she attempted to clean up the crumbs that had fallen beside him on the floor.

"Don't worry about that, I'll have some to eat later on if I get hungry," he resounded cheerfully.

Thus, began 6 months of chatting while refilling his porcelain coffee cups. At times Eileen purposely would spill on the table just so she could linger a little bit longer while cleaning it up.

After weekly interactions of such light degree, Eileen had assumed she was in love. She felt herself peeking out of the window on break just before he would normally come into the cafe. And if he was late, or heaven forbid didn't come, she would wipe down the tables as if her favorite cat had just been hit by a train that morning.

One day Terrance made the grand gesture that would change the rest of her life; he asked her out on a date. It was awkward to say the least, but Eileen thought it romantic. Of course, the fact that she hadn't been asked on a date in a very long time had helped the situation seem a little more grandiose than it actually was.

"Hey cutie," he said to her holding his coffee cup back so she wasn't able to finish her pouring and scurry away as usual.

"I've been meaning to ask you some time now if there was a special fella in your life?"

Eileen pulled back the coffee pot, sitting it on the table so that it wouldn't spill.

"If you mean do I have a beau, then the answer is no. Why do you ask?"

She blushed not having meant to rhyme when she spoke. Continuing to wipe the table to look busy in case her boss looked over, she made no eye contact with him as he spoke.

"How is it that a pretty girl like you, and one with such a fine talent for poetry I might add, doesn't have a boyfriend?"

He cleared his throat looking at her teasingly.

"Well, I work here all the time and I don't have a lot of time to socialize."

As Eileen said it she feared it might sound like she didn't want to socialize. He looked down at his coffee and moved it over to her to get a top up so he could gain some courage.

"My name's Terrance. You've poured me more cups of coffee than any other woman in my life, and yet I don't even know your name."

"It's Eileen. Nice to meet you. Formally that is."

She drew her hand up to her hair to fix a piece that had fallen out of place while she spoke. "Do you live around here?" She asked folding her serving towel in the belt of her gingham apron.

"Yeah, I moved here on this side of town for work. I'm a mason by trade and there is a new building going up."

He pointed out the window even though the downtown section of town couldn't be seen from the café.

"My cousin got me a job for a year. But I live about a half hour from here with my family and normally work at a hardware store they own in town. Where do you live?"

"Just upstairs...well, I guess I don't normally tell strange men that..."

Eileen distracted by the fact that he might actually ask her out on a date wasn't thinking much how she had just divulged where she lived to someone she didn't yet trust. She had lived in bigger cities than this throughout her life and it wasn't recommended for a single girl on her own to entertain gentleman callers. The best way for her to remedy those moments of refusing to cater to guests was just not tell them where she lived.

"I was thinking maybe we could go out and then I wouldn't be a stranger anymore. What do you say?"

Terrance was pulling the money out of his pocket so he could pay. He planned on making a quick getaway in case of an embarrassing turndown.

Eileen held onto the table for fear she might topple over. It was the first time in a year anyone had asked her out. Eileen was your average looking girl; tallish, but not too tall. Her hair was dark brown and slightly wavy. Thinking to have it bobbed she wore it in a loose pony tail so that she could get used to having it hang around her face. Knowing it to be the fashion of the day, she desired to look the part. Maybe not the standard of some of the girls in the dime store magazines, but at least up to par with the ladies she saw shopping downtown on her Saturdays off. She wasn't what some would call a looker but she didn't make the dogs howl when she walked by either. Still, the lack of compliments throughout her lifetime left her a little lack on how to encourage attentions. Finding herself daydreaming about what to wear she realized that she hadn't yet replied to Terrance and he was staring straight at her waiting.

"Yes, I would love to." She said forgetting to wait for the when's and where's. She promptly took her coffee pot and walked off into the kitchen.

When she went back to clear the table she noticed a note sat down on top of a few small coins that were meant to be her tip. The note read, "I'll meet you this Saturday, outside of the cafe at 6:00."

It was raining Saturday night and despite having worn a jacket, a hat, and holding an umbrella, her hair was dead flat. Terrance was wearing a black hat with a matching trench coat. He wasn't the most handsome of men, but she found his stature to be appealing and he offered to hold her umbrella. He had thick brown hair with a roman nose which made him look taller than he actually was. His brow reflected lines from the sun making it evident he worked out of doors most of the time. It was hard to hear him speak over the rain, but since he didn't say much it wasn't a hindrance on the relationship.

They went out to eat at a diner in town. Eileen ordered the country fried steak with gravy, green beans, and a roll. Terrance ordered a hamburger with French fries and a coke. The evening was uneventful but not awful.

After that evening, began their courtship. Every Wednesday, Terrance would come into the cafe and ask Eileen if she was free to go out with him and she would in turn say yes. They then would meet outside the cafe and walk the half a mile to the diner. Sometimes Eileen would order the chicken fried steak and then other times she would just have soup, fearing she might be becoming too expensive for Terrance's taste.

One Wednesday Terrance asked her to go meet his folks. They lived on the other side of town. Mr. and Mrs. Sweetly, Terrance's parents were kind to Eileen and after that, instead of going out to the diner, Terrance would take her to his parents' house for dinner every Sunday afternoon, and then they would catch the last bus back into town.

It was on such a Sunday afternoon that Terry, as Eileen had begun to call him, proposed. His mother wasn't aware of his intentions that evening but guessed from his fidgeting that something was amiss. He barely touched the roasted chicken she made, or the buttery mashed potatoes that were dripping with brown gravy. But his peas and carrots had been tossed and slid across his plate the entire evening. This proved alarming to his mother's watchful eyes. She looked at her husband and didn't notice any concern coming from him. Rather he looked pleased staring at the plate full of chicken knowing that he would be able to have his favorite leftovers the next day; cold chicken on white bread, spread with butter and salt.

Eileen spoke mostly with Terrance's mother. The two of them had a lot in common. Both were fairly chatty women. They could defiantly hold their own in conversation. Terrance's mothers name was Dorothy Ellen which Eileen said was similar to her name Eileen Darlene Parker. To any other person, there would have not been that much of a coincidence in such names but Eileen was very determined to find things in common with just about anyone she met and so could make up something similar enough to keep the conversation going for hours.

Dorothy was also attempting to keep Eileen amused. Normally, she would try to create conversation with the entire table however difficult that was. Her husband was a quiet man by nature and her son had inherited those qualities. She was very much in love with him however, and knew that her son was composed of the same brilliant qualities if only Eileen could learn to be patient and draw them out. Dorothy excused herself from the table and went into the kitchen to bring out the dessert: lemon meringue pie. It was Terrance's favorite and she was very pleased that she had decided to make it since he was obviously out of sorts. Since he had been a little boy a good dose of sugar usually did the trick to get him to talking more than usual.

By the time she returned to the dining room table, Eileen and Terrance were gone onto the front porch. She looked at her husband who was finishing his last bite of mashed potatoes and said, "Where did everyone go? They always stay for dessert."

Not looking up from his plate, as he scooped up the last bit of his gravy onto his biscuit, he said, "I think Terrance is going to pop the question tonight."

"Well what on earth gives you that idea?" she asked her husband in shock. She then made the connection to the battered peas left on Terrance's plate and realized it was probably true. "How in the world did you come to that conclusion, I mean, it wouldn't be a terrible thing, and they have been dating for some time. But how did you come to know it before I did?"

Howard looked up at his wife of 24 years and said, "My dear, you have never had to battle an evening such as tonight. But I have. I knew the look on my son's face the minute he walked in the door and I recognized the beads of sweat on his forehead as he hovered over his dinner. And there was something bulging in his shirt pocket that could only be from the type of box that holds an engagement ring."

Dorothy rarely heard her husband speak such a long paragraph unless he was prattling on about some injustice taking place at work or how the political poles weren't curving to his favor. She stared in amazement and giggled a little at the thought that one time long ago, her husband had been Terrance sitting at her father's table ready to ask for her hand.

She gazed up at the ceiling, trying to picture that moment in her head clearly. "Yes, that was quite the evening. I remember you spilled the lemonade all over my mother's freshly washed table linens. And that's when you got up and asked me to go outside."

This thought made them both laugh out loud. Dorothy decided to take the rest of the dishes in to wash them and wait for the deed to be done before slicing the meringue.

Terrance and Eileen went out on the front porch and sat on the swing. Eileen looked at Terrance a bit worried that he had some bad news to share with her as he always waited for dessert before retiring to the front porch.

"Are feeling alright my dear?" she asked quietly gazing over at him with big eyes.

He was rocking the swing with his legs and then stopped. He stood up and without answering her question got down on his knee.

It was at this point that Eileen was aware of what was about to happen. Her heart began beating a thousand miles a minute. Never before had she been proposed to and so her mind raced for any reference had she to the subject. One of the waitresses had told her the story of her proposal and she had cried when her boyfriend asked her to marry him. Eileen was very bad when it came to crying at the appropriate moment and so she thought maybe a more jubilant approach might be better.

"Eileen," Terrance was still on his knee and must have been aware that Eileen's thoughts had wondered, "I have something important to ask you. Could I please have your attention?"

"Yes, Terrance, go head." She sat up straight as she could trying not to rock the swing back and forth as Terrance was now holding her hand and it was making him jerk forward with every motion the swing made.

"We have been dating for some time now. And I find you to be a solid woman that wants the same things that I do out of life. I don't have much to offer anyone. I work every day and try to make a decent living. But a life lived alone is well...lonely at times."

Terrance wished he hadn't strayed from the original speech he had been rehearsing all week.

Eileen took her free hand and grabbed his. "I want that too." She often found he needed encouragement to get what he really wanted to say out and this seemed like one of those moments".

"Eileen, will you marry me?"

Terrance looked up with a wrinkled brow honestly worried he might meet with a negative response.

She stood up still clasping his hand and said, "Yes!" He grabbed her tight around the waste and lifted her up off the ground in a hug she would often remember as one of the most romantic moments of her life.

That night was not much unlike any other. The two announced their engagement to their family which evoked hand shaking, kisses, and hugs from Terrance's parents. Then the four of them sat down to eat Lemon Meringue pie. The Meringue was runny and the lemon too tart. But Terrance devoured two pieces, smiling from ear to ear the entire time he stared down at his plate.

Eileen's parents lived out of state so she asked her boss if he wouldn't mind her using the telephone to call them. When she connected with the operator, she had to begin with explaining her reason for calling as Mrs. Beatrice Bradley was the nosiest operator west of the Mississippi. Her parents were both home thankfully, as she was sure she wouldn't be given permission to use the phone again anytime soon. Having come from a family of 8 children, Eileen didn't have any hopes that her parents would be able to make the long trip out for the wedding, nor did she think they would entertain the idea even if they could. Some people just did not venture out in life, and her parents were one of those people. But Eileen promised once they had settled down, they would plan a trip to see them on holiday. She was given a sound welcome to bring Terrance the first chance she was able and a brief update on how her younger siblings were doing.

Wedding preparations were simple. Eileen didn't have much of a savings so the wedding was dependent on the generosity of Terrance's family. While having stability of family income, they were not at liberty to spend lavish amounts on such things as a gown or a reception. The morning of the wedding Eileen slept over at their home so that she could be closer to the family church where they were to be married. Neither Terrance nor Eileen were regular church goers but for every holiday as well as weddings and funerals this was usually where they would attend to worship.

The morning dew was still on the tips of the grass blades when Eileen stepped out in her white lace dress she bought from a girl who worked in the cafe and had been married in it last year. It was very simple lace that came together at her waist with a satin sash. She also had some fresh daisies from the garden as a bouquet. Terrance's mother let her spray on some perfume a cousin had given her all the way from Paris, France. Despite the simplicity of the occasion, Eileen felt it her finest day.

Terrance had walked ahead to the church yard so as not to see the bride before the wedding march. His parents borrowed a motor car from the neighbor and they drove Eileen the 1/2 mile to the church that they normally would have walked. Along the dusty road lined with oak trees were people walking to and fro. A few were on their way to attend the wedding, but most were just doing their everyday Saturday business. Even so, once they saw Eileen in her white dress with a bouquet in her hands they waved, clapped and cheered. Eileen waved like the queen of England herself and was very happy. Would Terrance be happy when he saw her? A wave of fear sent goose bumps grazing up her arm; she was about to be his wife. This came with a string of expectations Eileen hadn't really pondered on as much as she ought to have done. With minutes between her and her destination, she compared how easy life had been at the cafe.

At the cafe, she would serve all day and eat for free, though they consisted of whatever was left over from the morning's starter meals. Now she would need to care for a home.

Terrance planned on moving back into his parents' house until they had enough money for a home of their own. He had been living with his construction team and they would move from place to place working on whatever home or building they had been commissioned for. While able to save a little living this way, it still wasn't enough for them to put a down payment on property or begin building a place.

Eileen paused to make sure her hair hadn't been ruffled too much by the wind. Tensions over housekeeping melted under the fear of the wedding night. Terrance had not been overly intimate to Eileen's relief during their courtship. But now the reward for his patience would need to be rendered and she wondered if she had really done enough research on the subject. In fact, Eileen had not; as her parents never spoke of such a taboo subject and she never had any girlfriends with more experience than herself.

A camera flashed and Eileen forced a smile as she stepped out of the motor car and onto the brick road directly in front of the churchyard. About 10 people were waiting outside and smiling making her feel even more self-conscious than her daydreaming had a moment earlier.

Terrance's father had hired a photographer to take a total of 10 photos the entire day which was quite generous and why the man chose to take one of her getting out of the vehicle alone she did not know. Glaring at him as she walked past in an effort to discourage him from taking another before the ceremony had begun, she took her soon to be father in laws hand and waited at the entrance with her eyes closed hoping to find some courage deep down inside under all her lace.

The organ began to play and two young boys about 12 and 14 opened the doors wide for them to step onto a red carpet. The cherry wood benches were filled with the remainder of the attendees, about 20 in total; more than Eileen and Terrance had expected to come seeing as they had not sent out any formal invitations and there was to be only a small garden party at the house afterwards. The phone operator was there! Mrs. Beatrice Bradley must have gotten it into her mind to come from the phone call Eileen had made to her family inviting them. Deciding not to be annoyed Eileen smiled at her as if she were her personal guest and kept up the march to the tune of the piano. It was a march that seemed to take forever.

Terrance's mother looked very pretty in a pale yellow silk dress that she rarely ever wore. At the end of the aisle stood Terry, her fiancé, boyfriend, and best tipper. Mr. Sweetly let go of her arm and gave her a gentle kiss on the cheek. Terrance took the other arm, holding his hand on top of hers and the two of them turned to listen to the bible discourse on the sanctity of marriage. After about 15 minutes it was time for the vows. Both got through without stumbling and when it came time to exchange rings they softly told the pastor that there would be no rings to exchange at this time. Terrance had given her an engagement ring made of aluminum and glass but he had some simple gold rings on order and they hadn't arrived in time. The pastor finished up the remainder of the ceremony and asked, "Would you like to kiss the bride?"

Terrance grabbed Eileen's shoulders and drew her quickly in as if sealing the deal. With a steady smack on the mouth those in attendance cheered and they turned to have their photo taken. It was a joyful ride back to the house with everyone chasing behind the vehicle giving wedding well wishes and the two spending the rest of the afternoon with blushing faces.

Back at the house there were finger sandwiches, lemonade, and

Dorothy's best dessert yet: a wedding cake made with confectioners icing and real flowers from her garden decorating it. There was enough for everyone to have some. Both of Terry's parents gave a few words to the newlyweds such as, "Keep each other warm or cold nights, and cool on warm ones."

Then his father said, "Don't go into debt over silly things, keep a good head on your shoulders and you'll fare well."

By 4:00 in the afternoon everyone had gone home and Eileen and her mother in law were cleaning up the dishes in the kitchen while Terrance and his father dismantled the table and moved it to the back of the yard where it usually sat.

Dorothy and her husband retired early that night leaving the house to the two of them. At about 8:30 they decided to go upstairs and go to sleep. Without too many frustrations they made their marriage vows everlasting. It was much like Eileen had thought it would have been and she was glad to get the wedding night jitters over with.

The next morning, Dorothy had made a beautiful breakfast with all Terrance's favorite things; bacon, ham, biscuits, and scrambled eggs. They had taken their breakfast very early so the two newlyweds could have the house all to themselves that morning when they went off to church. It was a beautiful way to begin their married life Eileen thought in the quiet surroundings of the Sweetly estate, as the family called it despite its very small property line.

Built in 1867 the house had been Terrance's great-grandfathers when he came to America from Ireland to begin farming. The family had kept it very well maintained all these years and never ran into any trouble with debt during hard times. The trees that his daughter and her husband had planted were well grown. Outside each window was a lilac bush that, when in season, sent its aroma all throughout the grand old white house. Having two floors it was spacious enough for a family of 6 and so Dorothy was very happy to have her youngest son home again.

Terrance had one older brother who had died of the influenza 3 years earlier. It was very difficult for Dorothy to bear even if his name came up in conversation. It was with a hope that life would feel whole again now that the house was full that the Sweetly's suggested Terrance and Eileen settle for their first few years with them. This was under the guise to save money for a place to call their own one day. After all, despite the good economy, there were some experts saying that it was due for a plunge. So, cautiously, the four of them began their life together under one roof. A life that, ten years later would still be carrying on as if it had been the week after the wedding day.

Terrance had finished his job building the shop in town soon after the wedding and returned to working at the hardware store, and only taking on odd jobs as they came up. Howard had owned the shop since his uncle had left it to him at the age of 16. Dorothy worked at the cashier counter. The family decided it would be best for Eileen to take care of the home. Dorothy worried the first year living with her in-laws after having lived on her own might be suffocating for Eileen. And Eileen assured them she was ready to take up housekeeping in an attempt to repay them for all they had done for her and Terrance the past year. Dorothy would cook on the weekend and Eileen would cook during the week and do all the housecleaning. Eileen did her laundry during the week, including linens in the home. And Dorothy did her and Howards wash on Saturday afternoons, while Terrance and Eileen would work the store.

Fast-forward ten years. *As nothing exciting had really happened during that time, it would not harm the story to just begin with Eileen making biscuits in the kitchen.*

The smell of homemade biscuits drove Terrance up out of his rocking chair on the back porch and into the kitchen hoping to sneak a bite. She was too late in swatting his hand with her spatula and he ran out the front door while tossing one that was too hot back and forth. Attempting to do this at the same time as he opened the door to give his mother a helping hand with some groceries she was bringing up the steps, he dropped the biscuit but quickly picked it up and blew it off in time to eat it under what he termed the 3 second rule.

"Looks like you bought enough to feed an army" he said smiling and chewing his biscuit savagely.

"I must admit I was a bit distracted by the latest and greatest the other ladies had to share and just kept putting things in my bag while I listened."

Dorothy said eagerly entering the house wanting to share the gossip.

"It seems a new shop is opening in town. It is a woman of independent means."

Dorothy said this as if she knew what it meant, but it was obvious that she was just quoting the other ladies in the store.

Eileen shaking off flour from her hands grabbed the grocery bag from Terrance and began wiping off some of the goods before she put them on the shelf.

"What's this about a new shop?" she asked. Dorothy expounded on all the details true and untrue that she had been told at the end of it all she was so tired from prattling on that she flopped herself down in a chair and Eileen poured her a cup of lemonade.

Eileen decided the next day when she went to the vegetable market she would try to find out more about this mysterious new person in town.

GOSSIP

They were the type of people easily swayed by the newest bits of gossip available. To the common passerby it would seem harmless enough. But to a person who sold, bought, and lived in such a small town, their form of gossip could do damage that would last for months or even years. These women were the farmer's wives who came into town and sold their goods each week. Since they had no wealth or education to give them the sense of pride they carried, it was their foreknowledge before anyone else of the town's goings on that kept them in the proper societies and an integral part of the social circle of the day.

Eileen walked up slowly to the group of women selling their goods. They sported large straw hats and denim overall dresses of every color. Mrs. Leighton was cleaning off green beans to sell at a higher price to those who were buying on their way home from work. Mrs. Payton was taking the green tops off of her carrots and placing the orange batons in uniform piles to be sold by weight. She was older than the rest of them and Eileen often wondered if the weight of her piles was accurate, although no one ever had the nerve to ask her to re-weigh them.

The youngest of the bunch was a new bride from out east. She sported a thick Irish accent but was married to Mrs. Leighton's son Charles. She was sitting just one seat behind the two, doing some knitting. Her work was to help with transport. The farm was a good 5 miles from town. The three women all lived very close together. The other sellers Eileen didn't personally know but they too all had a story of their own. Farm life was hard but satisfying. Although they were the poorer of the town's residents, their life style gave them an air of confidence that would often leave the women of the town feeling intimidated.

"Good morning to all!" said Eileen with a mock air of cheer.

"Good morning to you Ms. Eileen" said Mrs. Leighton while continuing to slice the seeds out of her beans without looking up.

Mrs. Leighton still insisted on calling Eileen 'Miss.' What Eileen wanted to know so badly about this, is was she saying 'Miss' spelled 'Ms.' As if often done in the business world? OR was it 'Miss' as if she wasn't really married? This was what Eileen could not for the life of her dearest relation figure out and it succeeded in driving her to be edgy for at least a half hour after Mrs. Leighton spoke with her. Everyone else who married in town was Mrs. or Mame. But Eileen was still 'Miss' and she had the strangest feeling Mrs. Leighton did that on purpose because of not approving of her marrying Terrance. She never understood why Mrs. Leighton disliked her so much, but there it was. The more you wanted to know something of these women the less they would tell you. The trick to figuring out what the latest yarn they were spinning was simply waiting, and catching them when they were off guard. At times one could even eavesdrop when they figured you weren't looking. Eileen began to browse a different group of seller's vegetables nearby so she could still be in earshot of what these infamous three were saying.

"There's a new shop being put up in town," Mrs. Leighton remarked to her fellow vendors as if everyone didn't already know that in the first place. When a town only sports five shops it's easy to see when a sixth one opens up.

"Is that so, Mrs. Leighton? I wonder what they might be selling there?"

Mrs. Payton kept cleaning off her carrots as they spoke and only so often would their eyes meet for a brief encounter.

"I heard it was going to be the latest fashion for women's clothes from Chicago" chirped in the new daughter in law.

"Now what do sensible country folk like us need with a clothing store or townsfolk either for that matter? Not only do our women folk not have a desire to keep up with the big city fashions, we got hands of our own to be able to sew whatever clothes we like.

Everyone knows there's a recession going on. That's just for the lazy women who want to waste their husband's money!"

There is was. The new shop was not going to be approved or supported. It could have been according to Eileen's hope, that Mrs. Leighton was trying to train her daughter in law in how she wanted her son's money to be spent, but in an effort to convince her that this was indeed the proper course of action, it would seem the entire town would suffer the consequences. Eileen left with satisfied with the information she had accrued. As she walked out of hearing distance, Mrs. Leighton huffed and whispered out of the corner of her mouth to Mrs. Payton, "Why in the world would a nice young man like Terrance go and marry a girl from nowhere when he has an entire town full of respectable girls right here in front of his nose!"

Mrs. Payton gave a gut laugh in agreement but kept right on piling her carrots without the slightest pause to her routine.

Eileen used to live near the Chicago area. And although they didn't have much extra money, her mother had never learned how to sew and they would often go shopping in town on a Saturday afternoon. Where Eileen grew up it wasn't looked at as frivolous to buy an occasional dress. The shops were usually reasonably priced and some shops even sold used items that wealthier women would donate for the poor. In her single days she always tried to keep up with the latest fashion but since moving to this town, she rarely felt any efforts would be appreciated. In an effort to be neighborly, and to welcome the person who would establish a much needed shop, Eileen decided to see what it was like.

The bell on the front entrance of the shop rang hard against the wooden frame as Eileen opened the door just wide enough to peep her head inside.

"Well, don't just stand there gaping, come on in!" The words would've seemed harsh but the tone was very kindly.

"I didn't mean to gape, I was just wondering if the store was open yet." said Eileen trying to mask her apprehensiveness.

"It's no matter, gaping is for free, but the things for sale don't fall too far behind that. I got the best deals in town even though I'm the newest store around!"

The rhyme of her sentence caused Eileen to feel a little more at ease and she smiled while taking a few more steps forward.

The woman standing behind the counter had bright red hair; the kind Eileen had only seen in the magazines. Although the women sometimes colored their hair in the Chicago area, none of the local women would ever think to do something so bold. Eileen being more curious about the owner of this bright red hair more than the clothes, fronted as if she was browsing. Every few seconds she would lift her head up and smile while inching a bit closer to the owner while faining a smile.

"No need to go on fake lookin'," she said to a very startled Eileen. "I know everyone in this town wants to know where I's come from first. Did they send you to spy on me?"

The woman had her hands on her hips as if she was annoyed but Eileen could see the sparkle in her eye suggesting there was an air of teasing going on behind her words.

Eileen looked down at the shirt she was touching not knowing what to say at having been caught in her attempt to get a dish on the woman. She felt the insinuation that she 'had been sent' to be a slight injustice. Since this was not true she attempted diversion by means of self-defense. "No one has sent me here. I came because I wanted to see what the new store was all about. But you are right; you are the talk of the town at the moment."

"I knew it!" said the woman slapping the counter top smartly.

"Don't' worry," said Eileen reassuringly, "it's a small town; in no time everyone will find something new to talk about."

Eileen took a brave step forward and held out her hand.

"My name is Eileen Parker..uh I mean, Sweetly. It's nice to meet you. Welcome to Strasburg."

Had it been that long since she had a girlfriend that she reverted to using her maiden name? Eileen wondered at this mistake while gazing closer at the bright red curl dipped down over this woman's left eye brow. An eyebrow which had evidently been plucked bald and then re-colored to match the fake beauty mark that rested comfortably to the right of the woman's ruby red lips.

The red headed woman came out from behind the counter to shake Eileen's hand with a firm grip and several swings back and forth before she let go.

"Aw gee, I'm sorry I came off so cranky, it's just all week the townsfolk have been walkin' in and out without so much as a word, and not buyin' nothin' either. I guess I figured you was just another one coming to gawk at me and then make me feel like an alien from outer space."

Eileen smiled as she pulled her hand away and placed it on the counter trying to look relaxed, but in reality making her look a bit awkward.

"That's okay. I used to work with customers before too and I know sometimes people just have a way of making a bad day worse."

Clearing her throat she added, "So as I said, my name is Eileen and it's nice to meet you...Ms...?"

"Oh heaven's sake I have completely forgotten my manners. Hey I got some coffee brewin' in the back, you wanna come back and have a seat and get to know one another?"

The red headed, ruby lipped woman, began walking to the back without waiting for a response from her most recent shopper.

Eileen followed her new friend to the back of the store room. It was a small little room with a back door on it. There wasn't much in it but a couple of empty boxes, a table with a single burner on it that had the coffee brewing on top.

"I hope you don't mind the coffee black, I don't have much here and that's how I always takes mine."

Eileen wondered if this person was ever going to divulge her name or where she was from. Her clothes definitely depicted someone from a more influential city. But her manner of speech seemed like someone from the countryside. Eileen held out her cup as the woman poured and tried to think of more interesting things to say to draw the woman out. The woman however, was clearly in need of some female companionship and it only took a manner of time before she let all her secrets free.

"My name's Patricia Wellen. I comes from Pittsburgh out East. My father was a wealthy coal miner you might say. But he died young; guess all that diggin' gots to his lungs. Anywhose.... my Granny used to live in this town before they went out east to settle. She left me a little piece of property right north of here and I decided not being married at present, to try my hand at the country life. And that's what's brought me here to yous."

The bit about 'not being married at present' led Eileen's mind to trail a bit. Trying to compose herself so as not to stunt more delicate details, she posed some innocent questions about life in general.

"So have you settled in nicely? Do you need any help unpacking? When did you arrive?"

Having answered all the boring questions Patricia herself looked relieved when the doorbell rang out front.

"Hang on a minute darlin', I'm just gonna go see who that is. Who knows, maybe it's my first paying customer."

Eileen wanted so badly to be able to purchase something from Patricia's store now that she had exposed herself as a curious window shopper, but as she searched her change purse the stark truth of only 35 cents left her stumped as to what she could find to spend it on. Granted, there were probably some stockings or other tidbits she could buy with that amount. But a visit, with coffee and everything seemed to be worth at least a purchase of .75 and Eileen had nothing else in her bag but some lint and one button that she had not yet re-sewn on Terrance's best Sunday shirt.

A few seconds passed and Patricia came back into the store room looking glum.

"I guess it was just another gawker. By the time I got out there, they were gone. Oh I didn't mean to suggest you was a gawker. You knows what I meant right Honey, what did you say your name was again?"

Eileen took her last swallow of the black coffee with a bit of a grimace. She always took hers with cream and sugar but didn't want to seem rude by not drinking it down.

"It's Eileen. And I know what you meant. I do plan on coming back to buy but I was just passing by to introduce myself today. I really must be going."

Patricia held out a firm hand again swinging it back and forth.

"It sure was nice gettin' to know you Honey, I mean Ms. Eileen. Just call me Patty. Come back anytime. In fact, I'll make sure to set aside some nice things for you and I won't hike up the price neither."

She winked solidly to fix the deal.

Eileen walked away with a wave and never looked back. For some reason the way Patricia said 'Ms.' hadn't bothered her like it did when Mrs. Leighton said it. She wondered if it had been obvious to Patricia that she didn't have much to spend or if Patricia was just honestly a generous person. Looking forward to going back and purchasing something, she began to think of ways she might cut the grocery bill so she might save to have a little extra cash.

That night Terrance's back was hurting from work that day. Eileen rubbed some peppermint oil on it and left him there lying on his belly to go to sleep. She turned off the light and crawled under the cool cotton sheets blowing out the little gas lantern by her bed. They had electricity but it was still considered in frivolous taste to use it at night for something as simple as newspaper reading.

She went to bed thinking of what excuses she could come up with to pass by the store again. The idea hit her to bake some extra corn muffins in the morning and take them over to Patricia's store. Even if she couldn't yet buy anything, surely corn muffins would be a good welcome gift for anyone and it would personally help her swallow more black coffee if offered. Eileen was really hoping Patricia would offer.

The next day when Eileen brought in the corn muffins, she set them on the counter pushing them towards Patricia and said, "I was thinking they might serve you better at your home but it dawned on me I don't know where you live so I brought them here to you. It's just a little welcome present."

Eileen hoped this would mask the fact that she was secretly hoping to be invited to sit down for more horrible black coffee.

"Oh it's easy to find, just go up the hill past where the ladies always sells their veggies, turn left, when you see the big Willow tree you take the path to the right of it and follow it all the way back until you come to the water pump. At the water pump you turn right and mine is the first house on the left after the old school house."

"Yes, that sounds as easy as pie!"

Eileen spouted out and both women laughed at how funny all those directions had sounded. "It's a small town so I'm sure I can find it."

Eileen said this still giggling at the extent of Patricia's directions.

"No matter Honey, I'm planning on being here every day but Sunday and the store will stay open until 6:00pm every night."

"Really? Aren't you afraid to walk home at night at 6:00pm, the streets are so quiet by then?"

Eileen held her hand to her mouth in a bit of a shock that Patricia would think of spending so much time in the store. How would she ever get her washing done or care for the home, she wondered.

"Oh lord no! Back in Pittsburgh the trolley busses used to run until 11:00. My husband and I would go out to eat as late as 9:30 so we's could make it home on time before there was no busses. But I know this town isn't Pittsburgh and so I've been thinkin' of putting a cot up in the back room in case it's rainin' real hard one night and I just wants to sleep here in the store."

"I noticed you said you weren't married at the moment, did something happen to your husband? I'm so sorry if the question is too personal."

Eileen asked in a way that she was hoping wouldn't sound too cold in case Patricia had been widowed.

"The only thing that happened to Stan is that he had eyes in the back of his head! Pardon me but I and my ex-husband aren't on the best of terms just yet. He ran off with a woman that used to ride the bus home at the same time as he did. They still live right there in town! Can you believe that? That's why I just had to get out and start me a new life. Do you know what I mean, Honey? I mean, Ellen...that was your name wasn't it?"

Not wanting to sound too uptight with regards to her name Eileen said, "Here's my name written down for you on a piece of paper along with my home phone number. I know how hard it is to get settled into a new town and all. If you need anything just call me and I'd be glad to help."

"Thanks...oh Eileen," Patricia humbly muttered looking down at the paper, "I'm sorry; I'm always getting everyone's name wrong. Just this morning a Mrs. Coppersmith came by and had to correct me three different times on how to say her name 'Coralline was it?"

Eileen gave a gentle nod although the full name was Corraline-ann and she always went with the full name and never half. Patricia continued, "Well, after the last time I gots it wrong she says to me, 'You can just call me Mrs. Coppersmith.' and then you know what she did? She put what she was gonna buy back on the rack and walked out of the store! I tell ya, Eileen this town is gonna be a tougher crowd than I thought. Back in Pittsburgh all the local people's used to talk to one another even if you's was from outta town."

Although not having been raised in the town, Eileen felt a flush of embarrassment in her cheeks from the lack of warmth Patricia had been shown. Not being surprised either as it was the same type of welcome she had received, she only gave a tidbit of advice, "After a time, you'll get used to it. It's just the way people are around here. They don't mean any real harm by it."

Patricia seemed to like that idea and cheered up.

"Aren't you just the ray of sunshine Eileen? You are welcome here anytime. Just let me know if you'd like to stop by the house too and who knows, maybe I'll close up shop early and we can have coffee there."

"Okay I'd like that."

Eileen took her little basket that had been emptied of the muffins, and left with a merry skip to her step. Eileen had finally made a friend. The timing was indeed much appreciated as the slow moving town was about to drive her to tears of boredom. And Eileen typically was not a hard person to please.

IDEA

Thus began a daily appointment of Eileen coming into the shop as if she was going to purchase something and Patricia inviting her in for a cup of coffee. They would discuss the weather or any general information that might have been discussed on the news that morning.

On one such day the subject of marriage came up.

"So tell me your secret girlie. You've been married a lot longer than I was ever able to manage. What's your secret?"

"Oh I don't know, I'm not as clever as you are, I guess I couldn't really think of anything else to do."

Eileen laughed bitterly trying to make light of her present emotional frustration.

Patricia thought this over for a moment and then said slowly, "Surely there is more reason in life for happiness than just to marry because there was nothin' betters to do? And I know for certain, there is more than that to keeping a marriage intact for ten years. Not to mention under your in-laws roof? Now come on, aren't you going to share? What do you mean you're not clever? You just might be one of the cleverest girls I know to be able to pull that off!"

Patricia knocked her fist in her hand as if to seal her judgment of the situation.

Eileen responded by knocking her head on the table and leaving it there as the tears rolled slowly down her cheeks burning with every drop.

"That's just it. I don't know why he even married me in the first place! It was like we had nothing better to do. And now I am so bored I can't stand it. Life was more exciting when I was waiting tables then it is now. You're life seems so much more appealing than mine that I just can't think of a single happy thought to share with you on the subject. It's not like he beats me either. He's a good man. I'm just an ungrateful girl who's bored to tears, literally."

She sat up wiping her tears solemnly, but with a bit of a dance in her eyes said, "I don't suppose you could share with me some of your excitement in life. You know maybe I could live through your eyes."

Patricia laughed mockingly, "Excitement? Why it's no excitement to be alone at my age after having given my heart to someone. But the choice wasn't mine you see. You have the ball in your court. Not only is he happy to continue with you, you are the only one who is unhappy. So it's up to yous to make yourself happy!"

"What do you mean?" said Eileen, "How do I make myself happy?"

Patricia stood up and went onto the shop floor bringing back several pieces of clothing in her hands and sizing them up to Eileen as she spoke.

"Believe me, it's a lot easier to make us women happy then you think. All you need is to spice it up a little. You're just feeling dreary. You need a new outfit, maybe a new haircut, and I've got some make-up and perfume in back that would make the dullest of girls feel like they spent the day shopping in The Big Apple."

Eileen said, surprised at the offer, "Oh I couldn't think of imposing on you like that. And I don't have the money to pay for all of those unnecessary things."

"Unnecessary? Look, if you're starting to admire other people's lives more than your own, then it's time to do somethin' about it. You can pay it off by doing some work for me around the shop, how's that? Then you wouldn't be taking charity."

Patricia held out a light green dress with taffeta ruffles around a low lying collar.

"I might as well take up a fight with the man on the moon then try to argue with you," said Eileen sheepishly as she picked up the dress and put it up to her chest.

"I'll take that as a yes then. I'll take you're measurements first. And if you want you can wash up our coffee cups and we'll count that as you getting started. You're not above washing coffee cups are you?"

"Coffee cups just happen to be one of my specialties."

Both women laughed and spent the next two days working on Eileen's new outfit. There was a church picnic that Sunday and they decided it would be the perfect time to show off a new wardrobe.

The Sunday of the picnic the church was packed out more than it had been last Easter. Some of the children in other towns were off school and so had come to stay with their relatives. This accounted for the extra bodies. The church benches looked like they were filled with butterflies as everyone was so hot and stuffy they were fanning themselves with any bit of paper they could pull out of their bags and pockets. Terrance had gone ahead of Eileen as she had pretended needing to help set up for the picnic. The reverend was half way through his sermon by the time Eileen came running up the church stairs.

"Love is long-suffering and kind. Love is not jealous, it does not brag, does not get puffed up, does not behave indecently," the reverend stopped and gapped his mouth open wide as the doorway to the church was filled with the presence of a new attendee. Only it wasn't a new attendee. It was Eileen.

He quickly gathered his thoughts and continued extolling on the subject of love and the peace of the congregation. But his slight pause caused the others seated to turn their heads and see what he had been staring at. Eileen realized that this might have not been the best time to show off her new look. Several of the older women in town gasped and nudged their husbands with their elbows to get them to shut their mouths from gaping open and turn around.

Eileen walked slowly to where Terrance and his parents were sitting. She was wearing new high heeled white patent leather shoes with a Mary Jane strap that buttoned in the middle. Patricia let her borrow a pair of fish net stockings in the shade of rose that matched nicely with the flowing taffeta rose wrap she had on. She insisted on wearing a wrap because the dress Patricia had given her was held up only by thin silk straps. It fit tight around her body but flared out nicely at her knees. She looked like nothing that town had ever seen on two legs. Only possibly in the magazine catalogs had the women even seen fishnet stockings. It was a long sermon but everyone must have been hungry because they quickly left their pews to head for the picnic. Eileen and Terrance were almost the last ones out when he stopped her in the coat room before they descended the stairs of the church.

"What in God's name are you wearing?"

Terrence pulled his coat off the rack and wrapped it around Eileen's waist as he spoke.

"Don't be silly Terrance" said Eileen blushing while she ripped the coat out of his hands and held it in place, now feeling very self-conscious about what she was wearing.

"It's the new style. Surely you've seen it in the magazines your mother keeps in the sitting room."

"Well, where the heck did it come from?" he asked nervously.

"Don't worry, I didn't buy it if that's what you're worried about!" she snapped. "I never thought I would be interrogated about my new outfit as if I had been robbing the cookie jar to pay for it!"

"I didn't mean that!"

Terrance said in a desperate whisper, looking around as he spoke, "It's just you don't normally wear something that short. I can see your knee caps when you walk!"

"Terrance, you've seen my knee caps before, in fact, my normal clothes aren't that much longer so I don't know what you're talking about. It's just a newer fashion and not all plain and beige like most of my clothes. This is a shiny new material and it was sewn in Indianapolis."

She said this thinking it would show Terrance what a good quality garment it was and thus appreciate its fineness since apparently her knees were not convincing him of its beauty.

"Eileen, I know I've seen your knees before! In fact, we can go home right now, run up the stairs and I can see whatever part of you I want."

He lowered his voice towards the end of his sentence and leaned into her so as to make his point.

"But I do not think all the people in town need to see your knees. Now are you gonna tell me where you got this dress from or are we gonna need to go to the police to hire an inspector to get it out of you!"

Eileen rolled her eyes and sighed, "I had no idea you would be so dramatic about it. In fact, I kinda thought you'd think I looked...pretty."

Seeing no sign of a compliment coming, despite fishing for it, she sighed and said, "Patricia gave it to me."

"Patricia? Now what did she go and do that for? She thinks something's wrong with your normal clothes?"

"No, of course not! It's just I helped her at the store and she wanted to show her appreciation is all. She even did my hair up for me, see?"

Eileen did a half turn to show off the curls in back making her normally shoulder lengthened hair look somewhat bobbed.

Terrance was looking down at the ground when she turned back around causing Eileen's shoulders to slump in disappointment. After a typical moment of awkward silence where she had no idea what Terrance was thinking she too began to look down at the ground and roll her shoe over a loose pebble that was on the hardwood floor of the church. Terrance looked up after a moment and asked, "Did you take on a job at Patricia's store or something?"

Eileen now knew the real source of his irritation, Terrance! I did not take on a job. But what if I did? Would something be so wrong with that?"

She put her hands on her hips causing her skirt to rise up even farther. Terrance looked down with wide eyes and leaped forward grabbing her by the elbow and ushering her onto the street and towards the house. They walked briskly past the path leading to the picnic, Terrance kept speaking to her while holding onto her arm in case she escaped.

"Eileen, you don't need a job and you don't need to be hanging out at that store with the likes of Patricia. She ain't a good friend for you, she's too independent, she doesn't like to be married, and what's with all that red hair?"

They entered the front door of the house and stood in the hallway for a moment as Terrance locked the door behind him protecting the house from unwelcomed intruders who might learn of his wife's temporary stint of insanity.

"Don't try to lock me up in here Terrance! I'm not working for Patricia, and even if I was it shouldn't be a matter of concern as long as I get all my housework done. Now stop being silly. You are just going off of neighborhood gossip that you've overheard your mother talking about on the front porch. Patricia has not discouraged me towards my wifely duties. As a matter of fact, you have! Who would want to be a wife to some ogre who can't even stand his wife having a new fancy dress? What do you want me to do just spend the rest of my days in this house, dusting and cleaning up after your mothers baking dishes? I need a life too Terrance, do you understand?"

Terrance wiped his brow causing the skin on his forehead to wrinkle against his hair line. He continued standing there but didn't say a word in reply to what Eileen had just said to him. In his mind, she seemed to be acting very irrational.

"I'm going upstairs to change my unsightly garb and change back into my house coat, said Eileen breaking the silence, "Then I'll make sure to get down in the kitchen and make you a cup of tea so that you can get back to whatever it is that's more important than talking to me!"

Eileen stomped up the stairs and shut the door soundly leaving Terrance wondering what he should do next. It seemed that the argument was over. Eileen was clearly going to get out of that short dress, which had been his main concern in the first place. But for some reason he had this nagging feeling things weren't better between them but rather worse. Worse for what, he had no idea. It wasn't like he was the only man in town that wouldn't want to share his wife's knees with people. Thinking it was safe to stick with the routine; he picked up the paper and walked out on the back porch to read it.

Eileen walked down the stairs quietly hoping for the first time in her married life that he wouldn't speak to her as she couldn't bear to fake happiness at such a time.

"What's for dinner?" he called from outside. Eileen knew he had every intention of just sitting on the back porch and reading his paper so she wasn't up for small talk in a lame attempt to make peace. She did have a meal she could serve him but since they were supposed to have eaten at the picnic it wouldn't be ready yet for some time.

"Roast beef, mashed potatoes, carrots and gravy." She called even louder not wanting to go towards the door to invoke more conversation.

"When will it be ready, I'm starving?"

He called this out thinking Eileen would be tickled at how much he was looking forward to eating her good cooking.

"In about an hour, there is some potato salad still in the fridge if you want it before supper." Eileen couldn't believe how quickly Terrance had forgotten how upset she was and went right on doing what he had always done every Sunday for the past decade.

"That would be great!" he cried out, trying to be cheery and light but secretly fearing that Eileen wasn't over the fight they had just had.

The silence that ensued, left Eileen with no doubt that he expected her to retrieve the potato salad and bring it to him. She opened the fridge, took a spoon, and jammed it in the bowl with the potato salad. Opening the screen door, she set it on the table next to him and went inside.

A muffled, "Thanks" was heard as he put the first bite in his mouth.

"Would you like something to drink with that?" she called out in her sweetest voice.

"Sure, I'll take some more of that lemonade if you still got some!" he called out with a voice filled with hope that the storm had passed. That hope vanished as he felt the cool sweet lemonade dripping off the top of his head and onto his paper. Eileen stood over him with the empty glass upside down and still dripping.

"Let me know if there's anything else my dear that I can do for you. The roast is in the oven, it'll be done in about an hour. You can take it out and serve yourself. I'll be upstairs in my room the rest of the evening. Oh and dear, if you need anything, I'm sure your mother will be home soon and will more than happy to help you with it."

When Mr. and Mrs. Sweetly came home Eileen did not come down to dinner. Terrance ate alone as his parents had eaten at the picnic. Mrs. Sweetly went up to Eileen's room to talk with her a bit, knowing she must have been upset over Terrance's lack of enthusiasm about her new dress and hair-do. The conversation only added to Eileen's torment. Mrs. Sweetly despite the best of intentions always came off as rather patronizing, making Eileen feel like she was a teenager getting over the disappointment of not having been able to attend some late night function.

Terrance had no idea his mother had been up in the room, when he attempted to go to bed. He kept saying things like how hot it was this time of year but that the cooler night air always made him sleepy. This vain attempt to excuse himself only made his father follow him into the house. Inviting Terrance to sit down and join him for shot of whiskey, Mr. Sweetly was secretly trying to get steal some time away to warn his son that as of late his wife seemed to be somewhat unhappy. Ironically, as Mr. Sweetly had just uttered the words, "I noticed Eileen's pretty dress today," Eileen came rushing through the threshold of the kitchen where they were sitting, hesitating to enter all the way in, she said stammering, "I came – I wanted to say something to you – I will come back later!"

She had obviously been crying. Mr. Sweetly's least favorite thing in the world was an emotional scene, but he couldn't bring himself to repel the girl. He smiled and held out his hand saying, "No don't do that I've just poured myself a night cap, come and join me my girl."

"Eileen, leave pops alone, this is our affair and we shouldn't involve my parents any more than we already have. Let's go upstairs to bed."

This made Mr. Sweetly burst out laughing, knowing full well his son was not going to get the night's sleep he was hoping for. This outburst of laughter prompted Eileen to leave the room quickly out of embarrassment but not before turning and saying darkly, "Good night then!"

"Doesn't look like it's going to be a good night for you son," said Mr. Sweetly, still laughing and pouring himself another shot.

Terrance still hot from the words spoken earlier between he and Eileen shouted to his father, "She would have had a good night if I hadn't told her what you said about her needing to be more under control! Now instead of just suffering the sulks, she is sure to indulge herself into a flood of tears."

"Well son, that's as much your fault as it is hers. Why in the world would you have told her what I said? Come on, sit down and have a shot, maybe she'll cry herself to sleep before you get up there, and if not the liquor will help calm your nerves."

By the time Terrence went back to bed, it was nearly an hour later; well past midnight, and he was feeling quite exhausted and was tempted to crawl into bed without changing into his night clothes, but of course he didn't. Just as he was about to shut off the light he heard a gentle tap at the door.

"Terrance, darling, its mother."

In silence he waited hoping she would just go back to her bedroom but decided to open the door and walk out into the hallway for fear he might wake up Eileen who appeared to have collapsed from emotional exhaustion some time earlier.

"I feel just terrible for the way I've acted," said Dorothy with swollen and red eyes from crying.

"It's okay mother, I think it's best if we all can just get some sleep and talk about it in the morning."

Terrance tapped her on the shoulder hoping it would make her leave but it did not.

"I don't want Eileen hating me but you're my son and I love you, I only had your best interests in mind when I spoke to Eileen about not spending so much time with that woman at the shop. She's become a sort of bad influence on Eileen in my opinion. It seems she just isn't content here anymore now that she has that new friendship."

The only thing he could think to do was give his mother a kiss on the forehead and coax her to return to bed.

"I understand Mom, now go back to bed and calm your head. Where's dad?"

"Oh he hit the sack so hard it nearly knocked me out of bed. He's the only one that doesn't seem to suffer much in times like this. He has ways of calming himself."

She seemed to Terrance to be in a good enough spirit to sleep so he uttered one last 'goodnight' shutting the door behind him hoping she would go back to bed and not stay up all night in the kitchen. He could hear her bedroom door shut as he turned off the lights.

The next day Eileen woke up and quickly got dressed and left the house. She wasn't up to speaking to anyone in the home. Not only had all her efforts the day before went unappreciated when she arrived home she was driven to madness with everyone's efforts to persuade her to think she had been wrongly influenced by the poor innocent Patricia. Nonetheless, she decided to reduce the time she spent at Patricia's store. With a lump in her throat, and an arm full of clothes to return to her friend, she walked slowly through town wishing somehow she would just be hit by a car rather than have to tell Patricia all her efforts had been for nothing.

The bell hanging on the door of the shop rang causing Patricia to bounce out of the stock room with open hands and wide eyes waiting to hear what the reaction was.

"Well, darlin', you gonna keep me waitin'? Tell me what he said?"

Eileen being determined not to cry like a scolded school girl kept her words crisp and clear. "He didn't say a single thing. I think I rather embarrassed him. When I came home he said I have plenty to do around the house without having to keep you from your work."

Patricia gulped and clasped her hands together gently and said, "Well, you weren't no trouble, in fact, it was like you was workin' here."

"That was another cause for high spirits last night, he says, 'no wife of his needs to be working.' He then went on to say, 'As if it isn't bad enough we still live with my parents, you gotta go off and embarrass me further by getting a job behind my back.' That's pretty much the gist of what he said last night. So I've brought back your clothes. Thank you so much Patty. I really did feel beautiful that day. I'll never forget the kindness that you've shown me."

Patricia put her hands on her hips and creased her brow, "You don't mean to tell me yous gonna stop comin' by here just cause your old man don't want you to anymore?!"

Eileen set the clothes down on the counter as it didn't seem Patricia was going to take them and replied, "I'll thank you kindly Ms. Patricia to not give me anymore marriage advice. I have no idea what I was thinking taking advice from a woman who couldn't keep her own man and clearly has no intention of getting married to one again!"

And with that Eileen stormed out leaving Patricia standing there mouth gapping open.

No sooner had she uttered those acid words that she regretted them. Eileen blaming herself bitterly for having been betrayed into saying precisely what she never meant to say took the long walk home so that she wouldn't run into anyone before they left for work that morning. She could only hope that Patricia would forgive her selfishness and come to understand that she had not meant to hurt her.

It was an empty hope. On the following morning, she went to Patricia's shop and it was closed for the day. Deciding to walk all the way to her home, she arrived forty minutes later in a pile of sweat. The morning sun was already high overhead and the road to Patricia's didn't provide much shade.

When she arrived at the front door she could see that the house was shut up but in hopes that Patricia might be hiding inside she knocked anyway. After several efforts she went out back in hope that she might be working in the garden. A young girl who was playing in the field behind the house noticed her and shouted, "Ms. Patty's not home."

"Do you know where she might be?" yelled Eileen feeling too tired to walk to where the little girl was.

"Nope."

The little girl skipped off with a handmade jump rope made out tied up rags.

On her way home she saw Patricia walking out of the post office.

"Patricia, please wait!"

Eileen called out to her and hurried her step when she saw that Patricia had attempted to ignore her calls.

"Really Eileen, I'm very busy, I don't have time for one of our talks today."

Patricia was pretending to look for something in her bag but Eileen knew she was just trying to avoid having a conversation with her.

"I don't want to talk with you I want to give you my apology. You can do with it what you please."

Eileen attempted to put her hand on Patricia's shoulder but Patricia stepped back a pace letting Eileen's hand drop to her side.

Patricia stopped looking through her bag and stared at Eileen blankly waiting for the apology. Eileen not expecting she would actually stop had to think for a moment what she had originally meant to say.

"Thank you for giving me a moment," she said with a dry mouth needing water from her long walk.

"I was very rude yesterday Patricia. You are my friend and I did not mean to hurt you. I am just so desperate to improve my own situation that my thoughts led me to draw comfort from others pain, and that was very bad of me. It is my hope that one day you will be able to forgive me."

She was about to walk away when she saw the look in Patricia's eye soften. Eileen waited hoping Patricia might respond in kindness, and she had not hoped in vain. It was against Patricia's inner nature to hold a grudge against anyone, let alone a dear friend. With an opportunity given her to attempt to replay like for like she was thankful for the freedom to forgive.

"Thank you for that, Eileen. I do appreciate your honesty. But really there is nothing I can do for you now. You have to decide what you need to do. No one can give you that advice. And in the end you will be the one who has to live with your decisions and the merciless comments of others when they talk about your life as if it were just a header in the newspaper column."

Eileen could see that her words had hit a wound a lot deeper than she had realized. She asked pleadingly, "Patricia is there anything I can do to make it up to you?"

Patricia looked back at the post office and with a heavy sigh said, "I myself have often acted presumptuously and I'm afraid I must live with its consequences. The manager of the post office offered to buy my place and I've just signed the deal handing it over to him. I don't fit in here Eileen. You've been a good friend to me and I can see you mean to stay. I'm happy for anyone who is able to find contentment, as it isn't something that has come easily to me in life. But I'm going to head back east. Not sure where yet, I have an aunt who has offered for me to stay with her for a while. Here's the address," she said handing Eileen a piece of paper with an Ohio address on it.

"When will you go?" asked Eileen feeling her throat tighten. She hadn't expected to lose her friend so quickly.

"Can I please help you pack? I'm going to miss you so terribly."

Eileen through her arms around Patricia and squeezed her hard.

Patricia gave up a faint smile, clearly tired from the week's dealings.

"I'm going to miss you too. If you want to be burdened with packing you are more than welcome to help. Lord knows you'd be the only one in town to offer. I've got some phone calls to make but I'll be at the store this afternoon after lunch. See ya later honey."

And with that she left Eileen standing there staring onto the side walk wondering what could be done. She knew there was nothing. When someone like Patricia made up her mind to do something, there was nothing much anyone could do to dissuade her. Patricia had been the type of friend to alter Eileen's outlook on life for the better and she would always feel indebted to her kindness.

That afternoon Eileen came home to find Mrs. Sweetly home early and sitting at the kitchen table and sipping on what she called her cure for her rheumatism. It was oddly the same looking drink that Mr. Sweetly would drink before going to bed when he didn't feel sleepy.

Eileen braced herself for questions on where she had been, but the first words Dorothy Sweetly spoke were quite unlearning, "Come from seeing your friend, Patricia? She's a nice lady it would seem many of us had her all wrong. The town seems to be better for the progress of a new shop!" she said cheerfully.

"Would you care for a class for your rheumatism?"

She held out her hand with a tumbler half empty showing she had already progressed well into her afternoon's activity.

"No thank you Dorothy, but I don't have rheumatism."

"Oh yes, of course, that's silly of me to say. Well, at any rate, I was wrong yesterday when I said those things about your friend. You see, I think you're my only friend and I know you're my daughter in law which probably doesn't make you my friend. Or does it? Well, it's neither here nor there. I should not have said that about your friend and there's no excuse for what I said about you either. It's just maybe since I haven't really had a friend for so long I forgot how hurtful it might be if I said something like that."

She let out a puff of air as if she had been holding it in the entire time she had been speaking.

Eileen walked over and patted her mother in law on the hand.

"Don't worry. I understand what you meant."

Eileen hadn't understood but Patricia had been so forgiving of her just that morning she felt indebted to forgive others just for the sake of forgiving. Eileen took the bottle and capped it, setting it up on the shelf and said while walking towards the door, "I'm going to go upstairs and start changing bed sheets. Call me if you need anything."

Dorothy smiled limply and took another sip of her drink.

Eileen went to the store the next day to help Patricia pack. She felt she hadn't really given enough of an apology or at least enough of an explanation on why she had accepted Terrance's words so quickly. Eileen began to speak when Patricia interrupted,

"It's not really necessary to discuss all of this now is it? There is always tomorrow. And you have to get home to Terrance, I'm sure he's waiting for you, thank you for bringing these boxes and the tape."

"Yes, I suppose I should get going. I have to stop by the market to pick up a few things for supper. Tomorrow I have to go to the Doctor's office in the morning for a check-up but I can stop by after that if you like."

Eileen felt relieved at having had been given a way out of the already awkward conversation, although she had been expecting to spend the rest of the morning helping her friend pack. These next few days would be precious for Eileen as she didn't foresee ever having another friend in her life quite like Patricia.

Patricia took the boxes, smiled her biggest smile and said, "Stop by only if you like. I won't expect you though. But you are always welcome to come by any time of day or night, or even at my place up the hill if I'm not here." Patricia gave Eileen a gentle rub on the shoulder and went back into the storeroom leaving Eileen alone at the doorway.

Patricia had not been oblivious to Eileen's torn feelings on the matter of their friendship. But she had been gracious enough to allow Eileen a way out of extensive time together without looking rude. Eileen felt a lump growing bigger and bigger in her throat the farther she had walked from the storefront. She could barely keep her pace to a walk as she was skipping every second step in an effort to get in before the first tear fell. Deciding not to go to the market she went straight home, swinging the door open wide and leaving it there swinging back and forth as she ran up the stairs. As she shut the door to her bedroom, while still holding the doorknob tightly, she let the salty tears fall.

Patricia had been the closest friend she had ever had and as if all they had been together had been nothing, Eileen was ready to throw it all away due to public gossip and the dictates of Terrance. While wanting to keep peace within her family, Eileen feared her resentment would build with every evening silence. No other person in the house had the desire to talk with her about her day as Patricia had. There was certainly no one that felt Eileen had potential to do anything other than be married and live in her in-laws home. And now even if she wanted to change her mind, and she so badly did, it was too late. Patricia was going to be gone from her life forever. Eileen dried her eyes before Terrance came home. 'Those tears are for Patricia only' she whispered to herself in the mirror as she powdered her nose trying to blunt out the redness.

NEW JOB

Despite, all that had ensued by her supposedly having a job with Patricia, Eileen decided that it was time for a change. Maybe not the type of change that meant cutting ones and hair and showing off ones knees. As this type of change was so rudely dismissed as insanity, Eileen felt it useless to insist upon updating her fashion sense in order to please others. However, if she was going to spend the rest of her life in awkward silence she decided that it would be best for her to have a diversion, like a job. There was a new trolley line installed in town in an effort to get people from either side of town to begin to commute for work. Eileen took it one day and found herself at the counter of the café asking for her old job back. It had been 10 years since she had worked there and not much had changed, her boss gladly told her she was welcome and could start as soon as she liked. Since she felt she could still get all her chores done and work, she didn't really find it necessary to inform the rest of the family about it. However, it was only a matter of time before Terrance found out and came to the shop to investigate.

Eileen rose from behind the counter, and came forward, notepad in hand as if ready to take Terrance's order. He was seated at the same table he always sat at years before they started dating. Eileen held the pencil up to the paper, with a faint questioning lift to her brows. Nothing in her manner or in her voice could have given the most acute observer reason to suspect that her pulse had become very rapid, and that she was feeling strangely breathless.

"Hello dear, what can I get for you?" she said with a nervous smile.

"I have forgotten what it was that you used to order here."

This was far from true, but in her nervousness she was desperate to provoke a response of the smallest kind from Terrance as she had no idea why he had come except maybe to force her to quit at that very moment. Terrance picked up the menu that had been tossed over to the far side of the table by the previous customers and grumbled, "I'm going to need more time to think. Why don't you have a seat while I decide what I want?"

He then put the menu down in front of him, folded his hands and looked up at her.

She sat down and stammered, "Yes, I suppose I could, there aren't very many customers here right now."

Terrance just kept staring at her waiting for her to say something. Feeling the necessity to get to the point of his visit she allowed her apology to roll out of her mouth like water from a broken pipe.

"I know I should have asked your permission before returning to work here Terrance. But I also knew that you were sure to say no and that was something I just couldn't accept. I beg for you to forgive me on that indiscretion, but please try to understand that I very much want to work here again."

Terrance unfolded his hands and picked up the menu again. While scanning the breakfast specials he calmly asked, "Am I not providing well enough for you at home Eileen? Do you not have everything that you wish for, or at least desperately need?"

Eileen could see that this job was going to be more of a hit to his pride than his temper. She wanted to explain herself calmly so that he would understand.

"You have always given me everything I want and need by way of material things, Terrance."

For the first time in her married life, Eileen found herself without words to express her feelings. How could she tell her husband that she had become bored with caring for him? That she wanted something other than the price of flour to talk about when he came home from work. That she wanted people to talk to while she worked instead of sitting in an empty house, working only to find her family would come home and carry on the silence in the evening when they returned.

Terrance's brown eyes stared hard at her, penetrating her very countenance and causing her to feel a chill. She lifted her arms to fold them but before she could complete the task he grabbed her left hand into his and held it solidly in his. His fingers began to twist and turn her gold wedding band around her finger. Continuing to look up at her as he played with it, he asked, "Have I hurt you Eileen? I didn't mean to! Please don't give up on me as a husband. I will try harder. But if you're thinking of saving up enough money so you can leave me and go back to Illinois with your folks, you got to know that I just can't live with myself if that were to happen. That new friend of yours has put all sorts of ideas into your head, and it just ain't right Eileen. You are my wife! You are supposed to be with me for better or for worse!"

She drew her hand away, trying to reply as lightly as possible but the mention of Patricia caused her nervousness to turn to annoyance.

"Good grief Terrance, what things you have worked up in your head! I would no sooner cut off my right leg than return to living with my parents. What are you thinking?"

Terrance now embarrassed by his needless ranting, sat with his hands in his lap and his broad shoulders slumped over. His eyes were staring down as he inquired, "Then tell me why you are doing this? If you don't have a reason, or if you don't need the money, then why in the world would you want to work? And you can't tell me that it has nothing to do with that Patricia!"

His voice now seemed to be rising with frustration and he looked as if he was going to rise to go. Eileen interrupted, "Terry, you know I love you. And I love caring for you. But as we don't have any children yet, there isn't enough to keep me busy at home. Now if you really want to have a heart to heart about this, let's just go home and talk about it. You are mistaken in my intentions."

As she spoke she reached her hands across the table hoping he would put his into hers but he refused. Her eyes lifted swiftly to his face, and as swiftly sank again.

"Terrance, if it bothers you that much, I can quit this job. But I beg of you not to ask me to do that just for your pride. Patricia has not convinced me to do this. I just miss being useful. It's a decision I made all on my own. I do still have a mind to make some decisions regarding my life on my own."

Something between panic and indignation seized her; panic because her being forced to quit was clearly imminent, and she was far from knowing how she could approach her employer after having begged him to take her back despite not needing the help. Eileen stood up in a rush accidently hitting the table with her leg causing the napkin holder to rattle against it. Rubbing her leg she uttered explosively, "I'll let my boss know this will be my last day and I'll see you at home!"

She was half way across the room when Terrance gave a short laugh and said, "Wait just a minute hot head. You never wait for me to speak. I haven't made my order yet."

She turned slowly towards him again hoping that the color hadn't shown too badly in her cheeks, not realizing she was the brightest shade of tomato red he had ever seen, she smiled and said, "I see! Then what is it I can get for you, Terrance?"

He looked up at her with an amused smile knowing full well she would never have forgotten what he liked, "The usual, Eileen, I'll have the usual."

She wrote down on the paper that she would slip to the cook.....forgetting that she had told him previously that she forgot what he liked. She looked up as she hit a period firmly on the pad in her hand and said, "Should I bring a cup of coffee now or wait until your breakfast comes?"

"Coffee sounds good right about now, that would be real nice. Thanks."

She could feel his gaze following her as she took the paper back to the counter. She picked up the carafe and poured a steaming cup into the nicest porcelain mug she could find. Her hands were slightly shaking from their conversation. Terrance had never been a harsh man and so she didn't know why it was she stood before him in such uneasiness.

When breakfast was served up he ate with the same savage bites he used to take. She stood watching over him until the last bite as her anxiety was rising at how the day would end, still not knowing if she was to turn in her apron now or go home preparing to come into work the next day.

Terrance wiped his mouth with his napkin, put his money on the table, including tip from what she could tell. He stood squarely in front of her in a moment of silence. She had grown accustomed to his silent moments but this was a little uncomfortable. Eileen opened her mouth to speak when before she could utter a word, Terrence lifted her head up to his mouth and kissed her long and hard on the lips. Letting go he held on to her shoulders fearing she might turn and run. She stared at him with startled eyes, and managed to say faintly, "Terrance what are you doing? People are going to see you!"

He lightened his grasp slightly in case he was hurting her but still not letting go.

"I forgot how pretty you looked in your apron."

He said this with a twinkle of amusement in his eyes as he could see he left her utterly speechless, something which rarely happened to Eileen.

She broke off and turned her head to hide the fact that she was about to cry. He took her hand and held it to his heart and said in a whisper, "Eileen, you can work here as long as you like, just promise me you'll come home to me when your day is done. Don't ever think of not being mine. You have my heart and without it, I can't go on living."

She did not respond to this, but began to wipe the tears from her eyes. After a moment of watching her in silence, he asked softly, "Have I scared you off completely my dear? If you hadn't thought of leaving me before, I think that maybe you are thinking about it just now."

"No - oh, no!" she said.

"I think that if ever I have come to admire your words, now is one time that may keep me satisfied forever and a day."

The tears were now rolling down her cheeks uncontrollably but she didn't care. Eileen threw her arms around his neck and kissed him boldly on the mouth despite the fact that some customers had just entered the store and sat down. Terrance didn't really understand what she was going on about but got the impression she was happy and all was going to be well again. He wiped her cheek with his hand and then holding the back of her head to steady it for another kiss, said cheerfully, "Then you had better get back to work and make us some money. I think we should plan a trip to visit your folks this winter."

With that he gave her a goodbye peck and ran out the door with a new spring in his step.

Eileen feeling a bit tangled in thought, attempted to clear Terrence's dishes from the table. Gaining some measure of composure she took them back to the wash room. Feeling like the richest girl in the world, Eileen found herself regretting somewhat having to stay at the diner the rest of the afternoon.

About a month past and Eileen decided to walk past the shop where Patricia used to sell. Her job was going well and Terrance had just bought the bus tickets for them to go visit her folks. She looked at herself in the dusty glass window of Patricia's shop. Her hair was growing out and she was thinking of getting it curled upward on the ends. She wasn't quite ready to pin it back in a bun like her mother in law would have liked her to do by now. And besides that Terrance liked to play with it behind her neck when they sat on the front porch after supper. He wasn't aware that he was doing it. Eileen loved it when his finger would go through her hair although she was often embarrassed when he did it in public. She would never forget this summer and everything that had happened. Somewhere between spring flowers and apple harvest she found the courage to begin living life for the first time without fear.

As she walked past the summer vegetable vendors she noticed that Mrs. Leighton was sporting a short haircut! In fact, she had on tights with her dress and the dress was of the latest fashion. Eileen couldn't help but to approach her and ask what had brought on the sudden change.

"Mrs. Leighton, you are looking very fine today! Is that a new haircut?"

She bobbed it up with her hand as if very proud and yet shy all at the same time and said, "Well, I liked your new haircut at the picnic last month so much I decided to get one for myself. The husband really has taken a fancy to it you know."

Eileen smiled and said to herself in amazement, "Well, you just never know."

The End

A MORNING TO MEANDER

"Just great," whispered Fred as the rusted out screw broke in half inside the bolt he was trying to tighten. Not only was his tractor broken, but he was late for his doctor appointment. Still slumped over the engine, he could hear his wife's hurried footsteps entering the barn. Before she had a chance to speak, Fred looked up and said with a wrinkled brow, "I don't think it's going to happen today."

"But you promised!" pleaded Sylvia earnestly.

"I didn't promise nothin, you're the one putting words into my mouth!" replied Fred gruffly as he pretended to keep bolting the screw that he knew would have to be taken out.

"I specifically asked you if you would take the morning off and go visit the doctor, and you said...."

Fred cut in before she could finish her sentence, "I said, 'We'll see', and now I guess you see, that I'm not gonna do it!"

He turned back to the engine hoping she would go away, but knowing that he had no choice but to grab his oil soiled cloth and clean up the best he could before getting in their truck and heading to town.

Fred was the farmer of the old fashioned American type. He woke up each morning at the crack of dawn; sometimes before then, at 4am, and began his morning by pulling up his faded blue jean overalls that always hung near his bed on his old pine chair that he had hand carved 19 years prior. The alarm no longer needed to go off as after so many years of living the same schedule his body just naturally woke up at the same time. He and his wife, who he fondly called, 'Sylvie', had lived a quiet life over the past 55 years in the same house, on the same farm, and life had treated them kindly.

The doctor's office was empty when they walked in. Fred was glad for the emptiness. He didn't make an appointment because in the small town where he lived, the walk in clinic didn't usually have a line up. However, this being said, if there had been just one of the town's residents in the waiting room that day, he would risk the entire town knowing about it. At age 73, he didn't really care what anyone thought but he had heard of people going to the doctors thinking they had heart problems and it just ended up being gas. So why worry everyone and make him feel old when he knew he had years of work left in him? Fred and his wife sat in the empty waiting room for what seemed like forever and a day until a middle aged nurse in a white uniform cut the silence by opening a door that needed oiling.

"Mr. Pickens, the doctor will see you now."

Fred sat down on the cold examination table feeling the paper rip underneath his overalls. The nurse came in and took his blood pressure, checking his tongue, and asking a few simple questions that he often answered on his yearly physicals. Then the doctor came in reading the chart and while not looking up asked, "How are things Fred? It's been awhile since we've seen you."

Dr. Harris was not thrilled to have to see Fred on a non-annual appointment. Dr. Harris had been moved in from the big city and old timers like Fred didn't respect his position in life. Every time Fred looked at him he had the feeling he was thinking, '*what can this young punk kid do for me?*

It was the type of self-esteem barrier Dr. Harris hated, which made him nervous. Of course that ended up making him look even less competent than Fred expected him to be.

Before the examination was finished Fred asked abruptly, "What do I need to do Doc?"

Fred knew what the answer was going to be; high blood pressure. But he wanted to try to get things under control without taking medicine. He knew this would mean eating differently as his wife had been preaching the philosophy of a no fat diet for months now. Life on the farm could be hard work. In his younger years it never really mattered how much he ate because he worked breakfast off by lunch and lunch off by dinner. And dinner, well, he figured he slept that off.

"It seems your blood pressure has reached dangerously high levels," said the doctor knowing that Fred had already been warned about this at his previous visit.

"And your heart stress test showed that you are a future candidate for a heart attack. You need to start watching how you eat and learn to relax more."

The doctor looked at Fred empathetically as he knew for a man like him, a life change at his age would be a challenge.

"What do I eat that could cause me any trouble?"

Fred raised his arms up in mock confusion at the thought of having to change his diet.

His wife rolled her eyes and said in an undertone, "how about bacon and eggs every morning for the last two decades with the exception of biscuits and gravy on Sunday?"

"Oh." Fred looked down at his knees defeated. His wife had been on him for years to change his diet but it was only up until recently that he was beginning to see the need for it himself. He had begun to have painful tugging pains in his chest area and sudden shortness of breath.

She then added, "And full cream in your coffee."

All of the proof lay flat out on the examination room floor. Fred had to give up his life long battle and do things the *tree huggers* way as he called it.

"Okay okay! Fine! I told you I'd go see the doctor and I'm here aren't I? I'm not even really sick anyways, it's like he's saying I'm gonna be sick, but ain't there yet."

Now sitting there feeling vulnerable, he realized it was good he had come in. Not wanting to give his wife the satisfaction he simply said, "Thanks Doc, when do I need to check in with you again?"

"Not so fast," said the doctor trying not to laugh at his eagerness to leave, "Here is the name of a blood pressure monitor that will help you see if you're improving. Let Mrs. Pickens cook good healthy foods for you without a fight."

He looked over at her and she smiled gratefully for not having been reprimanded for having been the one to have cooked unhealthy for him all those years.

"And take a day off Fred, it won't kill you. Plenty of men your age are already retired. Just take some time to enjoy life!"

He patted Fred on the shoulder as they walked out, hoping Fred would take his advice.

On the way home from the doctor's office Fred and Sylvia drove their 1984 blue Ford truck to the drug store and bought the blood pressure monitor the doctor had talked about.

He and his wife had been married since they were 18 years old. Sylvia was a good wife who always made use of everything on the farm. They had fresh eggs, bacon, and milk topped with cream any time they wanted. It wasn't easy for her to begin cooking things made without butter and oil but she talked to her neighbor friend and got a lot of good tips. She even went and bought herself a steamer so that she could make their vegetables without any fat.

For months she had been sneaking in fat free things into Fred's meals but he obviously hated it. Most nights he would take two bites of biscuit before he could swallow one bite of broccoli. Fred loved eating his '*fruit of the land*' as he called it; he just loved it drenched in butter. Silvia couldn't help feeling some responsibility and remorse over having allowed him to eat that way all these years and now him having to suffer the consequences. She knew it would take a doctor's orders to get Fred to think on her side of the dinner table.

The life of a midwest farmer hasn't changed much over the years. There are fewer farmers to be sure, but the hard work and ethics that kept Fred's grandfather going so long ago is the same thing that keeps most going in present day. At any one time you may travel across the corn fields of Iowa, Nebraska, and Minnesota, and find the solitary dwellings of men who helped put bread on the tables of America for over a century. Fred was no exception. He liked his life the way it had been, and had he the chance to do it all over again, he wouldn't change a thing.

The next morning, while it was still dark outside and the morning dew sat heavily on the oak trees outside, he got up to make his morning cup of coffee. Putting on his overalls from the day before, as he had only done some light chores after his doctor appointment, he grabbed yesterday's paper to read over the daily news.

When Sylvia had found out the day before that her worst nightmare had come true and Fred was at risk of having a heart problem, she forced on him a conversation from every which way on how life on the farm was going to have to change.

"I want us to enjoy our Golden years Fred, and it's not going to be very enjoyable for me to drink my morning cup of coffee with you laying in a grave out back. I would much rather have you here beside me living and breathing."

Sylvia's hair style had not changed much since 1973, and even then, it was a little outdated. She went into town to get her hair done once a week at the beauty shop where she had her short hair curled up and pinned. Then all during the week, she would wear a bandana over it to keep it clean. Today she wasn't wearing her bandana and Fred took this as a sign that she was determined to keep an eye on him and his relaxing if it killed her. The notion was anything but relaxing to a man like Fred.

"What do you want me to do Sylvie, stop living?"

"No, I want you to take a day off every once in a while. You know, smell the roses. If you're dead that's all you're going to be doing anyway - pushing up roses, so why not just see how it's going to be and get a head start." Sylvia had always found that the best way to deal with Fred when he was being stubborn was to try and be as direct as possible. If he sensed her being over emotional, he would turn and run in the other direction of wherever her ideas were taking her.

Fred knew that his recent doctor visit had brought Sylvia stress that he didn't mean for her to have. But, in all honesty, he really did not know how to do what she was asking of him.

"What am I supposed to do with a day off anyways?" Fred asked his wife with a look that expressed sheer terror of what she might say. He had heard of one farmer, the next county over who went crazy in his old age and ran around the yard in his granddaughter's ballet skirt. Why bother going outside if you didn't want to work? This was a question that Fred had been pondering ever since that terrible day at the doctor's office when he told him to take a day off.

Why bother staying in the house if you weren't sick and didn't want to eat or go to bed? What else was there for a man to do but work hard with his hands and try to make something happen in life? Sylvia could see the stressful look in his eyes as he stared at her wondering.

"You could try a new hobby." She said cheerfully walking over to the kitchen pretending like she was drying dishes that had been sitting in the dry rack overnight.

He laughed as if that was never going to happen.

"Why don't you just meander around the yard for a while, the fresh air might do you good." She walked over to him and took his arm guiding him towards the door. He went readily but with a heavy sigh.

"What's that supposed to mean, 'meander'?" Fred asked pulling his arm away from her tight grasp but heading for the door all the same.

"Meandering is sort of like taking a saunter, you know, an aimless ramble." She said still trying to be light hearted about the concept but knowing Fred was dreading it.

Fred looked up at her like she was delusional. Sylvia could see that she was getting nowhere with him in trying to explain herself, but would need to throw him in the deep end of the pool in order to get him started. "Just take a stroll and get lost in your thoughts!" She said this with a bit of exasperation in her voice. After so many years of marriage, she had never seen her husband like this before. He looked like a broken man, walking with his head held low at the thought of having to take a walk for no reason. She looked at him putting a hand on his shoulder and said, "Fred, lots of people take a walk in their fields, stop looking so sad like I just said I thought you should move to the nursing home in town. Now get out of here so I can get some work done in the house!"

He put his hand on top of hers and said soulfully, "I don't think I know how to meander, honey. I never did it before."

She put her hands through his thinning gray hair and smiled. All his life he had worked so hard and now, when he could clearly slow down a bit, he was depressed at the thought of having to do it.

"Okay then, you aren't meandering, just think of it as inspecting the farm. You can't get distracted though by trying to fix something," she said with a sudden raise of her finger, "you just have to make a mental check list of what you can work on tomorrow, how's that?"

"I guess I can do that." Fred said putting on his red cap and shut the door softly.

The sun was just coming up and beams of red and orange were making the dew-laden fields sparkle like glittering snow. Fred always did like the smell of fresh morning air. He liked the feel of the soil when it was still cool to the touch before the warm summer sun warmed everything up. He wouldn't be touching anything today though. He would need to be satisfied with just looking. Deciding to walk down to the riverbed that lay on the left side of the property, he picked up a walking stick to shoo away any possible snakes that might be wandering in his path. It was slightly windy and so he was glad he had taken his hat as the river was lined with pine trees that would make it feel even cooler.

The path leading to the river wasn't one he often took as it was the farthest point on the property from the fields and the barn. The river is what made the property so lucrative though. Fred had never thought of selling the place, but had he wanted too, he could have made a mint on just the fact that it had a river going through it. The path was overgrown causing him to begin his mental checklist of things to do the next day, starting with cutting the grass that was growing over the footpath. Fred never fished much but sometimes guests would come who would want to and he didn't want anyone thinking he was getting too old to take care of his yard.

Fred's place was always clean but the one problem with having a river on the property was that you never knew what might be rolling up upon the shoreline. Seeing as he didn't bring a trash bag, Fred decided to try and use his stick to pull up some of the leaves and trash he might find on the shore so that it could be easily picked up the next day. The point in the river where Fred was standing had more of a creek-like appearance. The water was babbling over the slippery rocks and making nice morning music for Fred to hum along to. One rock in particular caught his interest. It was very near the shoreline and had something attached to it, something that looked like a gum wrapper. Fred slowly inched his way closer, leaning as far into the river as he could so that he could reach his walking stick in the water and pull the wrapper up onto the shoreline. A swift gust of wind made him totter for a moment and as he gained his balance again, a fish jumped up out of the water and almost in slow motion looked to be mouthing, "come on in, the water is fine!"

With no time for even a blink, Fred found himself sitting in the riverbed, soaked up to his shoulders.

The fish was long gone, the wrapper was still stuck on the rock, and Fred was wondering how on earth he was going to explain this to his wife.

He walked briskly back to the house, beginning to shiver from his damp overalls. Grateful he had just oiled the door hinges the week before he carefully took off his boots and tried walking slowly into the back room where he could change and make a quick exit.

"Fred, is that you? Why are you back so soon?"

Her voice was getting louder as she spoke giving Fred the impression that she was walking towards him. He quickened his pace and ran into the bedroom shutting the door. She heard the door shut and entered, "why did you come back so soon, you've only been gone a quarter of an hour?"

She searched the room only to see the back of Fred's head and the rest of his body in the closet clearly changing his clothes.

"Why in the world are you changing your clothes?"

Upon walking closer she saw the wet heap of overalls on the floor.

Fred turned in embarrassment as he had only made it past the overalls and his boxer briefs were dripping wet. "I told you I'm not good at taking a walk! I fell in the river bed."

"How did you do that?" Sylvia asked perplexed as the riverbed itself had an earthy shoreline that made it hard to get ones feet wet.

"I thought I saw something in the water and I went to pull it out." Fred said annoyed at trying to hide his secret from his wife, feeling like a little boy who had just gotten his hand caught in the cookie jar, he took a step away from the closet to fully expose how deep he had actually fallen in. Fred was soaked to the bone.

Sylvia put her hands on her hips and smiled empathetically. "You can't expect to be good at it right away; I suppose you tried your best. Maybe that's enough for today and you can just do some things around the house. But I'll tell you this, Frederick Pickens; Tuesday's are going to be your days to meander if it kills you. You can work Mondays hard like you want, then rest on Tuesdays, then work again on Wednesdays, then Thursday is the market day which will take the better part of the day so you can meander after, and that gives you Friday and Saturday to work the farm before church day. But you're going to have to start sleeping in until I get up, and coming in before dark. It evens out all your days to give you some balanced and much needed rest. Today might have been a flop but you'll just have to get back to the drawing board and figure it out for the next time!"

She walked out of the room leaving Fred to sigh in his puddle of clothes; Fred knew there was no arguing with his wife when she used his first and last name. He knew she was not angry because she didn't use his middle name, Emerson. Nevertheless, she was determined to make him learn how to take it easy and once Sylvia was determined, there was no stopping her. At least he had tomorrow to look forward to when he could work again.

That afternoon Sylvia said she wanted to go to town on her own. Fred would have thought she would want him along to keep an eye on him but instead she said she'd be back shortly and he was to stay out of trouble. When she came in, she had a big brown grocery bag filled with things that he couldn't see. He assumed it was filled with something that was going to taste bad, like broccoli.

Sure enough, that night they had a nice piece of steamed trout with a side of broccoli and a squeeze of lemon. It was a quiet but uncomplaining meal. Sylvia went to finish up the dishes and Fred moved into the living room to do some reading in his easy chair. He had a copy of the Farmer's Almanac for that year and was trying to decide if he should wait until closer to fall before he planted his winter vegetables or just risk it and do it early since the frost was supposed to come early this year.

Sylvia walked in the room with a long cardboard box. She held it out to Fred who looked up and put the ripped piece of toilet paper he used as a bookmark into his almanac.

"What is that?" He asked surprised as she put it on his lap.

"It's a telescope! Open it up and take a look."

"Well what's it for?"

"What do you mean what's it for, you look at the stars with it, I guess."

She got down on her knees in front of him with her reading glasses sitting on the end of her nose and began opening it.

"Since your walk didn't go so well, I thought maybe you might enjoy doing a little star gazing at night."

"Star gazing huh" he pulled the telescope out of the box and opened it trying to look uninterested as possible but secretly he was beaming. Ever since he had been about 10 years old he wanted a telescope of his very own but he gave up asking his folks for one. They never had the money and his Pa always said, "What do you need a telescope for? Just walk outside and you got all the stars right up above your head. You ain't never gonna be a rocket scientist anyway!"

But the stars were always so amazing to him. They shone so brightly and no matter how hard he looked there was always one that seemed to be way up there, just blinking and he wished so badly he could look just a little bit closer. He never told anyone that story.

He looked at his wife with a gentle smile that she took for him patronizing her. But what his smile really meant was that he was more in love with her than he had ever been. After all those years of just working the farm, and eating the eggs she cooked up for him. She somehow figured out the inner most desires of his heart. That sealed it for Fred. He was going to do his best to learn how to meander if it killed him. He wanted to live so he could take care of her in her old age the way she had been taking care of him his whole life.

The next morning, Sylvia figured she would break Fred in easy since he had been so good about the steamed fish the night before. She poached two eggs and cut up a cantaloupe, sprinkling it with a little salt just how he liked it. Then she put black coffee on the table and the 2% milk next to it, leaving it up to him whether or not he'd just rather go black and bitter for the day rather than taint it within anything less than full cream.

He enjoyed breakfast, only adding the milk in after his second cup. He found that it tasted better with the '*watered down milk*' as he called it, after you drank the first cup like, '*mud*.' It was no complaint to Sylvia's cooking, just the facts. Happy to get outside and do some real work he walked over to his faithful tractor.

This was his weekly project. It was now over 60 years old and beginning to resist repairs at increasing rates. He used to use it for farming crops that he would sell on the outside, but now he mostly just used it to maintain the one acre piece that they still grew things on for themselves and their stand near the mailbox during the summer time. 'Old Red' as he called her was an International brand Farm-all M series tractor. Fred had a feeling that there was a worn worm gear in the steering, which was causing the front wheels to shake in high gear. Even at low speed, no matter how hard he turned the steering wheel, the front wheels wouldn't budge.

No matter what he did, nothing seemed to work at fixing the problem. Fred was beginning to wonder if he and the tractor were sharing a parallel existence and if, like Old Red, Fred was going to see the day when all he could do was sit in the barn feeling useless. After spending about an hour on the tractor, as was his daily routine, he then went over to the next stall in the barn to milk Bessie, his prized milk cow.

Bessie was the best milking cow a farmer could ever want. She was the only cow he had left on the farm and she had plenty of good years left in her.

"Well, Bessie how are we doing today?"

Bessie milked two times a day, once in the morning and then once in the evening time. There was a sign out on the mailbox that read fresh farm eggs and milk and that alone brought enough customers to sell a couple bottles a week. If there was left over they either drank it up, or took it to town for their friends.

"Looks like I'll be drinking less and less of your fine cream Bessie. The Doc's got me on a diet."

A sound up the road told Fred that Rod Taylor was coming up the drive. Rod was a teenager in town, full of useless energy. In an effort to guide him in the right direction, Fred had been letting him come by every week and work on an old motorbike he had in the back of the barn. Over the weekend, Rod did his final work on it and asked to take it out for a test run. He had taken it the day before to tool around town and see if it was road worthy. He could hear voices like Rod had someone on the back with him but opted to keep milking Bessie until the need arose to have to get up and see who it was. If today was to be a workday, he couldn't take off time chatting with Rod like he'd been doing, he'd have to concentrate his time and get some real farm work done.

Rod pulled up the bike behind the barn planning on checking with Fred to make sure it was okay to keep it another day. The bike had been running good but there were a few noises he wasn't sure about and he wanted to ask Fred's advice. On the back of the bike was Suzy Baker, the prettiest girl in town. She hadn't given Rod a second glance until he pulled up in front of the gas station with Fred's motorbike. She was walking out with a girlfriend drinking a juice box drink when Rod was walking up to pay for his gasoline. He convinced her to go for a ride with him, put his helmet on her head, and giggling the rest of the way they headed for Fred and Sylvia's farm.

Rod had already told Suzy he needed to stop to ask his pops, if they could take a spin. Fred wasn't Rod's father but Rod's family wasn't the type he'd want to take Suzy home too. His father had never been around much since a very young age and his mother was overly critical of any girl Rod brought home. He always called Fred 'Pops' as a sort of nick name so he figured he would let the facade go for a while so as not to scare her off on their first date.

He got off the bike and helped Suzy off too. Then he leaned in close to her ear and whispered, "You want to get him started? Tell him you prefer John Deere tractors over International, then you'll get him so riled up we'll be able to take the motorbike for sure, he won't know if he's going or coming."

Suzy giggled like she had done since she first got on the bike and whispered, "I couldn't do that! He'll think I'm being disrespectful! You do it, and I'll learn for next time."

She poked him and he breathed in heavy ready to face the old bull in its stall. Both walked arm and arm into the barn where Fred was milking Bessie.

"Hey, Pops, did I tell you I saw a new John Deere in town? Man, was it nice. I think it might be a real game changer for old Man Bradley's farm, it looks like the next best thing to having yourself a brand new Ford pickup."

Fred turned slowly as if he was trying to control some inner fire that had just been sparked inside of him. Seeing that Rod had brought a lady friend he realized, his useless energies were at it again, looking for a show. Rod was a good kid at heart and Fred decided to help him out by inviting the girl up to the house.

"Son, I think we had better take this conversation out on the porch. A barn's no way to introduce company to the farm. Sylvia's got some fresh squeezed lemonade in the 'fridge. Your girl can help her bring it out. What I'm about to say regarding your lack of education on the finest piece of farm equipment this country has ever seen, the ladies don't need to be hearing."

Rod laughed and winked at Suzy and she giggled trying to muffle her laughter as Fred was obviously ready to school Rod on the defects of John Deere verses International tractors and it was going to be a whole pitcher of lemonade before he'd be finished. Truth be told,

Rod had run into Sylvia at the strip mall the day before when she went to buy the telescope. She asked Rod to not stop coming by just because the motorbike was fixed and explained that she might need some help distracting Fred from his work now that the doctor asked him to take it easy.

Seeing Suzy with Rod, who she knew from town, walking up the driveway with Fred already starting to talk his tractor talk, she tried to hide her prideful smile as the tactic of distracting him for a good hour while he went on about which tractor he prefers, had worked. Rod stayed out on the porch with him. The two of them sat back on the two white pine rocking chairs that were always dusted off nicely in case company came in. Sylvia met Suzy at the door and ushered her inside, Suzy still giggling profusely.

"Well, Fred. What do you have to say about that? John Deere has been around for a long time. How does International compare?"

Rod pretended as if he had never heard this conversation before, and Fred assumed he had just not paid attention the first time, and so he felt the need to repeat the priceless information for him again.

Rocking back and looking out into the grassy paths to the right of the house, near where he had meandered the day before, Fred said, "Rod, I will try to sum it up in simple words so that you can understand. Not being a farmer by trade, I realize the razzmatazz of a big company with shiny green tractors could sway anyone's good opinions. But this is what I know about the matter…"

Thus began a long dissertation on the original founding in the 1900's and its variety of letter series that ran well into the 1950's. Fred finished with, "basically Rod, if it's not red, it's dead!"

Rod had worked hard to shake off the small town reputation that went with growing up where he had been born. But when push came to shove he could chew the fat with the best of them, having grown up around farmers like Fred his whole life. However, one thing he could never get enough of was Fred's passion for International tractors. Talking about Old Red seemed to make Fred look young again.

Both laughed rocking back on their chairs as if they were 12 and riding their first roller coaster.

Bessie gave out a big moan due to the fact that she was still full and Fred hadn't finished his job. He patted Rod on the shoulder and said, "Excuse me Rod, I've got some chores to finish, you go ahead and enjoy your lemonade with the girls."

Rod not expecting this sudden change of the diversion plan, jumped up with his blue jeans, black leather jacket and fancy button up collared shirt and said, "Let me do it Fred, you stay here with the girls."

Fred looked at Rod like he had hit his head and lost his mind. "Stay with the girls? I'm not the one trying to woo one. What did you bring her over here for if you didn't want to make yourself look good with Sylvie's cooking? She's got a cake in there and everything like she was expecting your visit. Now you go on in there and learn a thing or two about women. I've got a lady out in the barn that will give you a good kick if you go poking around where you aren't wanted."

Desperate to not be caught by Sylvia alone without him, Rod ran after Fred who was already half way to the barn and said, "I'll do some learning then! I don't want my gal seeing me sitting with women while you're out working."

Fred chuckled as it wasn't like Rod to care much about work ethics. But as Fred's father had taught him at a young age, work ethics can be learned when the energy is right. And in Fred's opinion, Rod was coming along just fine despite his derelict father and lazy mother who had done their best to make a mess out of Rod in Fred's opinion.

Bessie had eyes as big as moon pies with eye lashes that gently swayed back and forth similar to those of a giraffe Fred had seen in a magazine once about the subject. If she ate more hay than he had expected that day he would joke that she had better be careful or she was off to the meat market. But his wife knew the truth; this calf was going to be one of their last projects on the farm. After years of having to farm and raise animals for food, Fred now loved his farm and everything that was on it, including its animals, as if they were a part of the family. Life was beginning to show signs of needing to take ease. They had paid off their home, and could now work for daily needs not having to worry too much about the future. But one thing Fred was not about to give up was his furry farm friends.

"Okay Fred, tell me how it's done." Rod said contently sitting down on the wooden stool Fred had been sitting on earlier. Bessie's head swayed over to Fred's general direction as if to say, '*You have got to be kidding me!*' Fred rubbed her head apologetically and said, "It'll be okay girl."

Turning to Rod he said in the most serious of tones, "You've got to rub your hands together and try to get them warmed up." Rod began feverishly rubbing his hands together, feeling nervous sweat collecting under his jacket.

"It's amazing how big a girl Bessie is, huh? I can see why she won all those awards you always talk about," Rod laughed nervously holding his hands out so Fred could see he was ready.

"Yeah, she's a big animal so you need to make sure and get out of the way if she gets cranky." Bessie had won awards for her milk, not her size, but he figured now was not the time to correct Rod on non-essentials. He walked over to Rod and squatted down, giving Bessie a pat on the side so she knew everything was going to be okay.

"Now take your hands like this" said Fred putting Rod's hands on the two front teats thinking it might be easier for Rod to start off that way, "You're going to want to squeeze, but do it gently as the milks has to fill up first before it'll come out. Do you understand?"

Rod now had his game face on and like he was going in for a tackle he said, "Yeah, I got this Fred, thanks."

He began working his hands in a gentle motion, pulling up and down. Fred slowly took his hands off of Rods and let him go at it alone. The first squirts of milk began to come out. Even Fred was surprised that the kid got it to work on his first try. He had about 5 gallons and Fred switched out his bucket. Usually Bessie could produce a couple more but a new milker like Rod would normally get tired so Fred asked, "You want me to take over there sport, it looks like you got the majority of it, I can get the rest of it if you want."

Rod, now having a rhythm and not wanting to stop almost sang out, "No man, I got it, don't you worry about it just sit back and relax, this is way easier than I thought!"

At that moment Bessie let out a groan causing Rod to jump, only when he jumped he didn't let go of her teats but fell off his stool pulling her with him. This jolt was more than Bessie could bear; she reared up knocking the bucket of milk all over Rod and his fine motorbike riding clothes.

Fred, who had stepped back behind Rod to watch, now grabbed Bessie by her rope and soothingly called out, "Down girl, it's okay, shhhhh."

He looked over at Rod who was now getting up and had hay stuck to his milk soaked jeans and asked, "Are you okay Rod, did you get kicked?"

Rod laughed and said, "No, only my pride. Wow, I bet I'll really impress Suzy with this story."

Fred sat down and began milking Bessie just quickly wanting to get it over with as she was showing signs of utter annoyance. Rod stared at her like she had embarrassed him on purpose and said, "Hey Fred do you mind if I rinse off out back before we go back up to the house?"

Still milking he said, "Sure, there's a tap out back that has hot water and you should find a brush that you can use to clean yourself off. Once we get in the house I'll let you borrow a pair of pants and we'll put your jeans in the dryer."

"Thanks Fred."

Rod walked around back leaving Fred and Bessie alone again as they were before. Bessie now having calmed down was chewing on a bunch of hay that Fred had given her when he was calming her down.

"Well, Bessie, it seems I'm supposed to take a day off tomorrow and go help Sylvie at the market, so I'm going to put out extra hay for you. But don't worry, if you decide to get fat off of it, then I'll probably meander over here mid-afternoon and give you some more. But don't tell the wife."

He picked up the scantily filled milk bucket and put the stool back where he always kept it, giving Bessie a wink before closing the barn door.

The next day, after they got home from market, but before heading out for his meandering, Fred looked over at Sylvia who was wiping down the counter top. She had never complained about not having had children. But he knew that there were moments in her life when she wished they had done so. Now that they were older, most of their friends had grandchildren running around the property and their lives were filled up with watching whatever it was their grandkids were attempting to do. Life on their farm was relatively quiet for them compared to all that. They had no little league kids to cheer on, or any elementary school performances to go to and pretend like they were enjoying themselves for the sake of the children. He looked up at Sylvia and said, "That Suzy is a cute girl ain't she? Seems to like Rod real well."

Sylvia nodded and kept wiping down the table and was moving onto the refrigerator.

"Who knows, maybe they'll end up married and bring their young ones over here to play on the farm."

Sylvia laughed and decided that Fred's conversation must be an effort to get out of meandering and so she put down her rag and said, "That would be real nice Fred. But what would be even nicer is if you would get on with your meandering today. What is it that you have decided to do?"

"I'm going fishing," he said getting up from the table and heading for the door, which was directly off their open dining room.

The lake that Fred used to fish at was a good two mile walk down the road. It had belonged to an older farmer who had long passed. He left the land to his children who lived in the big city, but allowed the local towns people to use the lake for fishing whenever they liked. The site of the old dilapidated farmhouse was always depressing to Fred and he never went back much after the last local family member had died.

Fishing seemed to be a pretty good meandering thing to do. Not ready to go back to the riverbed, he decided to revive his former childhood recreation and check the old lake out. The grass was tall but the road still had a two tracks leading to the broken down fence that was wide open at the lakes best beachfront shoreline. It wasn't common to have lakes in this part of the county, another reason why Fred found it such a shame the children didn't appreciate the property for what it really was; a real farmers haven. Not only could one grow their crops, but they could fish too. He didn't know why it bothered him so much that the farm lay empty seeing as it meant he could fish any time he wanted. Pulling out his coffee can of earthworms, and finding a rock to sit on, he noticed something nearby moving in the bushes. Thinking it might be a stray dog he put his pole down and went to look and see.

Out of the grass came a golden hair little boy about age 10 with freckles and bright blue-green eyes.

"Hello" said Fred not wanting to frighten the boy who was all alone.

"Hi."

The boy had some sticks in his hand and had dirty kneecaps, from having been playing in the dirt.

"What's your name?" the boy asked Fred.

"My name is Frederick Pickens, but you can call me Fred. And may I ask your name?"

"I'm Tommy. I live down the road."

He pointed to the Swanson farm; a family Fred had known for years. The little boy went over to the shoreline, picked up three rocks in one hand, and threw them into the water.

"What are you doing?" asked Fred.

"Skipping rocks."

He didn't look up as he spoke but kept chucking rocks into the water and before even seeing where they landed began scooping up the next ones.

Fred raised his hands up in the boys direction and shaking them said, "You're not doing it right."

"What do you mean I'm not doing it right?" asked the boy stopping to look up at Fred in the eyes for the first time. "You don't know how to play."

"Don't tell me about playing. When I was your age, I could out skip the best of them."

"You used to skip? You mean like a girl?"

"No, not like a girl! Skipping rocks, like what you're attempting to do, but failing at miserably."

He picked up a rock and skipped it across the water. The boy looked on in astonishment. "What's that? What did you just do?"

The old man couldn't believe that he was even asking, in his day every boy his age knew what skipping rocks was.

"You mean to tell me, you've never heard of skipping rocks? Where are you from son?"

"I've heard of it before, I just never seen it done that way. And I am from here!"

"No, I mean, where were you born?"

"I grew up here mostly, but I was born in Michigan, we used to live there with my grandparents."

"Oh well that explains it, kids in Michigan must lead boring lives because about the best thing in the world is skipping rocks how I just did it. If you want, I can show you how to do it."

"Okay!" the boy ran over to where Fred was standing.

"First of all, what you're doing isn't skipping rocks. You're just throwing them in the water, it's supposed to skip across and then you count how many skips you were able to make. Your rocks are just going 'plunk' and then sink down to the bottom. Let's go closer to the shoreline and I'll show you how it's done."

“How do you know how to skip rocks?” said the boy looking up at Fred, still a bit skeptical of his talents.

“How do I...!?!” Fred looked back, laughed as if there were some imaginary people watching who had knowledge of his rock skipping techniques, and could see what a ridiculous question that was.

“How do I know how to skip rocks? I’ll have you know that when I was your age, I was the number one rock skipper in this entire county.”

“Really?” His eyes opened wide as if he were staring at an Olympic athlete.

“That’s right. My buddies and I used to come out here every Saturday to fish when I was your age, and when the fishing was done, we would spend a good half hour just skipping rocks.”

“Could you teach me how to do it?” asked Tommy forgetting that Fred had already offered.

Without answering Fred began to look for what he felt would be a good specimen for training. He found a nice size rock that could fit well in the little boy’s hands, flat and smooth to the touch.

“What ya gotta do is, wait until it’s a quiet day.” Fred said in a serious manner.

“What’s a quiet day mean?” asked Tommy.

“No wind, no rain, not even too much sunshine, just…quiet, that’s the best day for skipping rocks.”

The little boy contemplated this and bending over picked up the first rock he saw.

“No, no, don’t pick up the first one. You have to look good and hard before you choose the right one to skip.”

"How do I know what the right one to skip is?"

"Well, on calm waters you don't want anything too heavy."

"I thought you said it always had to be calm"

"That's the best kind of water to skip on but it doesn't mean you can't ever skip on the other kind of days. Now don't get ahead of me on this one. Just sit there and listen."

Tommy obediently put his hands in his pockets awaiting further instruction.

Fred continued, "Now it depends on how many rocks there are near where you're standing. If you know you're going to skip rocks that day, then as you walk along the way you can look and shove a couple good ones you might find in your pocket. Like this one I picked up. But if you start off on a lake bank like this, then you'll have to look through the grass."

"It doesn't look like there's very many here" said Tommy looking around disappointed after his short search through the nearby grass.

"I'm told that near the Great Lakes," adding, "where you were born", knowing that Tommy probably wasn't familiar with that term, "the whole lake shore is filled with rocks, but here in Iowa, we got to work for our skippers. At least we don't have rough water here, so it's good for skipping."

Fred's eyes strolled along the grass as he kicked it and pushed it back. He saw just the perfect one and said, "Here's another one! Now take a look at this, Tommy."

He picked up a long gray rock that was flatter than most and smooth.

"Now this one's good for my hand 'cause it's not too big and not too small. That means we'll have to find you another one that's just right for your hand."

Fred raised his hand up above his head, bent back slightly, and threw it as if he was a competitive disc thrower. The rock hovered over the shore then descended onto the water, landing gently once, twice, thrice, then as if not ready to plunge to its watery end, took another three skips.

"Whoa! That was awesome. Let me try!"

Tommy quickly grabbed the first rock he saw and plunged it into the water sending it with one hit down to the bottom.

Seeing the dismal grimace come across the boys face, Fred pulled out of his pocket the original rock he picked up for Tommy that would be easier to skip and handed it to him.

"No one ever gets it right on their first try. That's the beauty of rock skipping you have to keep trying until you get it right. Hold this one with your thumb on the bottom like this and your middle finger on the top, making a c shape."

"Like this?" the boy showed him first. He didn't want to risk wasting a good skipper. Fred examined it, hoping to build confidence that this was indeed a good hold on your average variety skipping rock and then said, "Yup, that'll do just fine. Now you want to try to make it hover over the water like a space ship. Do you think you can do that?"

"Yeah! I got a toy space ship at home and I pretend to make it hover all the time!"

Tommy lifted his arm over his head but before he flung it, he made sure to listen to Fred's closing words of advice.

"Okay, well it's just the same as your space ship, only in rock skipping it really goes flying, no pretending about it."

The boy stood facing the water ready to skip his rock but asked, "Am I standing right Fred?"

Fred replied, "Stand just like you do when you throw a ball. You need one leg in front of the other like this."

He showed him the stance again that he had taken before and the boy copied it before Fred moved behind him again and said, "You got it, now lean over to the right a little bit, you don't have to lean over as much as I did because I'm tall."

Then Fred backed up and said, "You're ready, now skip that rock clear to Kansas!"

The boy took his stance very seriously, breathed deep and sent the stone flying through the air like he was Captain Kirk and the Starship was landing on a new planet. The stone flew farther than Fred had ever seen a rock hover before it hit once, then twice, then, 'plunk' down in the water. Fred stood still for a moment worried a two skipper might disappoint the boy, but Tommy jumped up with his fist in the air wailing, "Yeah! That was awesome! Did you see it fly? Fred, it went on forever! I think it might have gone farther than yours".

Clearly the boy was not getting the point of skipping rocks but he was happy and did get it to skip after all and so Fred let it go with that and the two of them spent the greater part of the afternoon skipping and hovering rocks over the lake.

The sun was starting to get auburn and it was time to go home. Fred picked up his fishing tackle that he had never even used and waved goodbye to Tommy who looked like he wasn't ready to go home yet.

"Hey Fred," Tommy called out to Fred as he was walking away. Fred turned and said, "Yeah?"

"Where do you live?"

"Up the road at the farm that has the sign for fresh milk and eggs."

"Would you mind if I come over and play tomorrow?" he paused to think for a moment then added, “If my mom says it’s okay?”

Fred thought for a moment and, forgetting it was one of the days he was allowed to work, said, “Um yeah, that sounds good. See you tomorrow.”

For the next few weeks, young Tommy would come over to Fred’s home every week.

One such morning Fred heard a knock on the door. It was Tommy holding a net in his hands. Fred opened the door and asked gruffly, “What do you think you’re doing?”

Tommy picked up the net as if he was the leader in a parade and said, “I want to go catch butterflies but I don’t have anyone to go with, wanna come?”

“I don’t know how to catch no butterflies” said Fred thinking that butterfly catching sounded like a girlish thing to do for a 10 year old boy.

“Don’t worry, I’ll show you, I know people here must not know how to catch butterflies, but where I’m from, they’re real good at it. So come on!”

Tommy ran off into the field before Fred could say another word. Hearing Sylvia coming around the corner he threw on his jacket and ran out the door. How the boy knew there would be so many butterflies in Sylvia’s garden, was a marvel to Fred. The honeysuckle looked as if it was flying away with the number of butterflies Tommy was flushing out of it. Every time one would land in his net, he filled the air with giggles. Sylvia looked out the window just in time to see Fred with a net in his hand making awkward lunges into the air. Stopping for a moment, wondering if he had lost his mind, she then heard Tommy’s giggle. She realized he must be out there in the garden but her day lilies had grown almost over Tommy’s head and since she left her glasses on the kitchen table, she couldn’t see his blonde hair jumping up and down in between her groups of lilies. Deciding to be happy that he had found a way to amuse himself without too much exertion, although she hadn't seen him jumping like that in some years, she went back to what she was doing.

Somewhat out of breath, Fred decided to hand Tommy back his net and sit on the rod iron bench fixed in the middle of the garden. Still gasping for air, he heard the sound of Rod's bike coming down the drive. Rod jumped off and ran over to the garden trying to make it over to Fred in time before he decided to get up.

"Hey Fred, would you mind if I took the bike in the barn, I just need to fix a little something on it."

Fred looked at his watch and said cheerfully, "Sure, no problem Rod. I got some time on my hands at the moment and I could help you if you like."

Looking at Tommy and not wanting to reveal the reason for his coming over, he said, "No, no, I can see you have company. I'll just be real quick and make sure to check in with you before I leave. That is, if you trust me to be alone in your barn."

Fred laughed, "Well, of course, I trust you to be in there! Go ahead, get to it, I have my own business to attend to here with Tommy."

Tommy looked up upon hearing his name but then seeing as he was only being talked about, something that he found adults did often in the presence of children he went back to the business of catching butterflies. Fred soon began to realize that Tommy was an expert meanderer as he was not only very skilled at catching his butterflies, but he would quickly release them so that he would have the joy of catching them again moments later.

Fred decided to go to the house and get Tommy and Rod some lemonade. Opening the front screen door and letting it fly back with a loud bang, he called out to Sylvia without taking off his shoes or going any further.

"Hey Sylvie honey, do we have any lemonade left for the boys?"

Sylvia, who was in the laundry room, ran out to the living room almost slipping on her way past the kitchen and needing to catch herself on the dining room chair that was facing Fred at the entrance way.

"What do you mean boys?" she asked in somewhat of a panic.

"It's just the boys, you know Tommy and Rod. No need to worry if you ain't got any, I just thought they might like to sit out on the porch after Rod's done in the barn."

"Rods in the barn? Oh, yes, that's an excellent idea Fred. I tell you what, I have a question to ask him about his sweetheart, why don't you take off your shoes and be a dear and see if there isn't any lemonade left and then pour it into the glasses that I keep in the hutch. But don't forget to wash out the glasses and dry them real good before you put them on the tray and fill them with the lemonade."

With that, she ran out the door towards the barn.

Fred was not used to Sylvia asking him to serve the lemonade and wondered if this was some new trick of hers to get him to settle down.

"Next thing you know, she'll want me to start wearing the apron around here," he said with a childlike grumble.

Sylvia knew full well, that the task she had just given Fred to do, would probably take him a good half hour to accomplish. She used it to buy time to go speak with Rod in the barn. Sneaking her head inside, she first called out, "Rod, are you there?"

Rod's head peaked over the corner, he was sporting some safety glasses which he had obviously put on in a rush and was causing his hair to stand up in every odd direction.

"Yea Sylvie, I'm here, come on in. Are you sure you're not being followed?"

Sylvia looked behind her to ensure that she wasn't and then shut the barn door putting a rock in its place to give warning should anyone enter unexpectedly. She walked past Rods bike and into the part of the barn where the old Red International stood. She asked hopefully, "Is it almost ready?"

Rod looked up again and gave a thumbs up, adding, "I just need about 10 more minutes. Do you think you can keep him distracted?"

Sylvia gave Rod two thumbs up and said, "Mission accomplished, we'll be waiting on the porch."

She ran out the barn door and past Tommy who was now sitting on the garden bench waiting for his playmate to come back, she said, "Come on, let's go wait for Fred on the porch."

About 15 minutes later, Fred came out sporting Sylvia's green polka-dotted apron and a tray filled with lemonade that had clearly over spilled as it was being brought out. Trying not to laugh she jumped up and grabbed the tray putting it down on the table.

"Thank you Fred, that is mighty kind of you to go to all that trouble. Look, your little friend is here and Rod said he was going to be out any minute and asked if we could just wait for him here on the porch."

Feeling completely exhausted from his time in the kitchen, Fred sat down, apron tight around his waist and grabbed himself a glass of lemonade.

Tommy looked up at him and asked, "Is that a bib you got on?"

Sylvia's eyes got big, but before she could protect Tommy from whatever might come out of Fred's mouth, all three of their heads turned at the sound of the barn doors swinging open.

A motor growled to life, and with a roar of an engine that had not yet seen its last day, the old International tractor came storming out of the barn. Rod, still sporting his safety glasses, was bouncing on the seat as he drove it clearly not one hundred percent in control but smiling from ear to ear as 'Old Red' pulled up the drive.

Fred jumped out of his seat spilling some of his lemonade down the front of his apron.

"Listen to her hum, Sylvie!"

He yelled out, loud enough for Rod to hear, "Look at Rod up there, just watching the world go by."

He swung his arm up in the air giving a cowboy like '*yahoo*' wave and Rod responded by doing the same but almost falling off the seat again. Rod had started in 5^{th,} as one could do on that type of tractor, but he didn't realize how fast it would make it go, and so rather than embarrass himself by falling off of the seat, he decided to park it so Fred could take over.

"Well, I'll be!" Fred cried untying the apron and throwing it onto the chair he had been sitting on and running over to the tractor calling out behind him, "Sylvie, would you look at that, Rod fixed the tractor!"

Rod parked it but still leaving the engine running, jumped off and gave a bow as Fred jumped up the other side to check out the machine from front to bottom.

"How in the world did you do this, son?" Fred said in astonishment, now turning off the machine so he could take a good look in the engine.

"I've been working on it a little bit at a time in the mornings before you would come out to the barn, trying to use some of those tricks you've been telling me about."

Fred looked up with sense of guilt and said, "And all that time i just thought you was running late."

Rod pushed his glasses back on his head and laughed saying, "due to my useless energy, right?"

"Yeah something like that," Fred said still trying to figure out how someone could pull a stunt like that without him knowing about it. Rod looked back and Sylvia who was clapping her hands in excitement over being able to pull off the surprise. Rod said, "Nope, Sylvia has been trying to keep you busy in the house later than usual under the guise of meandering or something like that. She's even been trying to make you sleep in later until 6:00, just to give me more time to work on the tractor. I wanted to surprise you and say thanks for all those lessons you've been giving me on fixing stuff. I even got a job down at the gas station working on cars once they heard I've been hanging out here with you and taking lessons. I hope you don't mind, me dropping your name in town."

"Mind!?! It sounds like you could charge me for the work you've done on Old Red here."

Walking back around to where Rod was standing, Fred extended his thick weathered hand and grabbing Rod's gave him a firm handshake and a pat on the back.

"Thank you son, this is just wonderful! This was quite the unexpected surprise and I think I'm speechless."

Rod shook Fred's hand back and the two of them just stood there for a while shaking hands and smiling, not knowing what to say next and not wanting the moment to end.

Sylvia seeing the need to intervene yelled out, "We don't just have lemonade here Fred, we got some special eats waiting for you inside, all your favorites. I even called and asked the Doc and he said one afternoon of splurging wouldn't hurt. Tommy was the first to run in the house once he heard there was food and Sylvia ran in quickly after him.

After a good home cooked meal of pepper-fried steak, mashed potatoes and gravy, with a side of creamy Cole slaw, they finished off the meal with a slice of apple pie and side of cheddar cheese slightly melted on top; just the way Fred liked it. Rod offered to take Tommy home on his motor bike and the two of them went on their way leaving Fred and Sylvia to clean up the dishes.

Sylvia smiled at her husband.

"So now that you're a professional meanderer, what's next?"

"I've been thinking about learning how to fly."

Sylvia saw from the look in his eye that he was very serious in this prospect which scared her half to death, thus prompting her to say, "You'd just end up crop dusting anyway, let's try to keep it on the ground shall we?"

"I guess we can compromise on the ground."

Sylvia always was worried he'd hurt himself with new ventures so Fred decided to decline informing her of the classes he signed up for due to start in two months time.

"One thing's for certain, I think I let my work distract me all these years from seeing what was most important."

"And what's that?" She asked curiously.

"People."

Fred had always loved his life on the farm, but he never felt he had a good relationship with people other than Sylvie. Recently, his life seemed filled with people and surprisingly, they weren't getting on his nerves.

"Imagine if you had never taken time to meander Fred."

Sylvia handed Fred the wet plates and he began to dry them.

"A whole lot of good has come from all your meandering. Old Red's up and running, Tommy's got a new playmate and the doctor said your blood pressure is at an all time low. I hope you see now that meandering has been good for you, and that your time is better spent than in just milking Bessie all day."

Fred put down his plate and gave Sylvia a kiss on the forehead just as he used to do when they were courting so many years back. Looking at her he said, "I don't know about all the good that's come from meandering but one thing's for certain, a lot of good's come my way from being married to you Sylvie girl."

She blushed a little and handed him another wet plate. After the dishes were done, Fred put the tractor back in the barn, and gave Bessie her last milking of the day. He went in the house and the two of them stargazed until their eyes were too sleepy to stay open for a minute longer.

The End

HAROLD'S HELMET

The Kitty Incident

"Do you have any idea how much that helmet cost me?"

I held the pointed plastic cap in my hands not knowing quite what to say.

"Well if you'd only remember to leave the door cracked Kitty would be able to go outside and do her business there. But no, you closed it shut with only your silly hat to come to her aid."

I said this hoping that my husband would take it well. However, I knew that he would not.

"It's not a hat, it is my helmet! You know that! And it's definitely not a potty for your cat!"

My husband, an avid volunteer actor at the local evening theatre tends to be on the dramatic side when it comes to disappointments. However, in this newfound reason for grief, namely, my cat Kitty's latest area for defecating was more than a disappointment. It seemed Harold needed his hat for this evening's theatre production. Now by the time I cleaned it out, it would still be wet and he would no doubt not wish to wear it.

I used my strongest disinfectant to wipe it out and then put my hair dryer to it. He had been packing up his costume bag in the bedroom when I walked in.

“Here you go, dear. Break a leg!”

“Thanks a lot!” he barked, grabbing the hat in his free hand and storming out the front door. The tires peeled out of the drive way as if he was Bo Duke and off he went.

We had only been married two years. Harold and I both worked at a plant nursery in the landscaping section of a general merchandise store located in the town where we lived. He had been transferred in from out of state and we hit it off right away. Our dating consisted mostly of dinner and a movie. Our sense of humor was similar and it was not long before we fell in love. Three months later, we were married. Harold had saved enough to buy a small ranch home.

Our work was not the most exciting of employment so in the evenings, Harold volunteered to work at the local theatre. At first I went to see him act every night there was a show, but after the first year, the managers of the theatre decided to re-do last year’s plays instead of come up with new ones. It was for this reason that I did not really deem it necessary to go watch them a second time.

It had been a long time since I had went to the theatre. Since he was so distraught over his helmet, I decided to play the supportive role of adoring wife and go to watch him act.

Tonight’s viewing was a version of the film, 'Red Planet'. The theatre was within walking distance of the house but since I was running late, I decided to take my car. When I entered the theatre, everyone was already seated, so I had to go to the candy counter to be able to purchase my ticket.

“Hello there Madison, how nice of you to join us this evening.”

Mrs. Madeline, a tall woman with ratted up blonde hair, had worked at the theatre since she was a teenager and was now in her 50's. She always wore blue eye shadow and hot pink lipstick. The smock she was wearing fit tightly around her thin waste.

"Thank you Mrs. Madeline, it's been a long time since I've watched Harold perform and I needed to get out."

"Well, there are still plenty of seats left and I don't think the curtain has risen. Enjoy!" She smiled and shut her cashier register.

"Um. Would you mind if I bought some Snow Caps while you're still behind the counter?"

She rolled her eyes and re-opened her register, un-locked the candy counter, and tossed the wrapped box of chocolate candies on the counter.

"Thanks a billion Mrs. Madeline!"

I happily picked up my box of candy with both hands not being able to wait to open it.

"Don't you mean thanks a million?" she snorted.

"Uh. Yeah, right. Thanks a million." I replied.

Apparently, I was the last customer for the night. She picked up her beige handbag and began turning off the lights. I did not mean 'Thanks a million' but rather 'a billion' because there was a billion things I would rather be doing than come to the old theatre on a night off. These candies were going to be my only salvation. Her obvious lack of enthusiasm about my purchase left me with the feeling that Mrs. Madeline only deserved a million thanks, and not a billion.

Some of the town's residents were real die-hards. They would come to watch no matter if it was a play, they had seen before. Or, even if there was a film running that they had never heard of and had no desire to see you would find them there. Despite loving my husband very much I had not been in about five months.

On the evenings when the theatre did not have a stage play showing, they would run movie reels and this kept the old theatre going despite the fact that other towns had begun to close down their theatre plays. I loved this little town but the humdrum of everyday life was beginning to wear on me. I would never tell anyone, but if it in the newspapers that the theatre had to go down to be replaced by a shopping mall I would not have protested.

I saw the usual attendees like Mr. and Mrs. Green who owned the hardware shop next door to the theatre. In addition, I saw sitting there unmarried Miss Caldwell who now in her 80's had been attending this theatre since it used to be a movie theatre for black and white films. Despite the popularity of the theatre, the lack of town occupants made a full house near impossible to obtain. On a Saturday night for example, even a new production or a new film would probably only end up filling half the seats.

However, tonight, even though it was a mid-week day, the aisles bustled with people from every corner of the town. I sat down with program in hand in just enough time for the curtain to rise. Not knowing the story, it took me until the second act to realize Harold was not there. I went in reception area and tried to call him, but there was no answer.

During the intermission, I went to the dressing rooms and asked if I might find him. The theatre had red felt carpeted walls sort of like an old time saloon. There were only two dressing rooms, one for men and one for women. When you walked behind the stage, there were a set of four steps that led to them on either side. I walked up the steps and saw an older man tying up the curtain ropes. His white hair was thinning and what was left of it looked a little disheveled. The play was still going on and for fear of anyone hearing me; I kept my question to a faint hush.

Tapping his arm, I asked, "Hi Mr. Charlie. How are you?"

"I'm fine dear, and how are you? Are you enjoying the play? Let me assure you, the view is a lot better from the audience."

"Yes, I know. But Harold is not in it and that is the reason I came. Have you seen him? He was supposed to be in the play tonight."

The Mr. Charlie replied while carrying on with his work. It was incredible to me how many ropes it took to pull up one old red curtain.

"He never came in to the theatre. We have one actor waiting in case of such an emergency and he was very happy to find that the part was that of a male role. Several times now he has had to dress up like a woman." He chuckled to himself.

"Well, do you know where he might have gone?"

I felt embarrassed having to ask that question about my own husband but since I never kept track of him on the nights when he acted, I had no idea what else he could be doing.

"No, I'm sorry I have no idea. You know these actors; they don't give us stage hands much mind."

He gave me a smile, turned, and walked away. I realized I did not know much about actors and since I had no idea where to look for Harold, I decided to go home.

The house was dark when I entered and the electricity was out. I lit some candles and went into the kitchen to make a cup of tea. I loved my old gas stove and I preferred to cook my water in a kettle on top instead of using an electric kettle like many of our friends used.

As I put the kettle on the stove, it began to shake. An electric blue light sprung through the window out of the backyard. I tried to look out the window but had to block the glare with my arm. The entire house was shaking. All the dishes in my cupboards were rattling against one another and I was afraid things were going to start coming off the wall.

Grabbing my candle, I ran outside. There was more fear in my heart that everything off the wall in the house was going to fall down on me than there was that I might be engulfed into the earth. We often experienced tremors in the town where we lived due to it being in an earthquake zone. Most people were injured by things falling down on them in their own homes more than they were from being swallowed by an earthquake. In fact, I had only experienced an earthquake once. But every year we would be plagued with tremors. This tremor felt unusually strong.

As I ran out the door, it not only came off the hinges but a gust of wind ripped it completely off causing it to fly over my head into the direction of the back yard. The sky was very dark and cloudy so it was difficult to see where it had gone too. As I tried to focus across the lawn, past the shrubs and over the trees there was an oddly shaped object sitting there. I rubbed my eyes imagining I was seeing things but as the wind died down the object became clearer.

It was a large metal vessel. It was only for a brief moment that I saw it there on our lawn. With another flash of light, the machine was gone. The earth stopped trembling and there was nothing. I could not believe my eyes. I rubbed them again and pinched my arm thinking that it was just a dream. Running into the house, I picked up the telephone and tried to call Harold but he did not pick up the phone. It did not even ring like there was no connection where he was. I then called the police.

"Hello! Hello! Please this is Madison Rowing and I am at 467 Shaffer Avenue. Please there has been some sort of tremor here at my home! I cannot find my husband and I don't know what to do!"

"Please stay calm Mrs. Rowing, a car is being sent out to your address as we speak and they will arrive soon."

"Was there an earth-quake tonight that you know of?" I asked thinking they would have the newest updates.

"No. I am sorry we have not been informed of any activities such as that. But we will look into it and radio the police before they arrive if we find out anything."

"Thank you very much. I will wait here for them to come." I placed down the telephone and went over to the kitchen table to try to calm myself. With folded hands, I sat and waited for the police to arrive. The minutes it took for the police to arrive felt like hours.

"Ding Dong!"

When I heard the ring of the doorbell, it made me jump. I rushed up, hoping that it was Harold but it was not.

"Hello Ms. Rowing, we received a call that there was some sort of tremor that occurred here tonight. Are you injured? Is anyone in the home injured?" asked a friendly looking man sporting a blue uniform. I recognized the officer next to him was a former schoolmate of mine.

"Julie, is that you?" I said, knowing that it was but I had never seen her in her blue uniform and was quite impressed. Seeing ones former schoolmates turn out to be successful always gave me a jolting reminder that we had grown up.

"Hi Madison! Yes, it is me. This is my new partner Fred. I hope you don't mind relating the evenings events to someone you know."

"Oh no, not at all. That is even better. Thank you for coming. Please come in."

The two of them were very professional as I related to them where I had been and what happened upon entering the home. Normally, I was sure Julie would have sat down for a cup of tea, but seeing as she had her new partner with her, she just wanted to investigate what had happened.

Their presence calmed me greatly. They thoroughly examined the scene of the incident. Although I gave them every detail, I neglected to tell them about the strange vessel I thought I saw in the back yard. It just did not make sense and I did not want them thinking I was crazy.

"I also went to find my husband at the theatre tonight and he wasn't there. It is unlike him not to tell me where he has gone. Is there any way you can try to find him."

"I'm sorry but it takes 24 hours for a missing persons report to be put into action. It might be that he was just delayed in traffic." He could see the concerned look on my face and then added, "But I tell you what, if he doesn't come home by morning, give us a call again and we'll send a patrol car out looking for him. We have the night shift tonight and you can be sure we will keep our eyes open just in case we see him. Do you have a photo we could look at?"

I showed the officer a photo of the two of us that we had taken when we were engaged. It showed off Harold's beautiful brown eyes and chestnut hair nicely. Julie winked at me when I showed it to her, as she already knew what Harold looked like.

"You cannot tell from the photo, that he is very tall, because we are seated. But he stands about 6 foot tall and sometimes wears glasses." I said taking the photo back.

"Thank you Mrs. Rowing. We will keep a lookout for him tonight. And if he does not come home by morning, call the station and we'll investigate further." The officer shook my hand and the two of them got up from their chairs in the living room.

The police officers were only in the house about an hour and could not find anything to report except what I had experienced. I waved them off, then shut, and locked the door tightly, still feeling nervous over the evening's activities.

I went back into the kitchen to put on my teakettle. The evening went by quickly and it was time for bed. After 3 cups of tea, and several attempts to call Harold with no success, I decided to try to go to sleep. In this, I was not very successful either. He did not end up coming in until midnight. I was in bed when Harold came under the covers quietly trying not to wake me. I was not about to let this go.

"Where were you?"

I asked sitting up very straight in bed. My aggravation had mounted and he could hear it in my voice. I poured out the evenings activities including the metal object in the back yard.

Harold listened to the story eagerly but then said, "I needed to go into work tonight and clear up some paper work before tomorrow. I did not feel a tremor at the shop but you know it is a common occurrence here. Just because the police don't know about it, doesn't mean it didn't happen."

"Yes I suppose you're right," I said, feeling only slightly better. "But what about the metal thing I saw in the backyard, what was that all about?"

"You never have liked being alone in the house. I'm sure the fright of the tremor caused you to see things."

He kissed me on my head, said, "Good night," and rolled over. Harold always did sleep very soundly. I on the other hand tossed and turned all night.

The next morning we both got up. As usual, we did our morning stretches. I made a cup of coffee for myself. Then I made a pot of tea for Harold. He was scheduled to be at work at 10:00 am but I was scheduled to be there before the store opened at 8:00. We always got up and had breakfast together no matter what time we had to leave for work. We watched a little bit of news on the television. I was disappointed there was no local news about the tremor the night before. I left Harold with Kitty sitting on his lap, watching the weather report and drove off to work.

The workday went well but Harold was late. He did not arrive until 11:00, which was almost time for me to take my lunch break. When he came in to work, I approached him but he looked very tired like he had just been somewhere.

I asked, "Harold, why are you so late? We got up together this morning. Did you go somewhere before coming to work?"

He did not answer me but kissed me on top of the head and said, "I'm sorry Honey, I did some work in the back yard and lost track of time. We can talk about it over dinner tonight; I have to get this report in."

He left me and walked towards the supervisor's office with his report in his hands. I walked over to the coffee machine and poured myself my second cup of the day. My restless night sleep left me needing the entire pot.

Harold being late and not showing up on time continued to happen for the next three weeks. When I would ask Harold where he had been, he would always come up with some sort of excuse. But none of the places he said could ever be proven. They were always vague such as, "I had to go to the Hardware store." Or ,"the theatre was having rehearsals on a night when I could not go so I went to practice alone."

I tried to express my worry over him but he did not notice that I was increasingly unconvinced of his whereabouts every time he came up with a new story. It was not like Harold to keep things from me, but I could tell something just was not right.

I finally decided it was time to have a talk. While we were getting ready for bed I asked, "Harold, can we have a heart to heart talk?"

"Whoa. This sounds serious. What's up?" He was unbuttoning his shirt so he could put his pajama top on. I was already sitting up in bed with our big fluffy comforter bundled up around my waste.

I began to talk about my growing concern for his newfound tardiness at work.

He shrugged his shoulders and said, "Our boss does not seem to be bothered with it. And my pay check hasn't been affected, so why should it bother you?"

This response only made me all the more paranoid as he still was not addressing what it was that he was doing. Without planning to bring up such a ludicrous subject as an affair, it came out of my mouth with full force.

"Well? Who is she? Who is the woman you have been seeing? I cannot stand to live knowing my own husband is sleeping around behind my back."

With that, I got up, swinging open the closet door. I pulled my black duffle bag out and frantically began putting clothes in it.

Harold, who was always quiet in the rare moment when I chose to be dramatic walked around to where I was and gently began putting my clothes back in the closet. Almost as if allowing me to take my turn in the dramatic arts he stood there for a moment while more ranting spewed out of my mouth. Soon though, my ranting lost its steam. I felt my breadth leaving my chest and I began to weep.

He held me in his arms and whispered, "I'll tell you everything. If only you can bare it. There is no woman Maddy."

He pulled my face up to meet his and asked, “Do you believe me?”

I nodded my head yes but then whimpered, “Then what is it that keeps you, Harold? I know these stories that you keep telling me are not true.”

He looked towards my duffle bag and sighed. Then said, “Maddy, Do you remember my helmet, the one you kept calling a hat?”

“The one Kitty pooped in?”

“Yes that very one. It is not a hat as I have been trying to tell you. It is truly a helmet. And can you guess what for?”

“Well I thought it was for the play and just a prop. Then when I went to clean out Kitty’s mess, I realized it was made of a very sturdy material. I felt bad about Kitty ruining it like that. Although it cleaned out nicely, I was thinking maybe that is why you were not in the play that night. But what does your going out all the time have to do with that hat, I mean, helmet?”

The words sat funny on my tongue. The only thing he could use a helmet for would be bike riding and I knew he did not own a bike so I was at a loss at what Harold would need a helmet for if it were not for the play.

I looked up at him with a blank expression and asked, “Do you rent a bike and exercise without me?”

Harold laughed as he often did when I asked silly questions. Then he took my hand and led me outside. Our anniversary was only a month away. I felt the excitement mounting, as I believed to have exposed a secret gift of riding bikes he had been trying to purchase behind my back. All paranoia began to dissipate.

We have a small yard. Filled with green grass and tall Maple trees. One would not think three large Maple trees could fit in a small yard with an aluminum fence. But they stood three in a row, right in the spot where I thought I had seen that metal machine during the tremors almost a month before.

Squeezing my hand and looking at me, Harold said, "Please stand here Madison and close your eyes. I'm going to walk over towards the Maple trees but I don't want you to move from that spot. Do you understand?"

"Yes I promise not to move an inch." I stood very obediently with my arms at my sides. A smirk crept up on my face as I anticipated what color my bicycle might be.

Upon closing my eyes, a gust of wind swept my hair off my back and nearly wiped me off my feet.

"Okay you can open them!" Harold shouted above the sound of the gushing wind.

I opened my eyes squinting as the same blue light I had seen coming out of the back yard was shining in my face. As the wind died down, I saw Harold standing there very robustly his one hand on his hip and the other hand extended to show me a very large silver machine.

It stood almost as tall at the Maple trees. I had seen the same object the night of the tremor. I could see it clearly now. It was round at the bottom and came to a pointed shape on top much like the helmet Harold had. There were no windows on the ship from what I could see standing on ground level. Placed toward the top was a tiny little door with a ladder leading out of it.

"What is that?" I asked, half hoping that he would tell me I was imagining things again.

"It's my space ship." Harold came closer to me and I took two steps back.

Clearing my throat, I repeated his words slowly, "Did you just say space ship?"

"Yes I did" Harold replied, "and I know that you think I've lost my mind. Just hold on a minute and let me explain."

"That's the thing I saw the night of the tremor isn't it? Oh Harold, I do not know if I want to hear this. I don't know what to say."

I hurried into the house, all my adrenaline coursing through my veins. Trying to calm myself to comprehend what just happened; I put the teakettle on the stove. Another gust of wind sounded loudly and the bright blue light filled the house once more.

Harold walked in the door in silence.

I asked with a nervous giggle trying to act as if I was not bothered by what he just told me, "Well, did you put it away?"

Harold did not respond but walked closer to me at the stove and put his hand on my shoulder. I stepped away from him and sat down at the kitchen table putting my head in my hands.

"Do you believe me then?" he said sitting across from me at the table with both hands placed flatly on it. I think he was trying to show me he was not going to make any sudden moves. He could see that I was scared.

"Harold I don't know. I believed that you were cheating on me and that is almost as ridiculous as this. How you are able to make a large metal 'space ship' vanish and reappear in the back yard, is beyond me. This leaves me with nothing else but to agree with you. But a 'space ship Harold'? I can see you are in possession of a unique piece of equipment but you sit here now and tell me it is a space ship. Can I ask you a simple question?"

"You can ask me anything Maddy, you know that." Harold stood up and walked behind me as I sat there.

He always rubbed my shoulders in times of stress. As I spoke, I kept trying to turn my head to look at him but his shoulder rubs always made me weak and so I just gave in letting my head drop down as I spoke.

"How did you get it?" I asked with the muffled sound of a person speaking into her chest cavity.

Harold, still rubbing my shoulders with both hands said, "I think this might be enough information for one night Maddy. You know I am not seeing another woman. You should also be happy to know there was indeed a tremor that night when I wasn't home, so let's just leave the subject to rest for a couple days and see where it takes us after you've calmed down a bit."

"Harold, while I appreciate your attempt to keep me calm, I still have no idea where you've been spending your time. Do you honestly think it's going to be possible for me to sleep tonight after I've seen you in the back yard with what you called your metal spaceship? I had trouble saying the word helmet if you would recall. And now this? I think I need a little more information, don't you? Where have you been going Harold? How did you get that thing? Please, I must know!"

He stopped rubbing my shoulders and sat across from me again at the table. I looked up at his brown eyes wondering what answer could possibly come out of his mouth. He seemed to be attempting to smile but his cheeks began to tremble and he grew pale. I wondered if he was going to throw up.

Closing his eyes tightly, he gripped the table at the sides and it began to vibrate. A slow creeping smile began to form across his mouth. He smiled and opened his eyes. But his smile altered. His mouth revealed that his tongue was no longer pink.

"Harold! Your tongue is green!"

It was not only green; it was divided at the tip in three places. As I stared at his tongue with my mouth gaping open, his eyes began to change color. The brown turned into specs that slowly faded into an iridescent yellow. There were also specs of green that, in my opinion, matched the new color of his tongue quite nicely.

I jumped up from my chair and he jumped up too. In a quick moment, I ran from the chair to the door. Harold leaped across the table, over my head, and landed squarely in front of me, blocking the door. He was still smiling with his head leaning downward but his yellow eyes fixed squarely on mine.

His chest was heaving for breadth. In addition, his skin was moving in waves as if still transforming into something else.

"Harold? Can you speak?" I asked sensing that he could not. His head jutted upward and he yelled out a high pitch howl similar to those heard at night by the barn owl that sits in our Maple trees.

"Harold, if you can understand me, please nod your head."

His head moved up and down. Tiny bumps began to rise from his skin and soon his entire body was covered with them. The pigment of his skin was turning into a yellowish green color and the hair was disappearing from his head. My head followed his eyes upwards as he seemed to be growing taller.

I felt myself becoming weak at the site and my body fell to the floor. After that, I must have passed out because the next thing I knew I was in the space ship.

THE SPACE SHIP

When I woke up, there was a faint whirling sound. Everything around me was metal except the pillow under my head. I always used that pillow when we watched television in the evenings. Harold must have grabbed it for me before placing me onto the ship.

My head was throbbing. I began to rub it and noticed a large bump that formed from when I fell on the floor. Everything in the room I was in was dark with only small bulbs in the ceiling causing some light to shine onto the top half of the room. There were hallways on all four sides of the area. From what I could remember of the shape of the ship, it seemed this was the core of it. I stood up and took my pillow in hand, holding it in front of me like a shield and chose the hallway in front of me to explore, hoping to find Harold.

The hallway looked more like an air duct of sorts. I walked down halfway from where I had entered and it just kept getting darker and darker. Therefore, I walked back and decided to go down one of the other passageways.

Once again, I found myself looking for my husband. This time, I did not suspect that he was seeing another woman. I now believed that he had a space ship. And the reason he had it was that he was not from the planet earth. My husband was an alien. I still had many questions I wanted answered.

Despite my predicament, I kept a calm mind as I returned to the center of the ship and took the Hallway to the right of me in search for Harold. No longer holding my pillow like a shield, I now held it close to my chest for comfort. I could feel my heart beating like a drum. I hoped the pillow could muffle the sound I felt my heart was making.

The second hallway was much brighter and there was a clicking noise coming from the end of it. As I got closer to the clicking, the noise was mixed with a tapping and whirling similar to that of electronic equipment running at great speed.

"Harold? Are you there?"

I began calling out to Harold hoping he would hear. Fear gripped me that I might run into others like Harold who might not have the same sentimental attachment that he did.

Having no idea, if Harold would even be recognizable, I just kept calling out for him. I assumed he was with me on the ship and had not placed me on it and left me there. With every step, the whirling noises got louder. I passed the reason for the noise. Many machines were going at the same time. It was the ships engine and it was obviously running. This meant we were in flight. I passed the engines and arrived at the end of the long hallway to see a cockpit.

Purple and green hews filled the room with a dark light. There were four seats at a control panel. Someone was sitting at the main seat pressing buttons. I called out in a hush, afraid to bother the thing, but desperate to find my husband.

"Harold, is that you?"

Slowly the alien, at the control panel stood up and then turned around. Standing about 7 feet tall, stood a creature roughly the same stature as Harold had appeared in the kitchen when I last saw him in my home.

However, this alien was white in appearance whereas Harold had been a yellowish green color. The alien had the same bumpy marks on its face as Harold did. As I spoke, the creature looked up at me with the same iridescent yellow eyes that I had seen in Harold. He was also breathing heavily.

I was immobilized not knowing what to do. With his head turning upward, he gave out an owlish cry. I covered my ears to block the piercing sound.

Within seconds, a flash of blue light filled the room and three other aliens were standing there. The shortest of the four was red and thick in stature. His eyes were green with no hint of yellow and his tongue flailed about in a hideous fashion as he stood there gazing at me. The last two were similar in color. The only difference between them was that one was more of a green hue than the other was. The other difference was that one with the green hue was approaching me slowly.

The first alien turned to sit back in his seat and continued operating the ship and the other two sat down. They were not the only ones that were yellow. I felt a yellow streak slowly growing on my back in the form of cowardice. I stood there face to face with an alien that resembled the creature that had been in my kitchen earlier. But I was too gripped with fear to utter a word.

He lifted his large hand and reached out to touch my face. Without meaning to, I jerked away causing him to pull his hand back again. Feeling badly for rejecting him if this was indeed my husband; I pulled out every ounce of courage I had within me to speak.

"Harold is that you?" I whispered looking into the alien's eyes for any sort of sign that it might be him. He nodded his head up and down.

"Do you work here, Harold? Is this some sort of place for research or scientific discovery?"

Harold again nodded his large head up and down.

The red alien turned in his seat at the hub and gave a hissing sound in Harold's direction. He then gave me a fierce look and pointed towards the exit door. It was clear that I was not welcome in the cockpit.

"I want to stay with you, Harold," I said as quietly as possible so the red alien could not hear me.

Harold looked around at the other three who were busy at the cockpit and called out to them in deafening high-pitched tones. The white alien and the one that looked more like Harold waved their hands up in the air in acceptance of whatever Harold had said.

The red one never replied but kept looking in front at the monitor that encompassed the entire wall in the front of the hub. He was holding onto a steering device as if he was piloting the vessel. Images appeared with readings and mappings of different planetary formations. Other monitors looked as if they were monitoring phosphoric levels.

We were flying through space. I could not tell if we were in the same galaxy or not but the monitor showed stars and planets sweeping past the ship in good speed. The luminaries that came onto the screen were the most extraordinary sight I had ever laid my eyes upon. Hues of orange, red and purple swept past the monitor in streams of light.

One formation seemed to flow into the next. When the color faded, there were billions of twinkling stars clustered together. In between the clusters were beams of aurora-like color, producing the grandest light show I had ever seen.

As they swept past the screen, I could feel Harold watching me.

One star looked as if it had just exploded and I jumped in reaction to what I saw and began clapping my hands as if I were watching fire works for the first time.

This fanfare caused all three of the aliens to now turn in their chairs and look at Harold with forceful stares.

“It’s wonderful.” I said and looked up at Harold.

Harold did not emit a sound but gently took me by the hand and led me to the core of the ship where I had first awoken after having fainted.

“They must have wanted me out of their hair,” I said to Harold as we walked down the hallway of the spaceship together. Knowing Harold, he was trying to figure out what to do with me. I had no idea how I came to be on this ship, but the fact that Harold wanted me with him after weeks of thinking he had grown tired of me, helped me over come any feelings of being distraught.

We arrived at the center of the ship once more. I had only been down two of the ships hallways. Well, one and a half since I had not summoned enough strength to finish the first hallway I began to walk down before finding Harold.

Harold now took me down a third and new hallway of the ship, holding my hand the entire time. Or rather, he continued to hold onto my wrist. His hand was now very large. Too large in fact, to hold anything as tiny as my hand. He had always commented in the past about my small hands and seemed somewhat mesmerized by them. Now I understood why. I also understood why there were no foreseeable key holes on the ship. Their big hands would have never been able to hold a set of keys, let alone put them in a tiny hole. Each door way had a panel of buttons that could lightly be tapped for the thing that was required to be done.

Feeling his hand against my skin was making me shiver due to its cold temperature. His skin was what I imagined a crocodiles would feel like. Almost damp and clammy but very thick. He had thick blue fingernails that took the shape of claws. I kept walking just one pace behind him to analyze the new shape he had taken on. There were six fingers on each hand. He was not wearing his ring. I wondered what he did with it in between transformations. That was if he was able to transform back and forth, as I had hoped.

At this point, I did not know if this was something my husband had been doing on a regular basis or if this was some new development in his life that he was sharing with me as he himself experienced it. The way he walked confidently through the corridor showed me that he knew what he was doing.

He led me to a room that was as sterile as the rest of the ship. The room did not have very many furnishings. There was a metal bed in the center of the cabin, which sat up on a metal pedestal. There were also compartments in the walls that looked like windows but there was no view to the outside world, just a metal plate. Lights came out of the ceiling making the room glow like a jewelry store. The metal trimmings and white walls made the room shiny.

Harold went over to one of the window like compartments and pushed a panel of buttons that was located next to it. It opened to reveal some white clothing. He pointed to it and then to me. Apparently, I could use these to dress myself with them.

Then he went over to another compartment and pushed a button that revealed a 3D image display. Lights and images from our home appeared like holographic images. Some were in the form of pictures and others were in the form of video coming in and out with sounds.

Three-dimensional images of our cat appeared. I could hear her meowing. The next image was of her brushing up against Harold's helmet. With that sore subject still sitting in the air, he pushed a button again to fast forward to videos of Harold and me together. This was clearly Harold's room and he was trying to make me feel at home.

I sat on the bed and began watching the slide show hoping to see some sort of image that would explain why this was happening. But there was nothing but images of our life together on earth.

Harold walked over to a larger door within his room that revealed a washroom. It was a small square room, white like the bedroom but with steam vents coming out of it. There was what I assumed a toilet and a sink. In the middle of the washroom was a circular plate.

I undressed and walked onto the plate in the middle of the room. Harold was always proud of me when I was brave enough to try new things but this was a test of even the bravest of persons. I stood there tense from anticipation of what was going to happen once he turned it on.

He pushed a button and warm steam came out. Then streams of soap splattered onto me and I began to lather up. I began to speak to Harold while I showering even though I knew he could not talk back to me. It calmed my nerves to pretend this was a normal way to spend the day with ones husband.

"Harold this had better not be some sort of plot to kill off my race," I said feigning laughter.

"Alternatively, you had better not be using me for the breeding of your species." This thought made me feel a little uncomfortable, as I did not want to put any new ideas into his head.

"I just want to take a shower and then we can discuss any sinister plans you might have once I've gotten dried off."

My attempt at making jokes was always lacking. Harold and I had always had the same sense of humor in that, I would laugh at all of the jokes he told. Now that I found myself trying to make light of the subject of my present circumstance, which was completely out of my genre, I was left with the realization that I was not actually funny at all.

A spurt of cold water came down on my head.

"Harold!"

I looked up at him with my brown hair all matted down flat on my face, using my hands to lift it out of my eyes so I could give him a dirty look.

Harold laughed exposing that horrible tongue again. No audible came out of his mouth when he laughed. His shoulders shook up and down and I could see it was he because he always pointed when he was laughing at me. This sense of humor that leaned on the side of wicked, was the only thing left to tell me my husband was actually him.

"Well, I'm glad to see you have not lost your sense of humor! More warm water please," I commanded.

"I'm not finished rinsing my hair."

He himself was not wearing any type of clothing. His skin had taken on a thickness that would not have fit any clothing we had back home. There were no signs of a human body anymore except for the two arms and legs that he possessed. His head sat on a neck that started at his shoulder and went all the way up to his ears making it difficult for him to turn his head unless he moved his entire body sideways.

He had no hair on his head but on the back of his neck was a tuft of hair. There were bumps all over, except for the bottoms of his feet. His feet looked similar to his hands, with a claw like shape and six toes. On one ankle, he had a metal bracelet that was thick like a handcuff and had little bulbs flashing on it.

Feeling as if new blood was running through my veins I wondered if there was not something more to this water, than I was used to. At any rate, I was finished showering. I held out my hand and asked, "Could you please hand me a towel?"

He pushed another button that blew warm air onto me drying off every bit of moisture left on my skin. I wiggled my fingers and toes enjoying the sensation of the warm air hitting my body. I was sure my love handles must have been rippling in the current but I did not care. Having Harold stand there so big and bumpy left me feeling much less self-conscious than I normally would have had he been watching me shower on any other day. He handed me one of the white robes from the compartment he had showed me earlier.

I wrapped the white cloth around myself like those women I have seen on television programs who live on islands. It was too long for me. As I walked back into the main room, I had to hold it up so I did not trip.

Harold put his big hand on my back and led me to the bed. I sat up on it feet dangling off the sides and said, "This does not seem like it's going to be a very comfortable night sleep. If you can figure out how to make a space ship, why can't you figure out how to bring a down comforter on board?"

With one press of a button on the side of the bed, thick green grass began to appear, much like pasta coming through a press. It was so thick I could feel it lifting me up slightly as it began to nestle under my legs and back. It was silky unlike the grass we had back home and I could no longer feel the cold metal underneath me.

I laid down on it feeling tiredness overtake me. With a faint voice left I said, "Harold however did you find this bed? It's magical!" He looked down at me and smiled then pointed to the image display. A photo appeared of Harold and me lying in the grass one Sunday last year.

"You remembered!" I gasped sitting up staring at the photo of the two of us.

It was a day Harold had off work – or so I thought at the time, now when I thought of any past absence I pictured him in this spaceship. He had come home from doing some shopping and we decided to go to the park and have a picnic.

I had made his favorite lunch, tuna salad with celery and black olives. We took white wine and banana cake that I had bought at a little bakery down the road from where we lived. I packed everything up in a picnic basket and we walked to a park nearby and laid out a blanket under a big Oak tree.

After we ate, we fell asleep on the grass. When we awoke, Harold held out his camera so that he could take a photo of the two of us.

We pulled our heads together nice and close to make sure we would both fit in the frame.

I told Harold that day that one day I wished I could have a bed made of grass. Being a restless sleeper, I said that I would never again keep him awake at night tossing and turning.

"Maybe we should just get a tent and cut the bottom out of it." I said to him, making him laugh.

After that day, whenever we had financial worries, Harold would always joke, "Well, at least you're happy to just sleep outside so we shouldn't have a problem no matter what changes life brings us."

As I sat on my metal and grass bed, those words came over the speakers attached to the photo on the monitor. I looked up at Harold who was looking down at me with soft eyes.

"I love the bed. Thank you Harold. It looks like life has given us a change, doesn't it?"

He nodded his head up and down and I could sense the worry in his face.

"Do not worry about me Harold. I must admit, I may have reacted poorly in the kitchen, but I feel better about it now. I would have hated you to leave me there all alone. I am sure I will come to understand what is happening before all this is finished.I am determined not to go crazy and jump off the ship or anything like that. I promise."

Harold pushed another button on my bed and the smell of lilacs entered the room.

"I would like so much to know what it is you do here." I said, my words fading away into whispers.

"Maybe tomorrow I can…" I yawned and closed my eyes before

finishing my sentence.

I was cognizant of Harold leaving the room, hearing the door shut. It made a sliding sound as it came down from a slot in the top of the frame and closed at the bottom of the floor. There were no knobs for opening it, but I went to bed unafraid. Glad to have found Harold I allowed my mind to rest and doze off into peaceful slumber.

I slept very well that night. Although I was not, sure what time it was by the time I woke up in the morning. The room looked the same as it had when I entered it the day before.

When I sat up the grass disappeared, sinking back into the metal mattress. It was a very convenient way to make a bed I thought to myself. I walked over to a shelf where my clothes were put away. They had been neatly folded and pressed. I looked at the shelf wondering if there was some sort of compartment that took the clothes to wash them but could not find anything peculiar. I got dressed again and went over to the door to push the button to get out and find Harold.

There was silence in the long corridors. I began to walk towards the hub I had been at yesterday but then decided to explore the hallway that I was hesitant to finish the day before. If I were to find Harold, first, he might make me stay put in that room all day and I wanted to figure out what was the reason for all this ship.

This hallway was darker than the others had been. I felt the walls with my hands and moved very slowly. When I was about a three-minute walk down, I heard a whirling noise that sounded like I was getting close to something. The next step caused something small like a cord to brush up against my leg. I lifted my leg wondering if I should run the other direction or scream for help.

I took one more step forward only to fall straight down some sort of airshaft. Huge gusts of wind were whirling all around me as I hung on for dear life. My one arm was holding onto the flooring I had just slipped from but each finger was slowly slipping at a steady pace.

I looked down but could see nothing but a black hole. Nothing would catch me if I fell. As my fingers continued to slip, one by one I let out a scream. I felt something grab hold of my wrist with both hands. The hands were large and cold. Screaming at the top of my lungs, I was lifted up by one of the alien pilots that I saw with Harold, the one that looked most like Harold in appearance.

The pilot lifted me up onto the platform but as I grabbed hold of him, he slipped off the ledge. He was holding on with both hands. I bent down to grab hold of him but could only get both of my hands around one of his wrists. I screamed again this time with the words, "Noooooooooooo!"

My hands were slipping away from his. His hands were too big for mine to wrap all the way around them. He was very heavy and I was attempting to pull him up but he would not budge. It felt like a thousand pounds of concrete pulling my arm out of the socket. I jammed my foot into the corner of the shaft and put my other foot on top of a screw that was in the flooring where we were falling. The screw was holding my heel steady but also ripping into it like a cheese grater.

I was not sure if he would understand me over the sounds of the gushing winds coming out of the black hole beneath but I screamed, "I can't hold you. Please try to swing your body upward, I'm going to slip and we will both plummet to our deaths!"

He swung one leg up and then another but when he swung his tree trunk sized leg up to the platform on his left, he landed squarely on top of me. As he landed though, his foot ricocheted off a spinning blade that was turning nearby. He cried out in pain and lunged further kneeing me in the head. At this point, I must have passed out again.

When I woke up, I was back in my sleeping quarters. Harold was standing there with his arms folding watching me. It was hard to tell if he was frowning as he had no brow but his eyes narrowed in on me as I awoke and I could see he was not happy.

"What happened?" I asked.

He pointed to me, then to the 3D monitor. It began depicting what I had missed after I passed out. The alien had indeed been hurt by a blade that was supporting one of the ships engines. And yet, he gathered up the strength to pick me up and bring me to Harold.

The screen turned off and I was left with Harold continuing to stare at me unapprovingly. He pointed again to me and then to bed and motioned with both his hand that I would not be leaving the area any time soon.

A bandage was wrapped tightly around my foot. Evidentially I had been out long enough to be dragged back to my quarters and cared for. Harold had always been very good at dressing wounds and it looked as if he had been the one to doctor up my foot for me.

"Thank you for bandaging my foot." I said sheepishly.

Harold got up to walk out after waving at me to stay put a second time. I knew he was not angry but was obviously attempting to ground me to the room for the rest of the journey.

In one last effort to free myself from being stuck in that room I held my hand out in a panic as he passed by the bed on his way to the door and begged, "Harold please doesn't make me stay in here! I am sorry I went exploring without your permission. I know that I put myself in danger. How is the other pilot? Is he hurt? Maybe I can help you!"

He paused at the doorway, hand on the button, and thought for a moment. Then he turned slightly still not looking at me and extended his hand for me to take it. I ran up to him, having to catch my step, still feeling slightly dizzy from fainting. I couldn't let him see that though lest he make me stay in bed. I still had my clothes on from when I fell down the shaft but I was now barefooted. "Just like Harold" I thought to myself as we walked hand in hand down the corridor. Only the patter of my feet and the thuds of Harold's could be heard as we walked down the hallways of his space ship.

Harold took me farther down the hallway where I had been staying. It was filled with bright white lights leading down its corridors. I could clearly see now that the metal ship was built with panels. The seams were very close together. I could see no difference in the floors, the walls, or the ceilings.

As we walked, I continued to hold Harold's hand and then glide my free hand against the walls of the hallways. This hallway had many doors. We passed two on our right and then entered one doorway on the left. Harold ushered me in first and then followed behind me shutting the door.

The entire room was white and very clean. There were no windows but it had a similar 3D image screen that my room had. Only the images on the screen looked like a series of x-ray images and heart monitors.

Laying there on a bed similar to mine but higher up in the air was the alien that had tried to save me. He did not look conscience. I walked closer and saw that his leg was bandaged. The injury from being caught in the air duct must have been worse that I realized. Harold put both hands on my shoulders and pushed me to stand farther away from the table. He then put a large light in my hand and showed me where to hold it facing the direction of the aliens injured leg.

Thus began 3 hours of surgery. Harold began by un-bandaging the leg. Purple ooze began spilling out onto a tray on the floor. Harold began wiping it off but it was very sticky. The room was so bright I assumed the light I was holding had another purpose, possibly a sterilization device. Harold took what looked like long strands of hair that had been woven into thread, similar to what was on the back of his neck and began to sew up the wounds with it, using a large needle. The entire time the alien did not move. Only his injured leg would rock back and forth, as Harold would pull the needle in and out of it stitching up the cut.

When Harold was done, he re-bandaged the leg. With a tap of his foot on the floor, a pole rose up out of it. Harold attached a sling to it and put the alien's leg gently inside. He then strapped in the rest of his arms and legs onto the bed. After taking the light from me and putting it on the table, he pushed another button near the bed where the alien was laying and an orange mist encompassed the body in a cloud.

As the mist dispersed, the alien woke up and let out a series of blood-curling cries.

"ARRRRRRRGGGGGGGGHHHHHHHHHHHHH!"

His body jutted up in a c-shape with only the bed straps keeping him down on the table. The floor vibrated underneath me as he continued to roar.

Harold now hit another button and a white mist came up out of the same vents that had produced the orange one. This time Harold covered his mouth and waved to me to do the same. I covered my mouth and watched as the creature fell back into a deep sleep, his body lying as limp as it was when I had entered the room just moments before.

When the patient seemed to be asleep, Harold released the straps. He then turned the 3D images on the screen into pictures of solar systems and led me out of the room so the alien could rest.

We closed the door behind us and Harold stopped and looked into my eyes, his hand on my cheek. He breathed a sort of chirping sound and I assumed it was his way of thanking me for my help.

"What do you do here Harold? Are you a Doctor for aliens?" I asked wide-eyed wanting so badly to understand what it was that he did here.

THE GREEN HOUSE

Harold then took me to the fourth and last hallway of the spaceship. He began to walk faster down the hallway more then I could keep up with as if he was very excited to show me something. I followed him to the end of the hallway. Where there were two sets of double doors. We entered the set of doors on the left.

A dozen different scents and smells entered my nose upon walking in a very large auditorium type room. The room was filled with rows and rows of plants and flowers. Encased in a clear plastic enclosure to my right was a case that looked void of the humidity. These were plants that I recognized being from the families of succulents that we had seen on our trips together to the islands of the Pacific Ocean. The dirt was sandy and dry with coral and rock lining its bed.

The walls of the cabin room had different types of monitors showing a variety of information that looked encrypted. Information was cursing up and down the screens too quick for the human eye to read.

In the center of the room stood a green house. We walked towards the green house to step inside. Harold pushed a button and a sliding door lifted allowing us to enter a tiny room that had a sliding door on both sides. When the door on the one side had shut, the door on the other side opened allowing us to enter the green house.

The air was thick and humid and a watery midst was coming down from the ceiling. Harold went toward the back of the tent and left me to looking at a Hygrometer nearby to see how much humidity was in the air. There was a variety of exotic plants in the room.

The studying of flora and fauna had always been a passion of ours. Now that I thought about it, although I had worked at the home and garden section of the store where we worked for 6 years before we met, it was not until we fell in love that I actually began to love my job. Always being embarrassed at working a minimum wage job, I never took the time to appreciate it. When I met Harold, he acted like it was the best job in the whole world, taking care of plants. As I walked slowly through the green house aisles, I was reminded of how special my husband really was.

One area in the middle had open trays of orchids of every type growing. Some had obviously just been planted whereas others looked as if they had been growing for some time. My favorite orchid was there; the Eulophiella with its Magenta colored flowers in full bloom.

Green leaves of every shape and size were climbing in vine like fashion along the interior walls of the green house rendering it equatorial in landscape. I had to push back large heart-shaped leaves out of the way for fear of tearing them as I passed by.

As I passed into an area that had ferns, I noticed several different kinds that I had never seen before. One of these looked like the Cycad tree fern however; instead of the typical leaves, it would normally have had; it sported ones that were yellow with coral specs. Another fern had sharp pointy leaves that went out in every direction.

Each plant was tagged with writing that I could not understand. I was about to walk to another aisle of plants when Harold came back out from behind the green house holding a small pot that looked like it had been made from the trunk of a mossy tree. Coming out of the pot filled with black dirt was a tiny red budding plant that I had never seen before. The entire plant was red including the stalk and its leaves.

"What is all this for, Harold?" I asked while searching every angle of the little flower in absolute wonder.

He pointed to one of the 3D monitors that were located behind him on the green house wall. Images of news items from home began to appear on it. One woman from a science channel began to give a report on a new species of fern that had been found. Above her head was a digital image of one of the ferns I had seen with Harold on a trip we had taken to the island of Madagascar on our honeymoon. I listened with interest as the woman spoke.

"A new species of Fern has recently been discovered on the island of Madagascar. While Madagascar has over 80% of its wildlife native only to the island, researchers are finding new species every year. This newfound species will spur on more aid from other countries. It is hoped that with more aid being sent from overseas wildlife conservation projects can continue to flourish here, helping preserve the beauty that is still left on mother earth."

The next news clip appeared in Spanish. I could understand enough of it to comprehend that another species of fauna had been discovered in the island of Costa Rica. Harold pointed to the screen as the man on the news channel spoke and then pointed to a tropical looking plant that was placed in a pot nearby where he was standing.

"What do you mean to say Harold?" I asked raising my eyebrows as far up my forehead as they could possibly go.

"Do these discoveries have something to do with you?"

Harold put down the little pot and picked up a bigger one that had a Pitcher Plant in it. Behind him, a news clip from somewhere in Asia popped up showing the exact same plant. A man was standing at a podium of a news conference holding the plant over his head like it was a trophy.

On the bottom of the screen were subtitles that read, "It's as if this plant came out of the middle of nowhere. Researchers felt every discovery had been made regarding this family of plant. Yet, unexpectedly, it seems there is still more to be discovered in Asia. Giving researchers new found momentum to continue their search and all the more reason to keep the preservation campaigns for our planets forests going."

"So this is what you have been doing all this time?" I said this while not taking my eyes off the screen.

Harold put down his Pitcher plant and took me by the hand to another aisle of the greenhouse. He reached his hand down a marshy tray of plants and with his, large fingers gently picked up, cupping into his hands, a bright orange tree frog the size of a peanut.

Holding it out to me, he placed his hand under mine. I cupped my one hand underneath it and the other hand over the top of it so it could not leap out onto the floor. I peered at him from the hole that my two thumbs made.

"Is this a new species too?"

I looked up at him completely in awe regardless if it was a new species or not. Harold was smiling, and nodding his head up and down.

Putting my hand to his bumpy yellow cheek, I said, "I'm so proud of you Harold. It must have been so hard for you to keep this all to yourself. Thank you so much for sharing all of this with me. I love you very much."

He nodded again and then put his large hands undermine so that I could place the tree frog back into his. He took the little frog and placed him safely back in his marshy home.

We walked back down the corridors of the spacecraft to my room. I wondered where Harold slept now that I was in there. He must have been worried I would be too afraid of him to be that close. He left me there to be alone with my thoughts. I had not a complaint in my heart. I felt like he had just given me the world.

That night in my grassy bed, I wondered how long our journey would take us. Would we go together to discover new plant life to bring back to earth? When would our journey end? Would it end? What if Harold was done with his mission on earth and not going back? I was filled with questions and it was hard not being able to communicate with Harold the way I normally did when things troubled my mind.

By day three, I had realized that I did not eat anything. In fact, I never really felt hungry until the third day when a horrible pain in my stomach came over me. I stayed in my room waiting for Harold to come but did not.

Promising myself not to go exploring again but only to find Harold, I walked out of the room in search of the cockpit. When I reached it, only the alien with the bandaged foot was working. He jumped up when he realized I had entered the room. We stood facing each other and I was not sure if he was angry with me for what had happened to his foot.

"My name is Madison. I am Harold's wife. Please," I said, desperately, "I am very hungry. Is there something on this ship I could eat?"

He looked at me tilting his head. A thin red beam came out of his eyes and began scanning me up and down. When the beam of light stopped scanning me, he walked over to a compartment in the wall.

Pushing a button, a tray popped out that had several bottles laying on it. He chose the one he wanted and handed it to me. I opened it and looked at him for further direction. He raised his index finger showing me to take one of the pills from the bottle.

Having no water to drink, I swallowed the hard little green pill feeling it linger down my dry throat. It tasted bitter and I tried hard to produce more saliva in my mouth to get rid of the taste. In seconds, my hunger pains had stopped.

"Thank you very much. And I am very sorry for what happened the other day. Is your leg feeling any better?"

The alien smiled and peeled back part of his bandage exposing the wounded flesh. It looked as if it was healing nicely. It was a relief to know that he would be all right.

Harold walked in with the other pilots. They spoke to one another in their native language and were gesturing with their hands.

He then turned to me and walked over to where I was standing. He held me by my shoulders looking into my eyes as he often did when he was about to be bossy. I had the sneaking suspicion that I was about to be put back into my room.

"I know it's so difficult that we cannot communicate." I said. "But don't worry; I'm a quick learner, Harold. Just let me stay and watch you, I'll be fine."

He led me over to one of the walls of the cockpit.

HAROLDS PLANET

Something important was about to happen. Three of the pilots were strapping themselves into their seats and had headgear on their heads.

Harold took me and placed me in a seat that came unfolded out of the wall of the cockpit. He strapped me in, including my head.

"Harold, what's happening? What are you doing?"

He did not answer but went and sat in the fourth pilot seat, strapping himself in, and placing similar headgear on his head to that of the other pilots.

A roaring blast shook the entire ship. I felt my skin stretching back from the gravitational pull. There was no sound in the aircraft but a heavy silence settled on my ears as if we had entered another atmosphere.

With a crash, we landed, causing all of us to shake with only the straps to keep us from falling out of our seats. Harold was the first to get up. He helped the others become un-strapped and then came to me but only took off my head strap. He bent over and tapped one of the lights on the metal band that was on his ankle. In the middle of the cockpit a three dimensional image appeared.

It was apparent that we had landed. They were now discussing a plan. The images projecting showed the terrain of another planet. There were not many other life forms moving and working about.

The display screen had no color. Everything was red but it looked like a rocky soil and very desolate. I still could not hear any sounds coming out of their mouths but they were motioning to one another to go.

The light display stayed up. Harold came over to me and pointed to himself and then to the screen. He then motioned to my watch, which still had been running but was not keeping proper time. He circled the face of the watch and held up his index finger to show me one hour. Then he pointed to himself and to the ship showing me he would return.

"Will I be able to know where you are going?" I asked not hearing any sound coming out of my mouth but hoping he could read my lips.

Harold nodded and pointed to the display.

This was to be my way of monitoring him. It would have been much easier if he could have set something like this up in the living room and I would not have had to come see it for myself dripping in anxious sweat, strapped to an uncomfortable jump seat.

Sitting strapped to that chair, on a space ship all alone, watching my husband go off onto a strange planet was not the type of undertaking I wished to pursue. Having no choice in the matter I said, "I love you Harold. Please be careful."

He left me there and I wondered if I would ever see him again. My heart pounded yet further as within ten minutes the four pilots, including Harold appeared on the screen of the monitor.

They were not wearing any sort of suits, which told me they were accustomed to the atmosphere on this planet. They walked as if there was no gravity bouncing from one-step to the other. The planet looked like it was in ruins. There were industrial type buildings that were falling apart. Smoke was rising from rock formations every few feet. It looked to be volcanic.

The image of the four pilots showed them entering building on the left of the screen. The screen then shifted to inside the building where they were. It looked as if the image was now being shown from Harold's viewpoint.

I could see the white alien, the pilot with the bandaged leg, and the red alien standing in full view. Only Harold's hands were showing as they entered a building. The walls of the building were badly damaged and looked like the inside had been ripped apart. There were no furnishings or signs of life inside.

The four of them began digging with pieces of jagged scrap metal that had been lying on the ground next to them. As they dug, the red alien kept looking around to see if anyone was coming.

After several minutes of digging, Harold's hand began to put something in the hole. It was one of the plants that I had remembered being in the green house. It was a common fern where we were from but apparently something new and undiscovered for this planet.

Harold's hand began gently pressing down on the dirt. A liquid was poured on top of the plants base. They each had special tools they were using to examine it making sure it would live in that soil. Harold looked to be snapping pictures on a hand held device while the other two were putting away their tools. The red alien raised his hand as if he was going to give Harold something. The screen went blank.

A few minutes later, the screen came back on again. It was again the view of the landscape I had first seen. Only this time I could see an image of only three of the pilots. Harold was gone! The red alien was holding out his hand and gesturing angrily at the other two who were shaking their heads in resistance.

I began trying to break myself free of the straps, but it was very tight and the more I squirmed to be free the tighter the straps became. The screen went blank again.

"Help! Somebody help me!" I cried out in a vain attempt to do something.

The screen moved back to Harold's viewpoint showing him coming out of unconsciousness. Every time Harold would pass out again the screen would default to the original image of the three aliens outside the building. Harold awoke again with everything in the room looking sideways. Harold's head was laying flat on the floor.

"Harold! Harold! Can you hear me?" tears were streaming down my eyes.

Here I sat helplessly watching my poor Harold wreathing in pain, being the victim of some sort of barbaric attack and there was nothing I could do about it.

His hand began to draw something on the dirt in front of him. His nails were sketching a flower, tiny in appearance. It was sitting in a pot. It looked like the tiny red flower he had shown me in the green house on the ship!

The screen blanked out again, Harold must have passed out. That was all I could let my imagination believe.

The scene shifted again to the three pilots. The red alien had tied up the white one and was pointing at him holding a sharp piece of metal to his head. He then held out his hand to the alien who had saved me and given me the pill to eat.

Pointing in the direction of the ship the red alien turned quickly and thrust the metal object into one of the legs of the alien who was tied causing him to fall hard to the ground. The yellow alien began to run past the building and out of the view of the monitor.

I shuddered at the thought of what might have happened to Harold. My tears were burning down my face in rage. I gave out an angry scream.

Outside the ship, a booming noise jolted me to stop screaming. I could hear the door of the ship sliding open. Soon the yellow alien was leaping into the room and over to the cockpit's operating hub.

"Please! Help me get out of these straps! I think Harold is hurt!"

I shouted out to him but he either could not hear me or was too concentrated on finding something. He was frantically pushing every button on the panel and along the walls, looking for something.

"I think Harold was trying to tell me something! I think he needs the flower in the green house!"

The frustration of not being able to communicate made my head want to burst and I began to beat my foot rapidly on the floor of the space ship hoping to get his attention.

The alien took one long leap through the air and landed in front of my seat. With one bear-like stroke, he slashed his hand down the side of my chair causing all of my straps to fall off. He ran out of the room and down the hallway to the green house.

I tried running after him, but it was more of a gallop as the atmosphere in the ship had changed when he opened the door and could I no longer could hold my weight on the ground.

We entered the green house and searched desperately for the red flower Harold had sketched that he needed. The alien began over turning every plant in his path. Finally, in a dark corner of the green house I saw the tiny red flower that Harold had shown me the day he had taken me there.

"That's it!" I cried in the shrilled voice of a desperate person.

I grabbed the tiny little red plant and handed it to the alien. He rushed past me and I attempted to follow him. Before I could make it out the door leading to the outside of the ship, he had reached it first and swiftly shut the door behind him leaving me nose to metal once again in solitude. I ran back to the monitor hoping it would show me how Harold was doing.

The scene was still on the two aliens. The red one was pointing the sharp metal object and yelling at the now injured alien who was lying on the ground.

The alien with the potted red flower appeared on the screen; he approached the red alien but was withholding the flower from him and pointing to the white one on the ground.

Now came the time for the ransom exchange. Who would be the first to let go? The red alien was shouting and holding out his hand as the alien holding the flower stood his ground and refused to hand it over. He had the pot firmly at his side much like one would hold a football and he was not about to let go until the other pilot, now attempting to stand up, was released.

The red alien slashed the ties that held his prisoner and let him go. Freed and weak, the white alien got up on one knee using his hands to balance himself and then slowly stood up on both legs. He walked towards the yellow alien who was still holding the pot in his hands.

They began to back up. Before they left, they sat the plant gently on the ground. Then they ran into the building where Harold was.

Next on the screen, all I could see was the monitor going in and out of view. It would flash in between the inside of the building and the outside. I sat back down in my chair feeling nauseous, as there was no sign of Harold having woken up.

The door to the spaceship slid open and the two aliens came in side dragging Harold behind them.

"Harold, Harold my love!" I cried.

I followed them trying to talk with him as they slowly dragged him back to the infirmary room where Harold had performed the surgery. The atmosphere was still very different. This made it very easy for the two aliens to lift Harold's large body and strap it onto the bed. Harold's body lay limp as hey buckled him in for takeoff.

"Please," I asked throwing myself over Harold's body in case they could not understand what I was saying.

"I want to stay with my husband."

There was no time to lose. The yellow alien pushed a button that generated a jump seat to come up out of the flooring. Knowing the routine, I sat myself in the chair and allowed the yellow alien to strap me in to it.

Before leaving the room, he pushed a button that caused a blue mist to rise up from my chair. I took a deep breath by now trusting that whatever they did would only be for our survival. They left the room, the door sliding down. And I began to feel drowsy. A few minutes later, a booming sound told me that the spaceship was leaving the planet.

With another rumble of engines, the ship took off at such speed my skin not only pulled away from my face but also so did. We shook in our seats, jarring every bone in our bodies. The pressure made my head feel like I was about to explode. The room became dark.

The next thing I knew I was in our living room at home.

HOME AGAIN

I woke up on the couch with the same pillow I had used on the spaceship under my head. Not sure if this was all but a dream, I took a moment to look around me for any sign of familiarity.

Sitting on top of our television was a little pot with the red flower in it! How did it get here? I stood up slowly, feeling very dizzy and trying to reach for the pot with blurred vision. I wobbled over to the plant and picked it up to inspect it closer.

A familiar voice behind me uttered, "Be careful! You are looking at the latest flora discovery this planet has known. You wouldn't want to knock it over."

"Harold! It is you!" I ran into his arms flushed with excitement that he had returned to me in human form.

"Oh my darling! I am so glad you are back. I was so afraid. Are you all right? What happened? How is it that you are back to your normal self?"

"Well, I don't know if I would call this my normal self, however, it is my new and improved self. I'm sure you would agree with that."

He kept me close to him as we walked arm in arm to the couch and sat down. I had not realized how boney he was before. I ran my fingers up and down his rib cage feeling every single one, making sure it was all there.

"What about the space ship and the planet? I have so many questions, Harold! You must tell me everything!"

"The entire planet that you saw used to be my home." Harold sat me on his lap, as if he were about to read me a fairy tale.

"It will soon burn out into nothing." A look of sadness clouded his eyes causing me to hold his head in my hands, running my fingers through his hair.

"A small team of botanists set out to rescue some of the remaining plant life left on our planet and relocate it to planet earth so that it would not become extinct. This was a very secretive work as the few remaining beings left there guarded the flora and fauna that remained with their lives. They had false hopes that the planet could be restored."

"When I first met you, I had newly arrived with several unique species of plant life that could thrive here on earth. I did not think I would be able to return to my home. However, we learned that there was plant life here on earth so rich in nutrients; they might actually be able to save our planet. Thus began a cycle of dividing and replanting. The goal was to divide both planets resources to help the other and in turn save their already existing plant life from extinction. But something went wrong."

I stopped rubbing my fingers through his hair and put my hands to my mouth in a gasp.

"What went wrong Harold? Was it that awful red alien?"

Harold chuckled giving me the impression that they did not use that expression to describe the life forms on his planet.

"Yes, the red 'alien' was one of our team mates. He started out as a pilot for the research team but then began to help us with our projects. He was always based on the ship no matter if we were in between planets. He had many inter galactic connections and began to set up the search and rescue projects in the various parts of our planet. Despite all of our efforts, we realized our planet was dying."

"We were left with one last mission before our planet was supposed to self destruct. A plant that was not of any benefit on our planet was recovered. But it was thought to have medicinal factors that could help improve the health of planet earth's inhabitants. This is when we began to make the preparations to return one last time, bringing with us a variety of plant life from earth in one last attempt to help the planet for those that were worried our efforts were solely for the gain of our new home."

"And is that when you began showing up late for work?" I said, now inspecting his neck, wondering if in the transformation back to human skin it would have left any remnant of the bumps I had seen on him before.

"Yes, that was about a month ago. What we did not realize is, our co-worker had become very greedy. Not only did he not want to give the plant to earth without cost, he did not want us endeavoring to harvest earth's plant life on our planet. Our mission was never one of commerce, and we weren't about to start no matter how much he argued with us. But he took matters into his own hands as you had to witness."

"Is that why we had to return the red flower? How is it that it came to be here in our living room? I saw you give that pilot the flower. How did you get it back?"

"We had divided two of them. The other two pilots, who you saw, realized that the third was up to something. So that final mission became a counter plot to get him back on the planet where he belonged for fear that his returning here could bring more harm than good. We figured we would leave him with that plant if things turned bad, as we had suspected. Our fears turned out to be true. When he hit me over the head and knocked me unconscious, he tied up one of the pilots for ransom in return for the red potted flower that you saw us give him. Thankfully, we had a second one, that you see sitting on top of the television" He pointed to it, with a look of satisfaction.

"Oh Harold! I am so sorry. You must have been suffering so much all this time trying to carry out your mission, knowing your planet was dying and I didn't even realize it."

I held him so tight it was straining my neck but I did not want to let him go.

"I had you to comfort me."

He smiled down at me, making me feel secure with his arm wrapped over my shoulders and his other hand holding mine into his. He stroked each of my fingers, and kept placing his own fingers into them. He was once again wearing his wedding ring.

"What will you do now that you have returned, Harold?"

"My co-workers convinced me to stay here. There is much work to do so that this planet does not have the same outcome as ours. And they could see that I had other interests on the planet that would make it very easy for me to stay for the remainder of my life time." He looked at me and smiled.

"And what about your friends? Have they gone back with the space ship?" I was a little worried we were going to have to keep that thing in our back yard.

"They have returned to their work on other planets that are facing a similar outcome as ours and if they discover anything worth saving, they will bring a specimen of it back here for us to place in an environment where it can flourish."

He lifted my hand up to his mouth and gave it a kiss. Then giving me a smile that no longer scared me as his tongue had returned to its normal color, he said, "What do you say? Would you like to carry on with me in my work here? This time, not in secret but hand in hand?"

I squeezed him again making him groan a little and said, "I can't think of anything I would like more!"

Harold laughed aloud. Kitty jumped onto my lap and curled up into a ball.

"We may have New Caledonia in our future for this little guy." Harold said pointing to the red flower on the television.

"But first things first, what would you like me to make us for dinner?" I asked, "And please don't say a little green pill." I wrinkled up my noise at the thought of that bitter green pill sliding down my throat.

"Why don't we just go out for dinner and a movie?" he asked.

"I think the theatre is still showing the play, 'Red Planet', do you want to go see it?" I said half laughing at the irony of the question.

"On second thought, let's just order pizza and stay home tonight.

I've had enough of planets for one day. Besides, Kitty has pooped in my helmet again. I'm not prepared for that type of travel."

Harold squeezed me tight, pulling me down next to his side and we laid like soup in a spoon on the couch as I called for pizza. Kitty jumped out of my lap and went off probably in search of Harold's helmet.

I grabbed the telephone to order the pizza. I could hear Harold begin to snore, his nose practically in my ear. He had fallen asleep.

I could tell Harold was glad to be home. Life might not be as exciting for him now that he was grounded. However, I would do my best to keep him happy. In addition, I would never again call his helmet, 'just a silly hat.'

The End

LANTO

Part I

"Not again!"

Hunched over a large blue washbasin, a thin young girl with dark brown curls sighed aloud. The water tap had turned off yet again. She was in the middle of trying to wash the laundry by hand. Lanto put down her soap and rinsed the white suds off her brown hands. The pile of wet clothes sat in the tub; without water to rinse them, they would have to wait for later. The tap seemed to stop working without warning and always when she needed water to finish her chores. Instead of waiting there for the water to flow once again, since experience told her that it might take hours, she walked around to the front of the house where she began to sweep the veranda.

A stiff breeze swept past the street where Lanto lived bringing with it a cloud of dust and debris. She continued to sweep the veranda even though she knew it to be a job she would need to repeat several times throughout the day because of the heavy winds. Cyclone season had just ended but the weather was still being temperamental. However, the clear blue sky gave hope of nice weather in the months to come.

Lanto had lived and worked at the residence of Monsieur Edmond since she was ten years old. Now at the age of sixteen she knew everything there was to know about the house that was in her charge to clean. Moreover, she was determined that no matter how many times she had to sweep that veranda, at the end of the day it would be the cleanest veranda in town.

Every morning at precisely this time, a boy came by with a bag of bottles for sale. He would also purchase unwanted bottles for a small amount from the residents. This was a common line of work for boys of his age, since there was no recycling on the entire island. It would have been hard to find a piece of plastic gone to waste in the rubbish piles. Most items were used until they had disintegrated into nothing. Even empty bottles were a prized possession that sold for only a few cents each.

Lanto heard the familiar call coming closer, "Bottles and cups! Bottles and cups!" She put down her broom and hurried down the veranda steps before the boy walked past the front yard. She needed to purchase one long plastic bottle for the oil she wanted to buy that day as well as two small tin cups. She dipped her hand into her blue-checkered work smock, and pulled out a silver looking coin.

"If I buy the second tin cup, can I have a little bit off of the price?" she asked tilting her head to one side and holding out the coin as if to bribe him with it.

"Yeah!" the boy said as he took the coin with both hands, put it in his pocket and held out his sack full of bottles and cups to allow her to pick which one she wanted.

"Take a good look Miss; sometimes the best ones are down at the bottom." The boy opened the mouth of the sack wide and jiggled it to make sure she could see clearly what her choices were. She found what she needed, nodded to the boy thankfully and turned to return to her sweeping, placing her bottle and cups next to the door. The boy skipped off with his sack over his shoulder looking very pleased with his sale. It did not take long for him to begin calling out for more bottles to buy or sell, attracting clients with the rattle of his sack.

A large woman with a floppy pink hat walked up to the veranda steps. Madame Muriel was married to the Chief of Police and was close friends with Monsieur Edmond. She had the habit of wearing dress suits that only served to prove to everyone that she was in complete denial about her true size. On this particular day, her choice of ensemble was a gray style with matching gray buttons screaming for a release from their valiant effort to hold the front of her suit coat closed.

"Hey there girl, is Monsieur Edmond still at home?" She was out of breath after her climb up the few wide steps that led up to where Lanto stood on the veranda; she placed her meaty hand flatly on Lanto's shoulder for balance and to keep herself from tipping over.

"No Madame Muriel, I'm sorry, he left over an hour ago. Would you like me to give him a message?"

"Yes, tell him that my son Rudolphe is arriving tonight from the capital. We are having a special welcome home dinner for him and would very much like it if Monsieur Edmond could come." At that, Madame Muriel turned and went on her way in a rush, apparently needing to inform others of her special visitor and the event in his honor.

Lanto went into the house and quickly wrote down the message in case she forgot. In reality, she never forgot. Coming from a poor country family in the mountains, it was not the norm to have paper and pen on hand. So one just had to remember the things one had to do. Since coming to Monsieur Edmonds' house, such things as paper and pens were always on hand. However, there were very few reasons to write things down, since Monsieur Edmond hated attending functions ever since his wife Madame Rosemarie had died two years earlier.

The day Madame Rosemarie died, the rain had been pouring down. A messenger had been sent to inform Lanto that the Madame had fallen. Lanto took a taxi from the house and went to the hospital as soon as she heard the news, but it was too late.

By the time Lanto had arrived, Madame Rosemarie had died of a heart attack. Monsieur Edmond came soon after. At first, he thought his wife must have had a bad fall due to the heavy rain. When the Doctor explained to Monsieur Edmond that his wife had left this world, he broke down into tears of shock. Lanto never saw a man cry so hard. The staff just left him to sit alone in that room holding Madame's hand so that he could have some privacy.

Lanto would not think about leaving him. Of course, it would not have been proper for hired help to hold their employers hand either. However, in the countryside village Lanto came from, no one would ever be left alone in such a time of need. In fact, a person who had just lost their wife would no doubt be surrounded by a room full of people for at least a month's time.

Food would be served around the clock to any visitors who might have come. The ones in mourning would sit in the room with the body while people came and gave words of encouragement to them. Each time someone would give his or her speech to those in grief, they would respond tearfully and sincerely; thus having dozens of opportunities to release their emotional burden a little at a time. So, by the end of the week, after so many visitors had come and spoken in like manner, it was as if the person in mourning had shed all the tears they needed to and would be ready to return to the duties of life as they must. Certainly, the situation Lanto found herself in with Monsieur Edmond bore no comparison to a room full of people, but Lanto could think of nothing else to do for poor Monsieur Edmond than to sit there quietly and watch him cry.

When the nurses came in and they took the body out, Monsieur Edmond apologized to Lanto for taking so long and said it was time to go. Wondering if her services would still be needed, Lanto had trouble sleeping that night. But Monsieur Edmond never talked about the subject of Rosemarie's death again. Lanto just went on with her work as if nothing had happened except of course when Monsieur Edmond needed her help in carrying out the funeral arrangements.

After the funeral, Monsieur Edmond had asked Lanto to pack up Madame's things and give them to the church. He requested that the items be donated to a countryside village, as he did not want to risk running into some poor beggar woman in Madame's Sunday best. Lanto doubted he would have recognized her clothing even if someone living in town had worn them.

Many of the poor in town could not afford the soap for washing laundry. And the river water often left clothes looking dull. Circumstances would be such that in a very short time Madame's clothes would have been unrecognizable. However, she made sure to pack it up and send it to her home village as there were many in need there and they never came this far to town. That was two years earlier and since then Lanto had grown into a young woman who felt confident in how to run a home.

Lanto set the note on the kitchen table and went on with her daily chores. She was well aware of the privilege of her situation. Being able to live in a fine plastered house, not a mud one like the village she came from was a dream for some girls. In addition, Monsieur and Madame had always treated her very kind, even letting her take some lessons at the local church so that she could finish learning to read and write.

Education for most girls in the area she came from ended at the age of fourteen. Many would end up working in the fields and marrying. However, Lanto's parents had wanted her to have other opportunities. Besides that, the money she made working in town gave them enough to put some of her younger brothers and sisters through school. Now that she was older, she felt her responsibility even stronger than before, and she was determined to do a good job and to make certain things kept going as smoothly as possible.

The water had begun to flow through the tap once again. Lanto filled a bucket full of water and then left the tap running so it could fill up the reserve barrel. The laundry would have to be done after the charcoal was lit, this would give the fire time to die down. She put the bucket of water on her head, picked up a bag of charcoal and walked towards the house to start preparing the noontime meal. The doorbell rang but Lanto did not hear it. As she walked into the house, she put the charcoal down next to the door and did not even notice the tall man standing in the kitchen.

Before she could put the water down, she turned to see two brown eyes staring right at her and screamed at the top of her lungs spilling the water all down the front of her smock and splattering water all over the floor in front of the stranger. The two stared at each other for a minute listening to the sound of the bucket spiraling in circles on the tile floor.

"I called out but didn't hear anyone so I decided to come in to see if anyone was out back," he said bluntly.

Lanto was still stunned from the feeling of the cold water dripping down her shirt but she had enough presence of mind to get down on her knees and begin wiping up the pool of water.

"What can I do for you?" she asked with a tone of annoyance in her voice.

"Monsieur Edmond sent me to fix the lights out back. He said they have not been working ever since the cyclone hit. My name is Cristo. It is nice to meet you. Do you need help?"

He held out his hand as he spoke but did not really step forward the way a person would do who truly wanted to help. Lanto pointed out back in silence rather than give him the lesson in manners she believed he sorely needed.

Cristo came and went several times that morning. He had to run back and forth to the hardware store to buy the parts he needed. Lanto made rice with a vegetable sauce for lunch and made sure to give him some as Monsieur Edmond always had her feed the workers when they came. Monsieur advised this for two reasons: first, if the worker is fed here, they do not have to go home for the noontime meal. Second, If the worker is here after the noontime meal they have no excuse not to return to work after eating.

Most of the people, who lived in town, went home for lunch every day. Monsieur Edmond worked at the bank across town and said his old legs had grown too tired to walk back and forth. A little restaurant served noodle soup down the street from where he worked. So, he would eat there every day instead of coming home. Lanto knew that the real reason why he ate there was that he missed his wife and just could not stand to take the noontime meal without her.

As Lanto washed the dishes, Cristo took a nap under the Loquat tree out back. Lanto was not prone to taking naps but her eyes felt heavy after having to finish her washing in such a short amount of time. She decided to lie down in her room located near the kitchen. When she woke up it was nearly 3:00, and far later than her usual time to go to market. She quickly looked to make certain that Cristo had gone and then locked up the house.

The market was bustling with people. Tuesdays were the busiest day, as all the people from the countryside came to sell their fruits and vegetables. Lanto passed several women waiting for a co-worker as the woman attempted to get her newborn baby tied up on her back. While balancing the tiny, sleeping ball in the crook of her back, she swung a cloth around it and snuggly tucked it in front while standing up. The baby remained sleeping the entire time. Within minutes, the woman had her baby safely wrapped. She put a basket full of avocados on her head as Lanto walked by. The woman once again pulled down her basket. The baby began to cry, and the woman took him off her back in order to breastfeed him. Lanto picked through the avocados to choose ones that would be ripe for eating later on.

Pumpkins were also in season, so Lanto bought three big slices to make some of Monsieur Edmonds favorite cakes. A little girl was sitting on the ground on a straw mat, slicing the large squashes to sell individually. Every once in awhile she picked up a homemade 'fan' or rather strips of a plastic bag tied to the end of a stick in order to fan away the flies with it. As Lanto chose her pieces of pumpkin, the girl never even bothered to look up. She sat with her chin in her hand; her elbow propped lazily on her knee, she used the other hand to take the money from Lanto's hand and put it in her little straw money basket.

Lanto then stopped to look at several chickens all tied up together. They looked like they would very much like to be bought as they were pecking each other in an attempt to get free. Rather than free them from one misery and take them to their grave, Lanto decided to wait until later to buy one as she had run out of time to clean and prepare it for supper that night.

"Well, hello there little Lanto!" She turned to see a familiar face from her younger years. He was a tall man with thin cheeks and graying hair; wearing a pair of sandals, shorts, a dress shirt that was only half buttoned, and a colorful blanket over his shoulders for warmth. The freshly carved walking stick he held filled the air around him with the smell of the eucalyptus wood. When the scent wafted into Lanto's nostrils, it forced her to take a deep breath. Lanto knew he must have come from the countryside since this was common attire there. She paused for a moment, trying to remember who he was.

"I'm sorry Sir, I have forgotten your name," she said as her cheeks darkened from embarrassment.

"I am from Four Rivers and worked with your father when you were just a little girl." Lanto recognized the name of the town as the one her father used to travel to for work so she felt quite sure the man was being truthful. As she did not often run into people from that area, and neither she nor her family had a telephone, she began to questions about how they might be doing.

"I'm sorry to say I haven't heard much from them in a long time. The cyclone weather drowned out several crops of rice and so the workers in our town didn't have a lot of harvesting to do, let alone enough to call over other workers such as from your Papas town."

Lanto carried on talking about the heat of the day as well as the price of the produce. When she could carry the pleasantries no farther, they shook hands and made their goodbyes. Lanto was always happy to speak with someone from her past. Yet, the brief encounter left her feeling anxious as to how her family might be fairing after such poor weather.

It was nearly 4:30 by the time Lanto walked in the door, only to see Monsieur Edmond had come home early from work. There was a serious look on his face as he read the note she had written about the dinner invitation from Madame Muriel that morning.

"Please sit down Lanto. I need to discuss something with you." She sat down obediently trying to think of how she could convince him to go to the party despite the fact that she knew he would not want to.

"Lanto," he asked, peering over his glasses, "is there something you need to tell me?" Lanto proceeded to relate the message from Madame Muriel as detailed as possible. Monsieur Edmond interrupted her rather abruptly, "Lanto, you know you can come to me if you are in any sort of trouble. I demand to know if there is something you are in need of that would warrant my help."

"No Sir, I do not want for anything." Lanto said, sitting very still. She was tempted to ask for phone credit to call her family but had the feeling that this might not be a good time.

Monsieur Edmond stood up in a rage, causing the wooden chair he was sitting on to tip over. The sound of his chair hitting the floor, made Lanto jump in her seat.

"Then why do you deem it necessary to take what is not yours? I came home early, Lanto, and to my surprise, the desk in my office had not only been broken into, but a good deal of money was taken out of it! If you hadn't returned home, I would have sent the police out looking for you but your honesty in returning has lent you time to explain yourself before returning to your former life in the field!"

Lanto could barely believe her ears. Never had she taken as much as one cent from Monsieur Edmond let alone dare to open his desk drawer and peek at anything inside. Lanto felt her throat closing up and her forehead beading with sweat. She could think of nothing else to say but "I did not enter into the office today."

Monsieur Edmond, who had remained standing, took her forcibly by the arm and marched her into her room where he nearly sent her spinning.

He turned to leave and without looking back at her and sternly said, "You have five minutes to pack your things. There will be a night bus leaving for your home village at dusk and you will be on it!" Without another word, Monsieur Edmond left his servant girl of the past eight years to stand alone in her tiny room with only the sounds of his footsteps climbing the wood staircase that lead to his room upstairs.

The ride to the bus station was quieter than usual. In a matter of a handful of minutes her life had turned upside down. Lanto tried to guess at what might have happened and what was going to happen. Thoughts of the reaction of her family kept overtaking her. She knew of things like this happening to other girls in her village, and once branded a thief it would take years if not the rest of her lifetime, before her reputation could be restored. She dreaded returning after her family who had worked so hard to get her to her current position in life.

The station was full of people coming and going. Several young boys at the station entrance were attempting to kick a ball they had made out of old plastic bags that had been tied together with string. The taxi driver beeped his horn to get them to move while yelling some words expressing his irritation at them. While moving out of the way, two of the boys attempted to jump on the back of the moving vehicle to catch a free ride, falling off and laughing as the driver entered the station. They entered the area of the station that had buses going to Lanto's town. Each town had its own booth. The booths were connected to form a square. Above the booths were wooden plaques, painted in a variety of colors with the names of various destinations.

In the middle of the square where all the buses parked and waited for passengers to fill them, vendors walked through the crowds of and clusters of people and even went on and off the busses trying to sell their wares. Some had handmade plaques with all of their items hanging on it. Items such as flashlights, children's plastic toys and combs were swinging back and forth, as the vendor called out an array of prices.

One small boy had a pair of glasses with a paper nose attached. The nose curled up and when the boy blew into a tiny tube, the nose flew out and a squeaky sound came out. Normally, such people watching would have served, as good evening entertainment for Lanto, but tonight her senses were not receptive to the environment surrounding her. Hoping this was nothing but a bad dream she tried her hardest not to look up at the crowds.

The bus that was going to Lanto's town already had men on top of it securing baggage. Monsieur Edmond asked the taxi driver to wait for him so that he could enter the station to buy Lantos ticket and then go home. Lanto got out too but stood just next to the taxi watching the men pack up the bus. There were other men below it throwing boxes to the ones standing on top packing the bus roof with the passenger's luggage. There was even a straw basket filled with quacking ducks on the end. The men were calling out to two other workers on the top of the bus next to theirs boasting, jeering and wagering that whoever was finished first had to buy the other a beer that night.

"Beg you for a coin Miss, I haven't eaten yet today," a little boy was looking up at her with his dirty hands out stretched. The one over sized purple sandal that he was wearing on his left foot caught Lantos attention. He had clearly gotten it out of the garbage. Yet, he had managed to match the color perfectly with the purple sleeves of his shirt. Since it was a shoe meant for an adult, its size enabled him to rest his other foot on top of the one actually placed in the shoe. To Lanto, he looked just like one of the egret birds found in the rice fields of the countryside. The boy was skinny enough to have not eaten for more than just one day. Lanto reached into the pocket of the work smock she was still wearing and pulled out her last coin. She sighed.

"It would not do me any good anyways," she thought to herself.

"Thank you very much! I wish you many blessings!" said the little boy smiling up at Lanto. Before she could change her mind, he ran off clutching the coin in his left hand and quickly holding up his right hand, called another child over to him. The two disappeared into a sea of people, mini buses, and stray dogs.

Lanto now saw Monsieur Edmond coming out of the station as if he were attending to business on any other occasion. From his left the gateman of Madame Muriel's house ran up with a group of men standing close behind him. Lanto could not make out what the crowd wanted but it seemed as if they had a man in the center and were holding him by the scruff of his neck. The men were all speaking at the same time, making it difficult to understand what the gateman was saying to Monsieur Edmond.

"We found this dog running off today Monsieur. When he went to buy his ticket out of town a slip of paper fell out of his pocket that had your name on it. When we asked him where he got that bank slip, he tried to run out and we grabbed him. He says his name is Cristo and that the money was his payment for work rendered at your home today. Is it true, Sir?"

Before he found out the answer, he gave the man a good slap on top of his head causing Cristo to free one hand in order to rub the spot.

Monsieur Edmond looked at the man closely but clearly did not know him. Lanto's eyes focused in on Cristo and suddenly it occurred to her what had happened.

"He came today to work on the lights!" cried Lanto in a late attempt to speak on her own behalf.

After briefly looking over at her, the group of men turned again to Monsieur Edmond. The gateman gave Monsieur Edmond a roll of money along with the bank slips with his name on them and waited for further orders on what to do with Cristo.

As the men spoke Lanto felt the breath come back into her chest. It seemed all would be right again and she could keep her employment. The men took Cristo off to the police station where he would no doubt spend an ample amount of time. Madame Muriel's gateman stayed to continue talking to Monsieur Edmond. Lanto felt a little sad for Cristo thinking he must have had really needed the help.

Monsieur Edmond was a generous man. But once crossed, he rarely took the time to reconsider.

Lanto once again focused on what the men were saying, as action of the evening seemed to be ending. She was anxious to get home as she had not been given the time to cook the pumpkin for Monsieur Edmonds' cakes.

"What in the world are you doing here?" Monsieur Edmond asked the gateman.

"I've come to fetch Madame Muriel's son who has just returned from the university east of here. I do believe the Madame said you might be coming for dinner tonight, Sir. Would you care to ride back with us to the house?"

It was the first time since he had initially asked her if she had something to tell him that Monsieur Edmond looked Lanto in the eye. Evidently, he remembered the note he had been reading upon her arrival and everything seemed to come together in his now calmed mind.

"Yes man! We will both be coming. Tell Muriel we will return home to get freshened up and that I will be bringing my right hand worker, Lanto, as my special guest." The gateman gave a nod and went off in search of the bus that was arriving with Madame Muriel's son.

Monsieur Edmond then turned to Lanto and said softly, "Lanto my girl, I owe you a great apology. As you know, these are hard times and things such as what I thought happened today, must be handled immediately lest too many emotions get involved. My Rosie would have taken care of things like thievery and whenever things come up that she would have handled I get very flustered and miss her very much. But all of that seems unimportant now. I feel it would be better if I were to show you my thanks. How would you like to accompany me to dinner tonight at Madame Muriel's house?"

Seeing as she had just heard him telling Madame Muriel's gateman they were both coming, she did not really view this as one of those situations where she could say no. She felt about as stunned as she did when he had accused her of stealing. In fact, the accusation had made more sense.

"Thank you Monsieur Edmond." Lanto responded despondently. He didn't really notice that there was no real joy in her eyes as one would expect for a girl of sixteen years old to have upon receiving such an invitation.

On social occasions, the mixing of servants and employers was not encouraged. There were things like church functions, political rallies, and festivals, which might warrant a communal meal together, but for the most part each person in the community knew their place.

There were those who could afford house help like Monsieur Edmond, and then there were those who could not afford to be anything but someone's house help, like Lanto. Now, here stood Monsieur Edmond, inviting his house girl to dinner at another person's house! If Lanto had any inclination of not forgiving her employer, it went out of her head when she realized he must have clearly gone insane at the thought of her having broken into his office.

It was not long before they arrived home. Monsieur Edmond swung open the door as if victorious and said, "Well, that settles it then. Your silence gives you away! Wash up, and put on your Sunday dress, we'll be dining out tonight, my girl!" With that, he bounded up the stairs, in a very uncharacteristically excited manner.

Lanto entered her room not knowing what was worse. Having just been fired and then rehired, was enough to leave a hole in her stomach. Now that empty stomach filled up with butterflies at the thought of having to dine at Madame Muriel's house. More accustomed to eating at the kitchen table at Monsieur Edmonds home, Lanto had never been invited to such a fancy home for dinner before.

The schedule of a servant was very full and rarely did one have any time off. Saturday afternoon was the day for washing ones personal clothing and Sunday was the day to go to church and rest. There was only one other servant girl her age nearby. Sylvie was Madame Muriel's house servant and since she was afraid to walk on the road alone, Lanto always ended up walking to her house. Sylvie's employers were not as friendly as Monsieur Edmond was and she was not allowed to have visitors in the house. Therefore, Lanto and Sylvie often would take a walk outside which meant getting in before dark. On a typical Sunday evening, Lanto would finish up by reading from, 'Say what?,' her favorite newspaper, and then go to bed.

Her thoughts must have taken her farther than she expected because before she knew it, Monsieur Edmond was calling for her to get moving. Lanto quickly pulled out a pressed dress. As her hair was standing up in certain areas, she tidied it up with her pink plastic headband and a ponytail in back, tucking in the end of her hair so it would look like a bun. It still looked very windswept, so she put some oil in her hand and tried to pat down the bits sticking up in back.

She took a brief moment to stare in the small frameless mirror hanging on the wall. As she placed her only pair of beads on her neck, she wondered if anyone else at the dinner party would be wearing plastic. No one in town really went around very showy but at this moment, she was feeling very self-conscious regarding what the appropriate attire for such an occasion would be.

Another call from the doorway quickly turned her thoughts to her green handbag. She thought to herself that green would go nicely with pink. This was actually the combination she wore every Sunday to church. However, she convinced herself that it was precisely the color combination she would have wanted, had she had many other choices. She whisked herself out of the room leaving the door to swing open behind her.

Monsieur Edmond and Lanto walked up the stone pathway of Madame Muriel's Colonial style home. They lived on a main street that had lights lining it. Most of the houses in town were similar. Madame Muriel had a veranda like most homes, but theirs encased the entire house, not just the front side of it. It had two stories, with staircases leading up to the second floor on both the outside and inside of the house. The second floor was also encased by a veranda that connected to all the bedrooms. Many homes had a place for the gateman to sleep. But this home had actual servants quarters equipped with their own kitchen areas for times when they were not working. The property was very large and included farming areas, a rarity in the center of town.

Madame Muriel's family had been some of the first settlers in that area and had done a lot to build up the town when it was first established. Her great-grandfather even had a stone bust built near city hall thanking him for all his contributions. Under the stone statue of this man, sporting a fashionable hat for his day as well as a thick mustache that tapered as far as his jawbone read the name, 'RASOANOMENJANAHARY JEAN-PIERE RIVO.'

The gateman let them in the big metal gate with a wave and a familiar smile as it had only been an hour prior, that they had met at the station. Lanto had been to Madame Muriel's home before, as her and Madame Rosemarie had been good friends. Madame Rosemarie rarely did any project without taking Lanto along. However, this time was different, Madame Rosemarie was not there, and Lanto had not come as a house servant. Lanto felt like she was being seen for the first time.

"Edmond, it is just like you to be late! We are so glad you remained un-injured with that beast of a man having entered your home today!" Madame Muriel approached the two hurriedly in the same gray suit she was wearing earlier but this time she had a silk scarf draped over her shoulders. She had braided her hair on the two sides of her head and pinned it back in a bun. In her ears were large pearl earrings that matched the pearl necklace, which fit snuggly around her neck. As she gave Monsieur Edmond her hand, he kissed her three times, first on the right, then the left cheek, and finally on her right again. He also gave a slight bow as he began to make his apologies.

"I'm sorry we are late Muriel. I believe you heard what happened at the station today with poor little Lanto here. I have been a terrible fool you see."

Madame Muriel never made eye contact with Lanto although she was obviously was aware of her presence as she pointed to the house so as to show Lanto where she could place the things they had brought to share with the dinner party. Lanto had three baguettes of bread and one bottle of wine. The baguettes were already showing signs of being too soft but the wine was Madame Muriel's favorite brand, being produced locally by a monastery nearby. The three of them walked into the house and Monsieur Edmond finished explaining everything that happened that day while they stood in the doorway and wiped off their shoes.

"So you see my good friend, I wanted to bring the girl with me as a sign of my appreciation for her respectful nature in light of my bad judgment. Please forgive me if I've intruded on your hospitality in any way."

All the Madame managed to say was, "It's just like you, Edmond to reward the staff after having slept on the job. But that's not for me to say, we are old friends and you may do as you please, come in and have a seat, there is plenty for everyone."

With a sigh of relief, Lanto followed her two elders into the dining room. She was seated near Madame Muriel's daughter Josephine. Josephine was Lanto's age but was still schooling and it was planned that she attend university next now that her brother had graduated. She had long smooth black hair with just the slightest curl in it. Her clothes were new and made of satin making her shine when the light hit her a certain way. Monsieur Edmond sat at the other side of Josephine, and then next to him was Monsieur Rakotomalala Noelson, otherwise known as Monsieur Malala. He was Madame Muriel's husband and well known in the community. His family had come from another town but he was transferred when still single to work for the police department. The two married at the local church and lived with Madame Muriel's parents until they died. After that, Monsieur Malala and Madame Muriel became the proprietors of the estate.

The guest of honor, Madame Muriel's son came in soon after. He began to introduce himself to everyone but since most in the room knew him, rather than introductions, it turned into more of an opportunity for comments on how he had grown and how old it made them all feel. By the time, he circled around to where Lanto was he shook her hand but was looking over at Monsieur Edmond who was talking loudly to him.

"So my boy," echoed Monsieur Edmond, "where will all this education take you now that you are free from the chains of higher learning?"

"As far as I can possibly go Sir, or as far as father would like me to go I should say," replied the young man with an air of mock assertiveness. He looked very uncomfortable when asked questions. Every time someone would ask him something, he would push his glasses up higher on his nose and clear his throat before answering. Lanto assumed he must have been very studious, as it seemed at a social setting like this one, he felt out of sorts.

Everyone else who had been milling around the dining room and chatting took his or her seats to begin eating. The table and chairs were made of rosewood. All the plates were made of porcelain and designed with mauve colored flowers. There was a brass candle bra that sat in the center of the table and was surrounded by freshly cut Mimosa's. Everything sat prettily on a lace tablecloth that matched the curtains.

Then, dinner was served. Madame Muriel's server for the evening was Sylvie. She carried in a large plate of juicy duck surrounded by candied oranges. Lanto's eyes met hers and Sylvie quickly bit her lip to hold back the laughter at seeing her friend sitting at the table. Sylvie served the meal, Madame Muriel dismissed her until it was time to clear the table and serve dessert. Before she left, she managed to look back at Lanto with a quick smile and then in an instant she was gone. Lanto's first reaction was to get up and leave with Sylvie, but she remembered that she was a guest and had to stay.

"Don't forget, Lanto, never turn down an invitation to a meal. And show your appreciation by eating well, but only take seconds if offered." This was her fathers' advice before dropping her off at the bus station so many years ago, and it was now ringing in her ears.

"Always have something to contribute to the conversation, Lanto, or else people will think you are arrogant. But do not command attention or people will not care for your general personality." Her mother had given her these words of advice while packing up her bags. Lanto was determined to put their words of wisdom to good use.

Often growing up, she had gone to bed hungry. When the harvest time came, it seemed everyone ate themselves silly, as if they were storing food away for harder times. There were always harder times. The older children took turns eating when there was not enough food for everyone. Now here Lanto sat, thinking how proud her father and mother would be to know their girl was sitting in town, in the home of the Chief of Police, eating duck, and having fine conversation. Well, at least she was listening to fine conversation.

"Please pass the butter." Josephine had yet to speak to Lanto and so this request helped her to break off from daydreaming and focus in on the conversation again. Lanto passed the butter and Josephine said thank you then turned her head to the rest of the adults sitting on her left as if to try not to notice that Lanto was sitting there. Josephine was very interested in whatever her brother had to say about university. Although in Lanto's mind, her questions really were not going to bring her any sort of benefit.

They ranged from, "What is the fashion among the girls there?" to "Is the music on the radio the same as the songs they play here?" Each time she would ask a silly question, before her brother could answer one of the adults at the table would answer with something like, "Well, what do you think the fashion is like among the girls there you funny girl?" or "There are only three stations in the entire country, why on earth wouldn't they play the same music?" Josephine was used to such criticisms and so it did not stop her from giving the person debating her questions a sharp stare and then turning her attention back to her brother. He would answer her while pushing his vegetables around the plate instead of eating them.

Lanto focused in on the rest of the guests at the table. On Monsieur Malala's right was Rudolphe, then a cousin, whose name Lanto never fully heard. Mademoiselle Therese, Rudolphe's high school teacher was next, then the minister, and his wife who were seated across from each other, leaving the wife next to Lanto. Seated at the foot of the table was Madame Muriel. This meant Lanto was sandwiched between the minister's wife and Madame Muriel's daughter, making Lanto feeling very nervous as to whom she could address. She opted to try to speak to the minister's wife as they had become acquainted already during church functions.

"Are there any new activities at the church I might be able to help with?" Lanto asked.

The minister's wife turned her head from her conversation and smiled at Lanto, understanding the effort she was making to join in. She replied, "Why yes, in fact, if you could come early this Sunday, I have an outing with the children that I need help with. We are going to forage the forest for plant life that was common in bible times."

This caught the table's general attention and everyone began to ask questions about what sort of plant life she would be looking for. Although finding herself out of the conversation once again due to the number and frequency of questions from the other guests, Lanto was very pleased she had come up with a question that was provoking such lively table talk.

Although being her first time eating at a table with such high quality plates and glasses, it was not her first time setting one. Her critical eye began to see where the cutlery was slovenly placed. The coffee spoons were touching the water glasses. The worst of it was several of the cloth napkins were folded inside out! Lanto was going to have to talk to Sylvie about this as she found it embarrassing for her friend to have gone to such insufficient efforts in the setting of the table on such a worthy occasion.

Madame Muriel had Sylvie bring in a beautifully decorated white cake with yellow edible flowers in celebration of Rudolphe's graduation. Everyone at the table ooed and awed as the candles at the center of the table were replaced by the graduation cake and Madame Muriel began cutting and serving big pieces of it. Sylvie would take the pieces one at a time and then place them in front of the seated guest. Lanto wondered if at one time Madame Muriel actually fit in the space, she was forcing herself in to. While she was perfectly able to cut the cake without spilling a crumb, with every slice she elbowed Rudolphe in the ear. At one point, the cousin turned and almost had his nose in the schoolteacher's piece of cake.

Lanto felt like her stomach was going to burst from the duck, green beans, and rice she had just eaten. Since no one else complained of being too full to eat cake, she too sat respectfully watching the three-layer piece of cake placed before her and wondered how she would ever get it down.

Everyone waited for the rest to be served before picking up his or her dessertspoon. As was the custom, Rudolphe's father gave a lengthy speech about how all the money that had been invested into his education would surely not be for waste, as he would work hard to return it with interest for the family. He ended by giving everyone permission to begin eating their cake.

The cake was dry in Lantos opinion and had evidently been store-bought. Monsieur Edmonds wife had instructed Lanto on how to bake a proper cake and would often have her make them for company or for taking when visiting those who had been sick in bed and in need of some cheering up. This past experience, or education, as Lanto liked to call it, left her a little snobby when it came to the eating of cakes. She was not accustomed however to eating so much white frosting and it seemed to her to be the very epitome of happiness.

Each creamy bite slid down Lantos throat and caused her eyes to close shut.

"Would you care for another piece my girl?" said Madame Muriel looking at Lanto for the first time with wide eyes and a slight chuckle.

Lanto looked up to see the entire table staring at her. Sylvie entered to take out everyone's dishes and noticed the reason for their stares. She quickly gestured to her mouth as a sign to help Lanto realize she had created a big white creamy mustache that reached all the way to the apples of her cheeks. Lanto quickly wiped her mouth as the guests got up from the table to retire to the sitting room.

Although not being given an opportunity to respond to the question of another slice of cake, Sylvie clearing the table could see the look in her friend's eye and quickly put another piece on a napkin and pushed it over in Lantos direction. "Quick, put it in your bag!' was all Sylvie managed to mumble before disappearing into the kitchen.

"Lanto my girl, come and join the rest of the party!" urged Monsieur Edmond from the sitting room.

"Oh Edmond, leave the girl to go sit out on the veranda and catch the night air. She doesn't want to be in here with a bunch of old stuffed shirts." Madame Muriel uttered the comment loud enough to let Lanto understand that this was a command more than an allowance.

Lanto quietly walked past the seating area. Monsieur Malala poured the men some rum. Everyone was slowly sitting down as if too full to make the long journey down to the bottom of the couch.

The large veranda had a wooden bench that rocked back and forth. Lanto sat down on it since it was closest to the sitting room window. She figured she might still be able to hear some of the muffled speech coming from inside.

"I don't really feel like being with a bunch of stuffed shirts either," said Rudolphe as he stood in the doorway. His hair was soft and combed to one side. Although fresh out of school, he was already sporting a very fashionable thin mustache. The navy blue vest he wore complimented his jeans and gave him the look of being conservative yet fashionable. The sleeve of his blue striped shirt met his wrist just in the right place to show off a nice shiny silver watch that had a large blue face. Lanto wondered if a boy his age could really go about picking out such nice clothes for himself or if his mother or sister had secretly helped him.

"You don't talk much do you?" he said looking at Lanto causing her to look down at her lap startled by the question. She had not really expected him to want to talk to her. She was accustomed to people speaking, happy for her presence in order for their thoughts to be heard, yet not really wanting a response from her in return.

"I like to talk" was all she could come up with to say. With that, Rudolphe sat down on the veranda step. He leaned against the post opposite of where Lanto sat so he did not have to turn his neck to speak with her. They began talking about where she was from and what brought her to be with Monsieur Edmond.

"I have been away at school for a long time I can see. There are so many new people in town; I barely know the place anymore. I wonder how I will fit into the general pulse of life here?" he said. He looked pensively up at the night sky as if throwing the thought up to the stars wondering if he might get an answer back with some foresight into his future.

"Returning home after a long period of time can make one anxious. I almost had to move back home today, in fact, I was quite worried about the outcome", Lanto interjected. Thus came to full light the story of what had happened earlier and how she came to be invited to dinner.

Rudolphe listened keenly. Raising his eyebrows and peering over the top of his thin black framed glasses, he asked, "Didn't you think to tell Monsieur Edmond that you did not take his money, and that there was a strange worker in the house that very day?" His question seemed more like a statement and Lanto felt herself becoming increasingly self-conscious, and worried that he would think she was silly. She knew that she had failed to give herself voice in the light of great degradation.

"It isn't easy to say what one might do in a situation of great shock." She said, straightening herself up in her seat and raising her head high, over compensating for her lack of pride earlier in the day.

"Well, one thing's for sure," he turned his head to look back up at the night sky and continue his thought, "Monsieur Edmond has a loyal worker in you. I would have never stood for that. Let alone went back to work for the person who had just wrongly fired me."

Lanto smiled at the compliment and the two continued to stare up at the twinkling stars. There were so many up there it looked like they were putting on a lightshow just for the two of them. There was hardly a sound on the streets. Every once in awhile muffled laughter from inside would cause one of them to look at the window where everyone was. Lanto thought that maybe Rudolphe would eventually want to go inside and join the others. But he never did. He sat on that step and just kept staring and talking to Lanto as if they had been old friends.

Soon Monsieur Edmond came out and told her it was time to go. She shook hands with Rudolphe who had stood up when she did to stay goodbye. Lanto and Monsieur Edmond shook hands with the rest of the guests and walked off in the dark waving to all that were standing on the veranda to see them off.

It was far too late to catch a taxi and the night air was just right for such a walk. Monsieur Edmond did not say much on the walk home. There was no need for words. In Monsieur Edmond's mind, the evening had been very satisfactory. Words would only risk spoiling the good outcome. He had his money back. He had his "little Lanto" back. And the best part of all; he had survived another one of Muriel's boring dinner parties and would not be expected to attend another for at least three months time.

That night Lanto thought hard about what Rudolphe had said. It never occurred to her to leave Monsieur Edmond after he had agreed to take her back. She fell asleep wondering what Monsieur Edmond would have for breakfast since she had not yet made him the pumpkin cakes she had planned to make for him that afternoon.

Part II

Rudolphe arose with a feeling of deep satisfaction over his new role as the family graduate. He greeted everyone with an air of superiority. He did not do so in a demeaning way, but rather as if to show, he was ready to take charge of his own life and future. This worked of course with the house help, the sellers he might have met on the street, as well as the children walking in his path. However, when it came to his father, he felt himself becoming increasingly incapable of wielding any sort of authority at all, even over himself.

"Well, what is your plan for the day?" his father asked, putting down the newspaper he was holding.

Knowing this was just an introduction to whatever his father had planned for him that day; Rudolphe simply replied that he was awaiting further instruction. Monsieur Malala then put down his paper and picked up a stack of papers with names of prospective employers. Monsieur Malala had each employer's address and location typed out along with the job description and name of the person who would interview Rudolphe.

Rudolphe graduated with full honors in business management. This meant applying to several of the stores in town that might need help in organizing their staff. A mobile phone store needed part time help. However, Monsieur Malala said this would be his last choice as part time work was useless. No one in town employed anyone part time in his opinion. There was part time pay with full time work for those employers who were too cheap to pay the already low day's wage that was standard. Monsieur Edmond felt there might be an opening at the bank where he worked that would fit Rudolphe's skill level, however Monsieur Malala felt this would look like he was just incurring favor from a friend.

"You'll need to start from the bottom up no matter where you work. It will mean no money for you, but if you can enter in a position of authority even over a few, then you will quickly be able to apply what you have learned and become a successful business man." Monsieur Malala kept counseling him with every paper he handed over to his son, handing them out one at time so that he could go over each one with Rudolphe individually.

The last place to go visit was the one for which his father was most hopeful. The Assistant Manager to Monsieur Boone's paper printing facility was open. Monsieur Malala liked the idea of his son having a title right out of university. Rudolphe made sure to put all the papers in his portfolio, giving his father a nod and excusing himself to begin his string of interviews.

He decided to go in the order by which he passed each business. The mobile phone store was first. Upon walking in, an older woman reading a newspaper, without looking up, asked what she could do to help him.

"I would like to speak with the Manager please," Rudolphe said while attempting to clear his throat of any remnant of nervousness.

She nodded, asked him to please wait, and came back in a few minutes time with a tall man, middle aged, with dark black hair, and a freckled complexion. The man conducted the interview right there at the counter. He had many questions to ask Rudolphe about cellular phones, the latest contracts, and his past work experience. Rudolphe feared that his lack of experience on how mobile phones worked had greatly decreased his chances of obtaining work there.

While in school, his parents felt it was a distraction to have a mobile phone. He was given a phone with no credit on it so that if they wanted to call him they could. But since the phone had no credit on it and he did not work while schooling, he was never able to call anyone with it.

When the interview was finished, the man shook his hand and informed him that he could call back on Monday to see if he got the job.

Next was Monsieur Edmonds bank. As it was nearly ten o'clock, and he knew men like Monsieur Edmond usually took a tea break, Rudolphe bought some pumpkin cakes a vendor nearby was selling. They had been freshly fried over the hot coals just minutes before. The scent of the cakes made Rudolphe hungry but he dared not eat one lest the grease from his fingers get on his freshly washed and ironed clothes. Rudolphe paid the woman who grabbed the money with one hand while still cooking with the other. He told her to keep the change. She looked at him strangely but gladly stuffed the ten cents in her pocket and kept flipping cakes making the hot oil crackle and sizzle.

The bank was the cleanest building in town. It was not the only bank in town, but for some reason, Monsieur Edmonds bank was the one most used by the town's inhabitants. Wondering if he should ask for Monsieur Edmond directly or just inform one of the workers that he was there for an interview, Rudolphe just stood in the middle of the reception area. Before he had made up his mind on how he would present himself, Monsieur Edmond walked out of one of the offices with wide arms opened.

He gave Rudolphe a solid handshake, making Rudolphe feel somewhat important in front of the customers waiting in line at the window. He was quickly ushered down a white tiled hallway that lead to Monsieur Edmonds office. Telling him to have a seat, Monsieur Edmond picked up the receiving end of his phone and informed someone, that he wouldn't be taking any phone calls for the next hour.

"So my boy, how is your first day home since arriving last night? You must be exhausted." Monsieur Edmond asked while gesturing Rudolphe to have a seat.

"No, rather I'm ready to find work so that I can get started before my enthusiasm begins to cool off. I don't want to start thinking that I'm only here on vacation. I need to make some roots and settle down."

With that, Edmond put a hand typed resume on the desk and said, "Here is my resume, although I do believe my father has already sent you one."

Monsieur Edmond gave a sort of chuckle, knowing that Rudolphe's father was a persistent fellow. What Rudolphe did not know is that Monsieur Edmond tended to be disorganized and he had no memory of ever seeing a resume. He gladly took the paper from his desk and began to read it while rocking back and forth in his big black office chair. "It seems you have quite a bit to offer any company," he said.

Rudolphe found these words to be very encouraging and thought he would be much more likely to stand on his own two feet with Monsieur Edmond despite his having been an old family friend.

"It says here you have done some intern work in a government office," Monsieur Edmond asked while looking up at Rudolphe. "Yes sir, that's correct, it was actually a land office that stamped documentation once proof of ownership had been provided." A short grunt by Monsieur Edmond gave Rudolphe the impression that he was interested in this and so he chose to expound on his duties in the office without any further prompting by his interviewer.

Rudolphe had nearly forgotten about the little cakes when they slipped from his lap and onto the floor and spilt out of their little plastic sack. As he bent over to begin picking them up Monsieur Edmond got up waving his hand and said, "Oh don't worry about that Ruddy my boy, we'll have someone come and clean that up soon enough. Now why don't you come with me and we'll take a look around the office and let you get a feel for the place." With that, Rudolphe followed Monsieur Edmond out the office door, but not before picking up a couple of the cakes that were wrapped in oil stained brown paper and placing them gently on the desk. He thought he had seen Monsieur Edmond eyeing them and was afraid after seeing him off he might be tempted to return to his office and eat one anyways.

After about twenty minutes, Rudolphe got the distinct impression that he was being given details of the banks functions because he had gotten the job. Monsieur Edmond did not seem to be a man of many words, but when he had taken Rudolphe back to the reception extending his hand while saying, "See you on Monday then?" Rudolphe knew the day had been a success and decided that would be his last interview.

As he walked home with a skip in his step, he tried hard not to think about his father. No doubt, Monsieur Malala would be disappointed that his son would not be holding the title of Assistant Manager for Monsieur Boone's paper printing facility. Rudolphe tried to figure out a way to make bank teller sound more successful but concluded that he would tell his mother first and let her break the news to Monsieur Malala.

The avocados Lanto bought at the market the morning prior were now ripe and soft for the eating. Lanto scraped several into a bowl adding some sugar and mashing them. This was one of her favorite desserts to eat. She placed the green mound in a glass bowl filled up to the brim and put it on the refrigerator shelf for later. She put the little pumpkin cakes she had made for Monsieur Edmond on the table and placed a small net over them to keep the flies away.

The doorbell rang and Lanto went to answer it, only to find Sylvie standing their crying.

"What's wrong with you? What happened? Are you hurt? Come in and sit down," Lanto asked, she ushered Sylvie into the kitchen and brought her some tissue to dry her red, swollen eyes.

"It's the most terrible thing in the world!" Sylvie lamented, choking back the tears. She still had her work smock on and was carrying an empty market bag over her arm.

"What is the most terrible thing in the world Sylvie? Please tell me what has happened."

"It's Johnny. He's going to join the army!" Lanto sat back in her chair with a sigh of relief at the revelation that this was just another piece of romantic drama in Sylvie's life. She quickly handed her friend a pumpkin cake knowing that she was fond of eating in times of emotional distress.

Johnny's family sold fruit from their orchard that was about an hour's walk out of town. Johnny and Sylvie secretly met and talked every afternoon when Sylvie went to get her employers' groceries from the market. Monsieur Malala preferred his food bought fresh everyday even though the family could afford refrigeration. It was only used to keep things like juice cold or maybe store some leftover food for the evening. This kept Sylvie's day very full and, as the house had several servants there was never a need for Sylvie to stay home and do other things.

Madame Muriel preferred to have her younger servant girl go with her on daily errands as she cost half price to travel with her on the public transport since she was still small. This afforded Sylvie time alone to chat with Johnny. They had secretly been meeting every afternoon for two years. Although he was not officially courting Sylvie, primarily because he did not yet have the money for the local formalities of engagement, they had exchanged words of commitment to one another and spent many a moment talking about their future together and making a family. Johnny's family loved Sylvie, but since the Malala's would not allow Sylvie to see boys while in their employment, Johnny and she met in secret. Well, as secret as one can be in a small town like this one. Everyone knew the two were in love except perhaps Madame Muriel.

"How could he do this to me?" she cried. "He's leaving in the morning to go for training! I'm not even going to be able to say goodbye." The tears that Lanto had thought were dried flowed afresh in big drops and she could think of nothing more than to put her arm around her friend and try to coax her to tell her more of how this all came about.

"I found out today when Madame Muriel was in the kitchen," sniffed Sylvie. The gateman, Joseph, came in with the news that several of the young men in town were accepted to join the new trainees for the army post four hours west of here. When I went to market this afternoon, I saw Johnny's mother and she informed me he would be leaving first thing in the morning with the new recruits. I came here as soon as I heard. Now I don't even have supper for tonight!"

Lanto got up to begin to gather some carrots and potatoes for her friend to take home. They often did this, if one of them had run out of time to do the marketing, making sure to exchange the next day for what they had borrowed. She had hoped that this would ease her friend's nerves but even as she sat the plastic bag down on the table, she felt her friend tense again. There was a sudden 'bang, bang, bang' that rattled the screen door.

It was Johnny. The doorframe was filled with his somber presence. His typically quiet nature made him a little intimidating to the average person. Now that he was standing there wearing the green and white uniform given new trainees before departing, he was even more so. He did not wait for Lanto to open the door but rushed in and hurried into the kitchen area to grab Sylvie as she was attempting to run out the back door.

"I tried to tell you this morning but you didn't come to the market," he pleaded as he held her close. Sylvie had buried her head in his chest and was crying. Lanto went into her bedroom and sat on the bed. She could not hear what the couple was saying but in between muffled sobs, she saw Johnny trying to comfort Sylvie by stroking the braided black hair away from her neck. He was hugging her and rocking side to side trying to say comforting things to ease the pain of their inevitable separation.

By the time Sylvie came around to being able to look up into Johnny's eyes, it was time for him to go. Lanto came out and walked behind them staying with Sylvie near the door as Johnny went away looking behind him every few seconds to stare at his brave girl. She was managing to swallow the tears but Lanto knew that another dam would burst forth again as soon as they re-entered the house.

Lanto wondered if it would just be best for her to leave her friend alone. How could she possibly come up with any words to comfort her? Lanto had never been in love. People who spoke of it said it was something wonderful and horrible all at the same time. Lanto figured this was one of the horrible moments.

"Are you going to be okay?" was all she managed to say by the time her friend came into the kitchen.

"Yes, I need to get the dinner started before Madame Muriel comes home" Sylvie said as she picked up the bag Lanto had set out for her. The fact that her friend looked so serious instead hysterical was a slight matter of concern for Lanto. Sylvie did not look back once as she walked toward home but rushed off with determined steps.

Lanto went back into the house and began to peel carrots all the while thinking about Johnny, wondering where he would move and how long he would have to stay there. They say that the military pays very well once you make it through the recruitment and training period. All the military men and police that come through town always looked tall as if they had eaten plenty of meat. Although they were always fit, their skin was fleshy not dark and tight like the skin of the farmers. After several years of training, the men were encouraged to marry their wives legally and were even provided with housing for their children. This gave their families a place to live when they went off on assignments sometimes for months at a time. "If only Sylvie could have a life of happiness!" Lanto thought to herself half-wondering if such a life would truly bring someone like Sylvie happiness. She hoped more that her friend could endure the lonely moments now that she would have to do her marketing without seeing Johnny standing there waiting for her every day.

After Lanto finished her cooking, she placed it in a warming bowl ready and waiting for Monsieur Edmonds arrival. Lanto locked up the house, picked up her plastic marketing bag and walked out the front door. Rudolphe had been sitting there waiting for her. He said, "well, it's about time you showed up!"

Lanto frowned with a look of indignation. Placing her free hand on her hip she said, "And what may I ask am I late for?"

"It's my mother's house girl. She has run off with some solider boy. I know you're her friend because I saw you smiling at one another at my dinner party and so I thought that maybe you might know where we could find her. Mama doesn't know yet and if she comes to find out, she might just call the police after the girl. I know it's not that the girl means to do the family wrong and I just want to find her before Mama does." Rudolphe said all of this in a rush while pointing behind him towards his home.

Lanto had no idea how this was possible as she had just been with Sylvie not that long ago. She looked down calculating the time again using her fingers to count and said, "I just spoke with her here at the house, and I gave her carrots for supper! How could she possibly be gone?"

"She left this note" and he handed it to her, still holding it while she read as if he did not want her to take it. The note read simply, "Gone with Johnny to the army. Will not be coming back. Thank you. – S'

"Where do you think they went?" Rudolphe said as he folded up the note and put it back in his shirt pocket.

"I haven't got any idea. The only place they ever met was the market and everyone has packed up and went home by this time."

"If she hasn't thought this through, she could get herself into trouble. My mother doesn't take to the help, or anyone for that matter, going off and making decisions without discussing it first, she'll lose her job for sure."

Lanto wondered at this boy from university. He was not like the other boys she had come across from town. Rudolphe had the look of a man brought up in another lifestyle, yet he had the heart of a person who knew what it meant to have a friend in need. In her short experiences, only one who was a good friend could possibly know what it meant to be a good friend. This caused her to trust him even though she could not figure out why he would care so much if her friend Sylvie ran off or not.

The majority of the time he was away at school, Sylvie had been Madame Muriel's house servant. Lanto barely knew who Rudolphe was and so she assumed Sylvie's interaction with him had been the same. When he came home for the holidays, Sylvie was permitted to go back to her village and spend the time with her family. The care he was putting into helping her find her friend left Lanto curious. Whatever his motive might be, he was right. Sylvie could not afford to lose this job. Even if she were to marry Johnny, she would need to wait until his training was complete before he even had a place to house a wife. Clearly, her friend had not thought this through.

"I think I should go find Johnny's mother and father; they might know where they have gone." Lanto looked at Rudolphe as she spoke; waiting for him to say that it was a good idea.

Rudolphe looked at his watch and gave out a sigh. "I would like to go with you but then I would need to explain to mother where I had gone. It will be easier if she thinks your friend has gone to the market. I will keep the note until I hear from you again tonight. How will I see you again?"

Lanto could see that he was clearly anxious about their interaction. Since she had just nearly lost her own job, she did not feel it appropriate to invite him to come to the house. Monsieur Edmond would wonder where she had been if she was not home when he arrived. With those thoughts lingering in her mind she said, "I will write a note and put it under the mat in front of the post office doors. If you make sure to go there to check your mail, then no one will suspect a thing. But you will need to go before it gets too dark and the watchman arrives." The two parted ways. Lanto headed for the market, running in between clearings of people returning home after work.

At the market, a man pushing a wooden cart, was desperately trying to do it one handed while puffing on the last little bit of his cigarette. The carts hand carved wheels did not have any rubber left on them and so it kept stopping abruptly in the potholes of the once tarred road. Lanto tried to weave in and out of the people but it was no easy task as everyone was heading home and despite being a small town, it made the streets seem very crowded. Her eyes scanned the crowds looking for Sylvie and before she knew it she had run right into the man pushing his cart causing him and her both to topple onto it together.

A group of children that came out of nowhere began laughing and pointing. Lanto got up first then gave the man a hand. The cart was filled with bags of charcoal, so it was not difficult to get out of it but it left Lanto covered in black soot. She dusted off her clothes as best she could. As she looked up smiling, she saw the man's cigarette sitting on the very top of his hat. She pointed to it while still giggling. He picked it up, took one last puff, and flicked it at the children who then dispersed. And with a wave, he was off.

Lanto finally arrived at the table where Johnny's family usually sold their produce only to find they were gone. She took a chance to ask a young girl who happened to be standing nearby, "Excuse me, do you know where the sellers have gone that keep this stand?" The girl shrugged her shoulders up and down as if to say, "I don't know," and then walked off.

Lanto continued to scan the market hoping she might see them but to no avail. She decided just to leave and head for the post office where she could hide the note for Rudolphe and inform him of her findings, or lack thereof. Just as she was about to leave, she felt a tap on her shoulder.

"Are you looking for Sylvie?" It was Johnny's younger brother. She looked down and quickly replied, "Yes, have you seen her?"

The boy looked around as if someone might be watching and whispered, "Come with me."

Behind the market stalls were alleyways where the vendors would keep their crates and baskets for carrying produce home. In between the booths, were little rooms that sold locally produced alcohol and a variety of greasy meals to the vendors before they headed home. Many travelers who might come there would take a glass of the sugar cane rum before traveling, to help them sleep on the bumpy roads. It was very potent however, and the smell of it proved so strong that Lanto had to cup her shirt in her hand and attempted to cover her mouth with it.

The smell of the drink had a dizzying effect on Lanto who had never even touched a drop. She closed her eyes for a brief second in an effort to clear her head. When she opened them, an older drunk man with only a few teeth remaining in his mouth was peering at her very closely. He began singing a song in French, swaying back and forth, holding his heart as he did it. She could feel drops of saliva spattering on her cheeks as he sang and so attempted to back up only to run into more men behind her. The drunkard saw the look of surprise in her eyes and tipped his hat hoping to spark a response to his love songs.

"Thank you for the nice song. You are really a very good singer in French," she said as she tried to slip away. He winked but was too drunk to follow her where she was going. Johnny's little brother had disappeared and it was now up to Lanto to locate her friend by herself.

It turned out that it was not that hard to find her, since they were the only two women in the room. There, sitting in a dark corner with a terrified look on her face, was Sylvie. She was holding a tiny hand-painted blue suitcase on her lap. Lanto had expected her to be shocked to see her but, Sylvie only looked up and said, "Thank you for coming to see me off, the bus is late, otherwise I think you would have missed us."

"Sylvie, where are you planning to go?"

Lanto pulled up a wooden stool and sat next to her friend speaking close and in a low whisper.

"Johnny says he has friends in the town where he is training and I might be able to stay with them." Sylvie was looking down at the broken handle on her suitcase, wiggling it to see how loose it had become.

"And what if you can't stay with them?" Lanto knew that they had not thought this through to the point of having a second option.

"I'll die if he leaves me Lanto-o!" and with that Sylvie buried her head in her hands and broke out in unrepressed sobs.

This time instead of just listening Lanto grabbed a hold of her friend's shoulders forcing her head up and firmly said, "You've got to let him go Sylvie! He'll get into trouble if they find out he's keeping a woman somewhere before he has permission. And you'll lose your job. Don't you want to save up so that you and Johnny can marry one day?"

At that moment, Johnny walked up with his bag in hand and nodded for Sylvie to get going. It was clear Lanto had lost the battle, as her friend could not take her eyes off him. She hugged Lanto goodbye and walked away, following Johnny through the crowd of men. With a sigh Lanto got up to leave; it was getting late, and this was the last place a girl her age wanted to be alone.

The post office was empty and the guard had not yet arrived. Lanto quickly jotted down the words: 'They're gone' on a scrap piece of paper she had in her pocket and ran up the post office steps to place it under the mat. As she walked away, a gust of wind came and carried the note away. Rudolphe walked up in enough time to catch her before she went. He called out, "Lanto, I'm here! What did you find out?"

Lanto explained all that took place.

"I guess we have no choice then, I have to tell mother," said Rudolphe with a look of defeat on his face.

"Yes, I think you had better. She will find out sooner or later and at least Sylvie did leave a note so she won't have to worry that some harm had come to her."

"I hope you won't be too terribly lonely without your friend Lanto. I know that the two of you visit every Sunday. I see you taking walks in the back field." Rudolphe cleared his throat while speaking as if embarrassed that he had been aware of her presence at his home.

This seemingly intimate piece of information in Rudolphe's mind did not faze Lanto in the least. Her business had been everyone's business for as long as she could remember.

"No, I will be fine. Monsieur Edmond allows me to sit in the living room with him on Sundays and listen to the radio if I like. The weather is going to turn cold soon anyways and I always have to be the one to walk to the house. Thank you for your help today Rudolphe. See you around."

With that, the two departed and Lanto went home to set out Monsieur Edmonds' supper.

Lanto had trouble sleeping that night due to a pack of dogs barking outside of the house. Normally it did not bother her but with the events that had taken place that day it did not take much to make her mind wander. "They must be hungry," she thought to herself. Monsieur Edmond always said that when the dogs are very hungry they would bark all throughout the night. She wondered if Sylvie was hungry as they would not arrive to their destination until late and no doubt, she would not know if she had a place to sleep that night until several hours later.

Part III

Rudolphe's new job proved more challenging then he realized. His lack of knowledge about the people who lived in the town severely limited his ability to be able to interact with them. Monsieur Edmond decided to put him behind the counter full-time to help him get to know some of the customers.

The last day of the month Lanto received her pay and then would go to the bank to put some of it into an account there that Monsieur Edmond had set up for her. Monsieur Edmond said that, "anyone under his roof would know the benefits of proper banking." On this particular day, Rudolphe was working at the counter. It had been three months since they had last spoken to one another.

"Hello there Lanto!" cried Rudolphe as if he had seen a long lost friend.

"Hello" she replied, "How is it going? Have you found that pulse you were looking for?"

"Well, it's going fine, I guess. But as you can see, I am not the most popular teller in town. I would say I've found the pulse but have not yet been able to match it." He used his chin to point in the general direction of the reception area.

Lanto scanned the bank reception only to see that of the three areas where a line could be formed, only one had a long line. That one lead to Mialy's window. Mialy was the woman's nickname. Her real name was Misho. She had lived in this town since she was a small girl and she knew everyone. She was gangly in appearance but her face was always smiling; and when customers came, she would flail her arms about as if it was the first time she had seen them in years, even though she knew that they had just been in her line the week before.

As the people came and went you could hear her calling out expressions such as "Greet your wife!" or, "don't forget to give the children a kiss from Auntie Mialy!" and off the client would go with a smile on their face, even if they had just come from paying on a large debt.

Lanto thought it was silly when doing banking, to show favoritism. After all, it is not like one benefited except for some pleasant conversation and in her opinion, time was more important than pleasant conversation when it came to business. In fact, she had not even looked up to see whom the teller was but rather, went to the place that had the shortest line.

"I can see your dilemma," was all she said to Rudolphe as she handed him her deposit slip and money. He took it and went back to the bank vault. As she waited, she saw Monsieur Clovis, a businessman who owned a Chinese restaurant. He was always friendly to Lanto, as they would often meet one another in the market and exchange tips on which vendor had the freshest produce. She decided to wave to him in an effort to get him to come over to Rudolphe's line. "Good Afternoon, Monsieur Clovis. How is business?"

"Oh it's going just fine. You know, times are changing. There are more tourists visiting town and the hotel across the street has been sending them my way. However, I have been told my atmosphere is a little, well…" he cleared his throat and broke eye contact while finishing his sentence with, "I'm told it's a little bit lacking in the modern charm". He looked up helplessly at Lanto scratching his head.

"Well, Monsieur Clovis, this is what I like about the new staff recently been hired here. You see, the teller that I am using came from a University in the big city and he has all the new ideas on how the businesses there are flourishing. In fact, he was just helping me with my finances. It might interest you to speak with him." Lanto made sure to point behind her to Rudolphe's teller window.

"Oh really, I did not know that! You know, when I was a young man I went away to university. I wonder if it might happen to be the same school. I just remembered there was something I forgot to ask the teller I used to check on. Maybe I'll just wait here until you're done, and speak with him. Pardon me, but what did you say his name was?"

"Rudolphe" Lanto said. As she spoke his name Rudolphe came back, and hearing her said, "Yes?" while handing Lanto her receipt.

"Rudolphe, this is Monsieur Clovis and he was just wondering what is 'a la mode' in the city these days with regard to restaurant atmosphere. Do you think you can advise him?"

"Gladly! Any friend of Lanto's is a friend of mine." Rudolphe shook Monsieur Clovis' hand and Lanto took her leave. She bid them both a good day. As she opened the door to walk outside she could hear

Monsieur Clovis asking Rudolphe who he was and where he schooled. Everyone in Mialy's line was listening intently to the conversation in great interest. It would not take long for everyone to want to have something new to say about the teller who arrived in town from university.

The next week Monsieur Edmond stayed home from work. He was not feeling well and wondered aloud if he was catching a flu that had been going around. Lanto made him some homemade chicken soup which usually always made him feel better. However, the week after when he should have been better, he was not, in fact he was much worse. His temperature had risen and he decided it best to go to the hospital in the city and see if they could find out what was wrong.

The hospital reported that Monsieur Edmond had typhoid fever. Lanto wanted to go up and be with him since he was too sick to travel back home by himself. But he wrote her a letter and in it he requested she stay and take care of things on the "home front."

"I will be better soon and then we can get back to life as we like it, everything is going as it should be. Please take no time to worry over me."

Lanto held the letter in her hands and wished so badly she had saved some of her monthly income to purchase that cellular telephone she had been thinking about so that she could call him. Monsieur Edmond had been talking about getting her one and now more than ever she would have liked to hear his voice and been able to talk to the nurses about how he was doing.

"They do not know how he likes things done just so," lamented Lanto. Since he did not have any children, Lanto worried that he might be feeling all alone in the hospital up in the big city. Nevertheless, he assured her in his letter that he would be getting better soon and since he was getting the medicine he needed there was no need to doubt that it was not true.

News came just three days later that Monsieur Edmond had died. Family would be coming to care for matters in town. Lanto did not know quite what to do. She spent the first two days crying. Lanto had been with Monsieur Edmond and his wife since she was a little girl. If she hurt herself, they came to her aid and dressed her wound. When she needed to learn how to do anything required in the home, they patiently taught her themselves what needed to be done. When Madame Rosemarie had died, Monsieur Edmond was still there for Lanto to care for. Now, Lanto felt more alone then she had ever felt in her entire life.

Madame Muriel sent Fano, her new house servant, over daily to be with her. This was most likely a way for someone to keep an eye on Lanto as there was no longer anyone looking over Monsieur Edmonds things. Lanto was glad for the support anyway. Fano was a few years older than she was and seemed to have a mothering nature that helped heal Lanto's broken heart. They went about taking care of the home and did what shopping they could with the little bit of house money that was left. In a few days time; one early morning, there was a knock on the door.

"Hi there, we have arrived!" said a tall woman, all alone and forcing her way through the door as she spoke. "My name is Patricia. I am the only niece of Monsieur Edmond and am here to set up the funeral arrangements, as he had no children of his own to do it. My brother Paoly is on his way here from the city to give his assistance. And what is your name?"

Patricia extended her hand to shake in a very professional manner once she was safely in the house. She was a tall lighter skinned woman with curly reddish hair pulled tightly up in a bun at the top of her head. A few strands of curls rested on her forehead drawing out her big brown eyes. Instead of wearing a skirt like most women in town, she wore a very tight pair of beige plaid pants. The red patent leather heels she was wearing looked as if they were making her feet swell.

"My name is Lanto. I have lived here since I was 8 years old. And if you need me to do anything, Madame, I am ready to assist you." Not sure on what the protocol would be in such a situation, as Monsieur Edmond never made such demands of her, Lanto did a small bow hoping that would look like what the woman would expect from Monsieur Edmond's house servant.

"Well, I don't know that you'll get paid any extra but your services will be needed. We have much to do and I'm not at all familiar with the town. Monsieur Edmonds brothers and sisters will be coming in and all the arrangements are going to be made to take his body to the family tomb. The funeral is to be here at the church. Then of course, there will be the matter of what to do with the house. Well, no matter discussing that with you. Please take my things to the guest room and make sure to begin preparing another room for my brother to stay. There is another guest room isn't there?"

"Yes Madame, there are two guestrooms and Monsieur Edmonds room of course." Lanto did not think it necessary to mention her quarters.

"Well, no one will want to stay in the dead person's room, now will they? In fact, anything personal of his, you can remove and put in his room. We will end up selling most of the things with the home when it goes anyway. The guest furniture in the sitting room is enough to receive any visitors that might come." Patricia gave a smile, then a nod, and then began her self-guided tour of the house.

Lanto did all she could to get everything done. She prepared the guest rooms for Patricia and her brother just as she had always done for any guests that came; although she could not remember Patricia nor her brother having come to visit in the past. A few cousins lived on the coast that had passed by on their way to the big city. And Monsieur Edmond had some great aunts who were still alive when she was younger that would come for a couple weeks out of the summer. Other than that, this was going to be the most visitors the house had seen in years.

Caring for all of the affairs proved to be very overwhelming. It was as if her life had changed overnight. She could not even think of what would happen to her once the arrangements were finished. Lanto missed giving Monsieur Edmond his tea and finding him later on that evening, sleeping in his favorite chair to the sound of the radio. Lanto would usually have to turn it off for him and wrap him up in a blanket in case he never ended up going to bed. But, to Lanto's relief, Patricia and her brother were rarely in the house. They only seemed to come home to sign off on papers or to make telephone calls. It was as if there was no one to care for.

The day of the funeral service at the church Lanto was in the kitchen cooking the entire day. Madame Muriel again sent her new house servant over with baked goods. Fano spoke a different dialect than Lanto, and had come from an area near the eastern coast. She had many stories about 'real' cyclone weather as she called it. And these stories were a welcomed distraction to Lanto's tired mind. Rudolphe came over to bring some table cloths that Fano had forgotten at the house.

"Do you need any extra help?" he asked looking at both the girls in earnest.

Lanto did not really have time to answer before Fano did. Fano was a master of finding work for others to do and quickly asked him if he would not mind to pull the tarps out of the attic so that they could set them up in the back yard. After the funeral, the entire family was planning to come back to the house to have a meal and then go over Monsieur Edmonds Last Will and Testament.

Lanto went into Monsieur Edmonds bedroom to pick out an outfit for the service. The smell of his aftershave was still in his favorite white shirt he always wore on special occasions. She put it up to her nose and immediately remembered the day Madame Rosemarie died. Lanto and Monsieur Edmond had picked out the clothes she was to use for the funeral. Monsieur Edmond sat on the bed in this same suit that Lanto was holding as she displayed different dresses to him from the closet. She held them out one by one for him to decide. He ended up going with a pink polyester dress with blue flowers that Madame Rosemarie liked to wear on special occasions.

Now Lanto had to decide all by herself what Monsieur Edmond would have liked to wear for his funeral. She chose his favorite tie, one that was green with a man riding a horse embroidered on it. Next, she selected a tie clip that Madame Rosemarie had given him for their 40th wedding anniversary. Finally, she tucked in the handkerchief that matched the tie, folding it the way Monsieur Edmond had taught her to do for him when setting out his clothes after ironing them

Suddenly, Lanto heard a scream coming from downstairs. She ran down the wooden staircase that leads to the living room to see what had happened. Fearing that Rudolphe had fallen from the attic, she scanned the hallway looking for him. No one had fallen. It was Patricia in the living room who had screamed. Rudolphe had already entered the room by the time Lanto walked in and Fano was peeking down the hallway from the kitchen while still drying a dish she was holding.

"No! This cannot be! He can't have done this to us! Why? Why?" cried Patricia as she paced the living room floor. A man in a blue suit, wearing a straw hat was sitting on the sofa with his brief case out. He looked a little anxious over the disturbance and his head was following Patricia's movement back and forth, as she paced.

Patricia turned to see Lanto standing there and said while pointing a shaking finger, "You! I should have known something funny was going on! You have taken our only reason for coming here! You are a little thief that clearly took advantage of a sad old man! You will be cursed for this!"

The man with the hat stood up and asked, "Are you Miss Lanto?"

"Yes, she is," replied Rudolphe knowing that Lanto did not do well in these types of situations where she was being accused. He held his hand out to encourage Lanto to step closer despite the ranting of Patricia in the background.

The man turned to Rudolphe and explained the reason for the upset.

"It seems that Miss Lanto is listed as the person who will inherit this place. It is all documented in writing. I just came to go over some of the paper work before the rest of the family came in for the funeral and the reading of the Will."

Patricia ran out of the room rushing past Lanto and giving her a firm bump with her shoulder. Rudolphe looked at Lanto and smiled. She looked at the man in the blue suit and said, "I can see no one has offered you anything to drink. And it's so hot. Could I get you a glass of lemonade?"

The man, thought for a moment and said, "Yes, that would be lovely!" He sat back down and began shuffling through more papers. Monsieur Edmonds nephew sat down next to him ready to sign any paperwork that needed to be completed.

Rudolphe followed Lanto into the kitchen. He held the cups in place as she poured the lemonade staring her in the face looking for any sign of emotion he could find. After what seemed an eternity he asked, "Lanto what are you thinking? Do you understand what this means?" She kept moving around the kitchen doing things such as getting the ice cubes, finding a straw, and then slicing a lime for garnish. All the while Rudolphe followed her around the kitchen with the serving tray waiting for her to answer.

"What is going on?" asked Fano putting down her dishcloth for the first time since all the commotion.

"It's Lanto, she's inherited this place!" cried Rudolphe in a mixture of shock and laughter.

Fano gasped at hearing what had happened. She excitedly grabbing onto Lanto's arm and said, "You have a home! You do not need to worry anymore. Lanto you are free!"

Lanto did not really comprehend the chain of events. She had never heard of anything like this being done before but she was sure that it would be resolved by the time the other relatives came. She went about her business sorting out affairs just has she felt Monsieur Edmond would have wanted. The funeral went well; the reception in the back yard afterwards was well attended. Only immediate family stayed for dinner that evening before they were scheduled to return home.

Lanto mostly stayed in the kitchen and kept the food and beverages going that evening, as the family debated on what to do about the inheritance. The man in the blue suit looked tired as he had only been permitted to leave for thirty minutes and then he came back pouring over papers explaining legal terms that most of Monsieur Edmonds relatives did not seem to understand nor agree with.

Finally, in a breath of exasperation, Lanto heard him say, "The end of the matter is that the little Miss working in the kitchen gets to have this house and there is nothing anyone can do about it! If you have any questions, feel free to contact me Monday morning at my office. Please accept my condolences for your loss." With that, he tipped the straw hat off his head, picked up his suitcase, grabbed a few extra papers he forgot to put in it, and hurried out the door.

Within a short amount of time, everyone including Patricia and her brother had left Monsieur Edmonds house. They had all planned to leave after the funeral originally but the news of Lanto inheriting Monsieur Edmonds home, left them no reason to linger. There were no orders for things to be done, no requests for help packing, and no one wanted the leftover food to be divided up for their long rides home. Lanto stood in the hallway and watched the last of them leave without as much as a goodbye. The key that Patricia had been using to go back and forth was simply left on the coffee table in the sitting room.

Lanto, Fano and Rudolphe cleaned up the last of the dishes from the guests.

"Lanto, I think you should come and sit out on the porch with us. Remember that night we met?" Rudolphe asked taking her by the elbow, "We sat and talked on the veranda of my parent's home. Well, I think it would be nice to do that again." She obediently followed sitting on the bench in the same place she always sat. Fano stood in the doorway leaning against the frame with her arms folded.

Lanto had not recalled ever having had two friends sitting on the front veranda with her before. Had she thought about it further, since living with Monsieur Edmond, she could not have recalled having had two friends at all. At this moment, sitting on the veranda without any fear of being forced to leave it, she realized what Monsieur Edmond had bestowed upon her. It was a most precious gift; his home.

The day she first arrived so many years earlier, Monsieur Edmond looked down at her holding her little hand as they left the station and said, "This is your home now, only if you want to stay." Now, as if Monsieur Edmond was asking Lanto that question all over again she wondered what her answer was. What would she do with her time now that Monsieur Edmond was not there to care for? How would she continue to support herself? What would the community think? Despite feeling very tired, her mind was racing with activity.

Fano put her arm around Lantos tiny shoulders and asked her if she would like her to stay. "I'm sure Rudolphe could tell his mother that you don't want to be alone tonight and she would understand. I could make it back in the morning before work time."

She looked at her new friend with a sense of gratitude. Lanto very much did not want to be alone. In fact, she had never spent one night alone in her life that she could remember. All she could think of to say was, "No that's alright, go on home. It's been a long day. I'll see you again in the morning."

Rudolphe looked up at the night sky and said, "What do you think Monsieur Edmond wanted you to do with his house, Lanto?"

"I don't know." Lanto looked up too while speaking as if hoping to find the answer up there in the stars.

"Will you bring your family here?" Fano asked, picking up her bag to go.

"I suppose I could do that. Then who would care for the farm? My father has always said he would never live away from the countryside. I don't think he would be very happy here while he is still healthy enough to work."

Rudolphe could see the anxiety in her brow and said, "You know Lanto, no matter what happens, you'll be just fine. You are a survivor. And no matter where life takes you, you're going to get through it." With that, he stood up and walked towards her. He bent down and gave her a soft kiss on the top of her head; looking her in the eye, he said softly, "Sleep sweet."

"We'll be here for you if you need any help," Fano echoed as the two walked away vanishing into the darkness of the night.

"Good night. Thank you for your help today." Lanto said a little late for them to hear her clearly enough.

Lanto opened the door, and quickly shut it behind her. She made sure to lock it and put the wood latch over the inside of the door to make it secure. She stepped into the living room to stare at the only photo hung in the entire house. It was a photo of Monsieur and Madame on their wedding day. She decided not to sleep in her bed that night but in the living room with their picture. She went up stairs to Monsieur Edmonds bedroom and grabbed his favorite rocker, taking it down the flight of stairs and putting it back in the sitting room next to the radio where it belonged.

"There, that's better," she said to herself.

She went into the kitchen and grabbed a banana. Then she took her banana, sat in Monsieur Edmonds favorite chair, and ate it. Then she fell asleep to the sound of the radio. Only no one was there to turn it off for her as she had done so many times for Monsieur Edmond.

Around midnight, she woke up, turned it off herself, and then went into her own bed. The old chair was not as comfortable as Monsieur Edmond had always made it look. She slipped under the cool cotton sheets and whispered drowsily as she lost consciousness, "Merci Monsieur Edmond. Thank you, I've decided to stay."

The End

FERDINAND'S MISSING RED HAT

'Zavona' is the Malagasy expression for a foggy mist that falls over the highland areas of an island called Madagascar. This island is situated in between the continent of Africa and the islands of the Indian Ocean. Zavona begins just after the rainy seasons have ended and brings in the winter season. When the zavona lifts, the sun beats brightly and the sky is a bright blue.

It was on a morning such as this that a young boy named Ferdinand lost his favorite hat. Not only was it the one hat that he owned, or had ever owned, but it was exceptional. What made it the world's best hat is that it never fit too tight, wasn't so loose that the wind might take it away, its bill blocked the sun entirely from his face when it stood hot at midday and it had perfect sweat absorption. It was also redder than the nose of a circus clown. Red was Ferdinand's favorite color. All these things added up together, made for the perfect hat. And it was now gone most likely forever in Ferdinand's opinion. Many might wonder why he wouldn't just go to the town market and buy a new one.

Not only did the market in an undeveloped country like the one where he lived change out what things they sold every other month when a new shipment came in from overseas, the new items that came in were never the same as what had been for sale prior. It wasn't just the new items for sale that was the problem; Ferdinand didn't have the money to buy another perfect red hat even if he were to see one again.

Although he went to work every day with his mother, Ferdinand was never given any money. He had a place to sleep, his house was located high up on a hill from where his mother worked. And they had at least one warm meal almost every day, but there was nothing in the world that gave him independent means to buy something new. He had received that hat as a gift from a man who used to live near his mother's fruit stand. The man gave it to Ferdinand as a keepsake when he left to move back to his home country.

Ferdinand's mother owned a fruit stand in the middle of town. Each day, at four-thirty in the morning, whether the sun had risen or not, the two of them would begin preparations to make the journey into town. The small house that they rented, since moving out of her mother's home was located in one of the outskirts of town where they still had mud houses. The mud was made from the dung of cows mixed with the left over stalks of rice after the grains had been beaten off. It was a one-room house where Ferdinand, his older sister, and his mother shared one bed. There was a straw mat on the dirt floor so that their feet stayed clean when they walked. To the left of the house sat one little window that let out the smoke from cooking when they chose to cook inside the house in the cold season.

They usually cooked using wood which made more smoke then charcoal but every Sunday Ferdinand's mother tried to buy some charcoal so as to create a lighter work load for them on that day. There was one little wooden table and chair where Ferdinand's sister Lisy did all of her school work. And a long wooden bench that was directly across the table for company that might stop by as it wasn't local custom for people to sit on the bed as their clothes might be dirty and thus bring fleas into the house.

They had no electricity but used handmade lanterns pounded from empty cans of tin that were filled with oil and a small rag used as a wick. Their walls were covered with a variety of posters such as a pair of Chinese twins, a home from abroad that had a table filled with food, and several pages of magazines from abroad that had models posing for hair color advertisements. The roof was made of the same rice stalks that went into the walls. And the inside of the ceiling had plastic nailed to it so that when it rained, the water didn't leak through the straw and land on their heads. Although their plastic was torn and at times this happened anyway when the rains were strong and it pooled in certain parts of the ceiling.

Most towns' people were embarrassed to have to live in what they called a countryside home, although almost everyone in town still had family who lived in countryside that they visited regularly when on vacation or when burying a relative in the family tomb. What made this type of house nicer than the town homes was that it had its own pit toilet.

Many of the homes in town also had pit toilets; however, you often had to share them with a group of people that were living in the same corner of town as you. As one could only imagine, this did not lend itself to the highest forms of cleanliness. Ferdinand's mother and sister were very clean, and kept their pit toilet immaculate. One could only find the occasional fly buzzing about. It was a mud pit toilet to the left of where their house stood, but farther out in the field than most. She surrounded it with a tree that produced three different flower colors and was very fragrant. And she had made a path made of stone so that even during the rainy season one could get to the pit toilet without getting too muddy.

The best part of the house was that because they were in a place all of their own, they didn't have to share a toilet with anyone. And their place was only a fraction of the cost as the town homes. Ferdinand's mother was more in favor of practicality than status and taught her children to never be ashamed of what their situation in life was but to be content and happy to be alive and breathing, as life in undeveloped countries was fleeting and one never knew when sickness or some other hardship might come their way.

Ferdinand's mother would usually awake first and begin by walking a half mile down to the rice fields with her daughter, where there was a water source, and fetch the daily water needs for cooking, bathing, and dish washing. There would often be a group of women there who lived in similar type homes surrounding that same rice field who would gather water as well.

They would carry one bucket of water on her head, and a bucket in each free hand. Now that she no longer had a baby on her back as she used to have so many years ago, she found the task much easier than before, although she was now older. Once home, she would prepare a dish of watered down rice and green leaves that can be found on the stalks of the sweet potato plant. They would eat before packing up the fruit to be sold for that. Tuesdays and Fridays were the big market days when everyone from countryside brought their wares.

While there was a market every day in town, on these days the town sellers would buy from the countryside people and then sell what they bought at a slightly higher price on Monday, Wednesday, Thursday, Saturday and if not enough money was made, then Sunday afternoon. Tuesday was the big market day when Ferdinand's mother would buy her fruit and prepare it for the week's sales. And Friday was the day she tried to do her clothes washing, providing there were no rains that day and the clothes could have a chance to dry on the grassy parts of the rice fields near where they used the water to wash their clothes.

It was Ferdinand's job to hold the fruit when they went into town. Ferdinand mostly watched his mother admiringly as she organized her things each morning. He wanted to help but she was so efficient at what she did, that by the time he could think to do something she already had it done. Mainly, his task was to keep his mother and daily companion in good spirits. This was a very easy task providing Ferdinand had no troubles. As trouble for Ferdinand seemed to be the only thing that truly worried his mother.

He couldn't find the words to tell his mother who worked so hard for her family that he had lost his favorite hat. Of course, she noticed immediately the next day when they went into town that the hat was missing.

"My word what have you done with your hat?" Was all she said as she looked in and out of her straw baskets that she kept the fruit in.

"It must have drifted off in the wind and I didn't notice," she lamented.

"Oh well, maybe we will find it at home." She said this with her usual optimism.

Ferdinand always kept his hat on the bedpost so that it was one of the first things that got put on his head before starting his day. He had his doubts that it would be at home. When they arrived at home that night, they couldn't find Ferdinand's perfect red hat.

Ferdinand didn't actually think he had lost it. There were some boys who came by that day and Ferdinand is pretty sure they took it. The zavona was thicker than usual that morning and he couldn't remember which of the boys it was that came up to him. He knew they had been there but he could barely see their faces through the fog. They were always harassing him and while he didn't recall them taking it off his head, it would be something they would do. It wasn't long after they stopped by the fruit stand that he felt the breeze on his head once the zavona lifted. And it was then he realized, his hat was gone.

His mother had raised him on her own ever since he was a baby. Meva's husband was never quite the dependable type. They married young and had to move to the city for work. When Ferdinand was born the pregnancy was unexpected. His father found himself without work that was sufficient enough to care for the family's needs. Under the guise of leaving town in order to find work, he left her one day with the baby in her arms and young Lisy standing next to her. It had been many years since that day.

Meva knew by the look in his eye he would never return. He looked at her and gave her a kiss on her forehead and patted Lisy on the head. Never even looking down at his new born baby that she was breastfeeding, he turned to walk away and never looked back. It was at that point that Meva decided to move back in with her mother until she could get back out on her own.

The family home was very small and so there was not a lot of room for her, Lisy and Ferdinand. Meva still had five younger brothers and sisters at home at that time. They could sleep in the same bed with two of the younger siblings, but as all the children kept getting bigger with each passing year, this became increasingly difficult.

She had met her husband while away on vacation visiting family near where he was from. When they moved back in the city it was because her family sold goods there and Meva could work with them while he looked for work building homes. Now that he was gone, it was one less mouth to feed and Meva continued working with her family selling produce on the side of the road.

That had been many years ago. They had learned since then to work as a family unit without the presence of a male figure. Ferdinand loved his mother. She never complained about taking care of him. Every day they would go together to the market and every day she would sell the same apples, or other fruit that was in season. Meva was not a complainer. She believed that what challenges you were handed in life was an opportunity for you to shine. If you let such obstacles as raising two children on your own get the best of you, it was a lack of faith.

Now Meva, being in her late thirties was beginning to show signs of her age. Her once black glossy hair now had specks of white jumping out of it. The brown eyes which used to attract so much attention, now had signs of sun spots speckled to the sides, and lines from her smiles stretched over her cheek bones like sun beams. At one time she had a full set of teeth, and despite a lot of apple eating, she had lost most of the ones in back but was thankful to have all her teeth up front. In the town where they lived it was not uncommon for women of that age to begin looking older before their time. And Meva was no exception. Her frame was still slight as in youth but she now had the look of a woman with experience and was very much respected by her co-workers in town.

Meva felt that people began to look like the things they sold. For instance the banana vendors were always a happy bunch with big wide smiles as if they had a banana stuck right in their mouth. The onion vendors were healthy and tall but looked a bit dark and dismal – possibly from all the crying. Grapes always came in clusters and so the sellers who sold them never seemed to be alone, but came to market as a family. Then of course, there was the seasonal fruit seller like herself. She liked to think of her as the 'mixed fruit' type, somewhat indefinable and original in her own right. She could be sweet like an apple, or tart like the lemons that she only sold one month out of the year. Depending on the season, she could make herself be refreshing or bitter.

Sitting on the side of the road with all the cars passing by, Ferdinand loved distinguishing between the many sounds. He could hear someone scrubbing the concrete in front of their store. He had never scrubbed concrete before but the sound it made was a bit like music. The man seemed to be going back and forth to the beat of some tune he had lodged in his head. With the rhythm of the brush strokes fixed firmly in his head, Ferdinand began to watch the people walking by and form their movements to the beat that was now in his head from the scrubbing. With each passing step there was yet another movement and the passersby began to look like they were dancing.

His mother had him sit in a different part of the street than normal due to his having no hat. Here there was plenty of shade but not as many people passing by as he would have liked. Being across the street from where his mother was he also wasn't able to speak with her about everything he was seeing. And he wasn't able to call out to her when something went wrong.

As he sat on that shaded side of the street, a group of boys began walking towards him. One of the boys it just so happened, Ferdinand suspected to be the hat thief. Boys like him hardly ever spoke a word to Ferdinand. He would have liked to hear so much as a hello but they had never done anything but tease and walk past. The boys stopped right in front of him as if they hadn't even noticed he was sitting there. He could see one of the boys had a backpack and it was opened slightly.

The sun was bright, especially when one wasn't wearing a hat and so despite the fact that he squinted his eyes the best he could he still was not able to see if there was anything inside of the bag. Ferdinand reluctantly gave up his search until the next day. For they were sure to walk by again. Every day the same people walked past. Ferdinand's peripheral vision was not good, so he could only see who they were when they were directly in front of him within about a three second window of time.

The next morning the same boys came by again where Ferdinand was sitting. Only this time they were eating some popcorn. Ferdinand's mother never allowed him to eat popcorn. She said it wasn't good for his stomach. But he loved the smell. The boys kept shoveling it into their mouths as if they hadn't eaten for days. All Ferdinand had eaten that day was some boiled sweet potatoes that his sister had cooked that morning and put in their things for them to take for lunch that day. It hadn't been a good week for selling and so Ferdinand and his mother decided to stay in town and work through lunch. He could smell the salt and butter from the popcorn every time the breeze hit just the right way.

Closing his eyes for a minute wondering what it might taste like he heard one of the boys say, "Look he's sleeping maybe we can pinch that keychain he's got hanging off of his belt."

Another boy whispered to this one, "Leave him alone, it's bad luck to steal from people when you don't need what they have anyways. And what do you need a keychain for? You don't own anything that has a key!"

Ferdinand not planning on waiting to see if they would attempt to steal his keychain or not, opened his eyes and yelled out a scream that sent the two boys running. His mother heard it and came running over.

"What on earth is going on? Why would you do that Ferdinand? You're going to scare the customers. Here, let's move you back over with me; there is shade on that side of the street now. Too much sun can make one uncomfortable and the zavona has made it feel a little humid this morning."

Ferdinand wasn't uncomfortable, he was mad. Those boys had wanted to take his keychain, the keychain his uncle had bought him last year after he went on vacation in the north of the country. That fact alone was proof enough to him that they might be the culprits who took his hat. But he would need more than that to convince his mother.

Meva always thought the best of everyone. Even when Ferdinand was much younger he was aware that not everyone in this world was as nice as his mother had made them out to be. She had raised him with words of sweetness about everyone who walked past. But he knew differently. He could sense which persons were genuine and which ones were hypocrites. The hypocrites always seemed nicer than they really were on the inside. And the genuine ones always came off the wrong way at first, but in the end, were the ones who could be trusted. Ferdinand prided himself in his keen sense of observation when it came to people. And now he had these boys pegged. All he needed was the proof that it was one of them who took his hat. And then he would need a plan in order to get his hat back.

Ferdinand's best friend in the whole world was Eddie Ranaivo. Eddie's family didn't have a home. But they were given a space in front of a hardware store to set up a sort of tent made out of cardboard boxes so they could sleep there in the evenings. The store was near where Ferdinand's mother sold during the day. In exchange for getting to sleep in front of the store, Eddie's family became guardians who warded off thieves. When the stores income was good, they might even get some change so that they might buy something to eat. The rest of the time was spent begging for money from the tourists or passersby. Eddie and Ferdinand had that in common. Ferdinand's mother also gave him a tin cup to have near him at all times for those who might have passed by. Eddie would walk by every morning and say hello to Ferdinand and his mother.

The day after Ferdinand's hat went mysteriously missing Eddie came by. He was wearing his usual grey, stained ripped t-shirt that he wore every day. The t-shirt may have actually been white at one time but seeing as they had only the river to wash their clothes, which was already muddy, and never spent money on soap when it could mean having another cup of rice in their already empty bellies, the shirt remained gray. His hair was short but in need of brushing. Eddie always seemed to have bits of straw or leaves sticking in it as if he had just come from taking a nap on the ground somewhere.

The people who lived outside in their town - meaning, without a home, acted as if the entire town was their living room. They didn't have a lot of personal space requirements and while they didn't mind others taking up space where they lived, they also had no misgivings about entering into others personal space should it be out on the street. Because after all, to them, these people were in their private space. The only place Eddie was never allowed access was inside the actual stores. Someone with his bare feet and raggedy clothes was a clear warning sign to most store keepers who needed desperately to ward off thieves.

Eddie stopped by on this particular day to give Ferdinand and his mother an update on the comings and goings of the town's residents. Since each morning when the store opened, his family had to move their cardboard boxes, he had no place to dwell all during the day. His family couldn't afford public schooling so he would make his morning rounds, ending up at Meva and Ferdinand's stand around the time when she might feel sorry for him and toss an apple his way.

"Good Morning to all! The evening has finished well. How is everyone's health?"

Eddie leaned over looking at Ferdinand as if he might whisper a secret to him. Ferdinand smiled and said he was well. The few sellers who were nearby gave the common reply that everyone's health was well and this gave Eddie the go ahead to carry on with conversation in a more direct manner with the person whom he actually wanted to speak to in the first place; Ferdinand's mother.

"Maman'i Ferdinand, could I please trouble you for your opinion?" Eddie asked Ferdinand's mother using the title that was bestowed upon her by local custom; '*the mother of Ferdinand*' – often used with the name of one's first born child, but in Meva's case everyone was so used to seeing her with Ferdinand, that she began to be called by his name since the time he was about ten years old.

Meva turned to Eddie as he spoke and rolled her eyes as Eddie was a bit of a rogue and she knew what ever was about to come out of his mouth would be meant to hoax her into giving him something.

"Yes, Eddie, what is it? I'm running late today so please hurry."

She carried on organizing her apples on her table as he spoke. It wasn't really a table but rather a wooden pallet where she would sit on the ground next to it on a straw mat. On the pallet was a lamba; a traditional type of cloth used for a variety of purposes including table clothes. The apples Meva sold came in shades of green, yellow and the typical bruised brown. Each pile had four apples in it. The apple that was farthest from a clear eyes' view always had at least one bruise on it. All the sellers hoped by doing this they could sell the good with the bad and make a profit, as almost always half the apples they received were already bruised. Some buyers were pickier than others, but most who were in a rush just bought the pile without looking too much at each individual apple in it.

"Did you know that right now at this very moment there are three busloads of tourists at the city hall? I have heard it said that some tourist feel if they eat one apple a day they will never have to visit a doctor again. Now I have no idea where this superstition came from, but it would be to your benefit to go down and check it out."

Meva raised her eyebrows and thought for a moment then replied, "I don't want to leave Ferdinand here alone; I think I'll just wait and see if any of them decide to pass by us here on the street."

Expecting such a response, Eddie said, "but you see, I have nothing to do and so the two of us can watch your stand here, while you go and take your apples to the tourists. It would behoove you greatly to take advantage of this opportunity. And you can trust me; I will never steal from my best friend here or his mother."

Eddie winked at Ferdinand who smiled and then looked up at his mother longingly hoping she would say yes. He loved the thought of him and Eddie working the fruit stand while his mother was gone.

Unsure of what to do, she stopped piling her apples and looked down the street longingly as if she could see the tourists standing there just waiting to sink their white teeth into her apples. She sighed and said, "Okay Eddie, I'm going to go out on a limb here. I will leave you two to watch the stand but you have to promise not to leave until I come back. Do I have your word?"

Eddie looked again at Ferdinand and then at her and said soundly, "I swear on my mother's grave."

Meva looked down at him disapprovingly and said, "Eddie, your mother is not even dead yet, so you can't very well swear on her grave now can you? I don't need your swears anyway I need you to promise to take this seriously. Can I count on you to watch this stand and barter well for me while I am gone?"

Eddie nodded yes and lifted his hand to salute as if he were one of the soldiers who stood post at the gendarme up the hill.

Meva turned to Ferdinand and gave him a quick kiss on the forehead and then quickly filled up a basket with apples. She rushed off so fast that her hat fell off in a gust of wind and she was seen running across the street after it. She grabbed it and never looked back as she kept on running up hill to where the city hall was located.

Eddie now turned to Ferdinand and said with a smirk, "Can you believe it my friend? I never thought she was going to leave. Maybe she will strike it rich and meet some gentleman from across the sea. Like someone from Paris, France! He will own a big house with a pool like that hotel near the city hall. And you and I can go live it up in his palace and spend our vacations somewhere the south of France, by the ocean. What do you say? You can be the prince and I'll be your trusted servant and we'll rule the world!"

Both boys broke out in laughter. Eddie always had a way to make Ferdinand laugh in a way no one else could. Ferdinand could not believe that his mother had left. He felt this must mean he was getting older and she could trust him to help every once in a while. The laughter was quickly interrupted by Lioka; one of the boys who had been there the day before discussing whether or not to steal Ferdinand's key chain.

"Hey Eddie, what are you doing with this looser!" He said this obviously talking about Ferdinand but never looked over at him while he spoke. Rather he rushed past where Ferdinand was sitting and got up in Eddies face, nose to nose. Both boys were roughly the same age, Eddie being 12 and Lioka being 11. However, Eddie was a whole head shorter than Lioka and so not only were they nose to nose but Lioka was looking down to Eddie as he spoke.

"Hey Lioka," Eddie replied bravely without the slightest hint of the fear that was lingering in the pit of his stomach, "why don't you try brushing your teeth before you leave the house? You're breadth smells like two day old fish!"

Lioka stepped back, blew his breadth into his hand and took a whiff. Redirecting his thoughts once again to the offense, he threw his head back, laughed and said, "Like you would know what fish smells like, you probably haven't eaten meat in months by the looks of you, unless of course you've been picking through the garbage again. Lioka said this while pointing to the garbage dump nearby.

It wasn't really a garbage dump, but self-made by the town people. Although there could be seen garbage such as wrappers at any given corner of the town at any given time, this was a special area for things like food garbage. And Eddie could often be found there with his brothers and sisters, as well as several stray dogs, in the later part of the evening before one of two things would inevitably happen. Either the night watchman of the house on the corner would come to burn the pile down to a controllable size or the drunks on their way home from the bar up the street would pee on the pile making most of the things in it inedible.

Eddie looked down at his stomach. It never dawned on him that his lack of daily sustenance showed to others. He was skinny but most everyone in town was as even if they had enough money for food everyday it was only a plate of rice and vegetables. Except of course the 'Uppers' as Eddie liked to call them. 'Uppers' like Lioka lived in the upper part of town. It had better housing, better schools, and thus was more expensive to live there which meant most who lived there had more money. Lioka was round and pudgy clearly having eaten meat most of his life and being proud of it, had nothing but bones of shame to toss at people like Eddie who only dreamed of having half the physical life that Lioka had.

Lioka noticed Eddie looking down at his clothes and remarked, "Why bother looking at those rags you're wearing, there's nothing new there, it's the same clothes you've worn every day for the last year since you're mom got them from the donated bin at the church last Easter!"

Eddie who was clearly about to cry, stood there in front of Ferdinand silenced. Every word Lioka had said was true and he could find no self-confidence within himself to defend what Lioka was saying or even make a joke about it.

Ferdinand could take a fair amount of goading for himself but there were two people in the world he could not stand to see made fun of, his mother and his pal Eddie. He felt the tin can in his hand, the cool metal calling out to him to do something about his rage. And with all the energy he could muster up he took that tin can and chucked it right at Lioka's big fat head.

"Ouch! Hey you stupid…." cried Lioka finally casting glaring eyes in Ferdinand's direction before finishing his sentence. He began rubbing his head and looking around him as several school children who were walking on the opposite side of the street began to laugh mockingly when they saw what had happened.

Before he could carry on with any threats he was interrupted by Eddie who gained a sudden sense of courage by Ferdinand's heroic move.

"Watch it Lioka, there's more where that came from!"

Eddie held up his fists and took a stance ready to fight. But Lioka was in no shape to fight the likes of Eddie who had far more street smarts than he did and Lioka knew it. Lioka left running off as if he was going to go tell someone what Ferdinand had done.

Eddie turned to Ferdinand and jumped up and down repeating the words, "Man! That was awesome! You chucked that tin can right at his big fat head! Go Ferdinand! You're my hero! I told you that you would be the prince and I would be your trusted servant. Now I'm indebted to you forever and the two of us can rule the world!"

Eddie said this while skipping back and forth in front of where Ferdinand was sitting. He would pause from this happy dance briefly if someone would stop by and ask about the price of the apples and then when they left he would carry on either chanting, 'Go Ferdinand!' or re-enacting what would one day be one of his favorite moments in time; the tin cup that landed squarely on Lioka's big fat head.

While Ferdinand was hoping hitting Lioka in the head would bring him the measure of satisfaction he longed for, one thing held him back from feeling a sense of relief. When Lioka's head flew back as the tin can hit it, his bag flipped open. In a flash of red, Ferdinand saw what could have only been his red hat! Ferdinand now had proof that Lioka was his arch enemy and needed a plan to get his hat back. It would take something more than his tin can to get that hat back. Not feeling he could say anything to anyone he waited the entire day, just thinking of what he might do the next time Lioka walked past his mother's fruit stand.

The city hall was located on the opposite side of the valley from where Meva, Lisy and Ferdinand lived. All marriages and divorces were handled there. It was also a historic sight, and the location of the only banks in town, many of the tour busses coming from the bigger city in the north and heading to the Oceanside towns would drive through and stop for the night. Vendors had to take advantage of the short length of stay and try their best to get a jump on sales before the bus load would leave and move on to other vendors in other towns.

Meva climbed up the steep hill, with her basket of apples rocking back and forth on her head. The beads of sweat were dripping in her eyes and the lamba that was wrapped around her waist wanted to come undone. She got there in time as three busses were unloading. She wasn't the only seller that got word of their arrival. There were other fruit sellers as well and they were all rushing after the tourist like a stampede. Some of the tourists were clearly afraid to get out of the bus and sat inside looking down as men and women held up their goods as high as they could so that they might buy something from the bus window.

The vanilla sellers were the most popular with tourists. They barely needed to pull the vanilla out of their bags to show it off as the scent of fresh vanilla permeated the small radius in which they stood. Selling vanilla was profitable but at the same time a risk as it was expensive to harvest and buy and most of the local people couldn't afford it. If one wanted to sell vanilla they had to depend solely on the tourist industry, which depending on the cyclone weather could mean many tourists or few, or worse than that, none at all. The cyclones didn't harshly affect the towns, but word of their existence stopped tourists from coming to the island.

One man was selling hand carvings of what he called 'foot massagers'; little spikey pieces of wood made from Eucalyptus trees, that the bus travelers could use to roll their feet on while they rode the ten hour drive to the coast. Two other sellers had piles of used clothes that some of the older women on the bus were looking through.

One of the men selling the clothes was yelling out the price in a quick succession of rapid beats that no one but the keenest listener could have discerned. This either scared the tourists or attracted them to buy as it was something quite different from the manner of buying that they were accustomed to in their home countries. Then of course there was your usual plastic gadget salesman. This person would have a variety of things from mirrors to watches. All of which had a life span of about 2 weeks per battery. They drained the already old batteries so bad that most people ended up wearing their watches even though they didn't tick anymore as it often became too expensive to keep replacing them with more batteries.

Meva scanned the bus loads and decided to go for the bus load of tourist's who had the least amount of sellers surrounding them. They didn't look like the mean sort that would yell at her to go away but rather were looking around their area people watching and therefore would be primed for some human interaction. She could see that they spoke French and so she tried her best to offer them her apples so that they would understand clearly.

"Pomme pour vous."

It was the best Meva could come up with to offer her apples. She was hoping it meant something like '*an apple for you*' but unsure of herself, she held out one of the nicest of her apples she could find and then showed the 200 ariary bill that it would cost them to buy one. Several of the tourists gathered around her picking up the apples and looking at them contemplating whether or not they should buy.

One older woman with short, curly, white hair, who looked to Meva to be some sort of giant, began saying in French, "There is nothing like fresh apples. I haven't had any fruit since I arrived here. Look at that one! Did you know there are over 70 varieties of apples in the world?"

She turned to her friend who unlike her was tall and thin with hair that had been dyed brown and was wearing a similar bag around her waist in which she carried all of her money and important documents. This tall woman also picked up an apple and said, "How many of our friends back home, have had this variety of apple, not too many I suppose."

The giant laughed and said, "None of my friends have that's for sure. Let's buy some, wash them up good at the hotel tonight and then we can compare what we ate to the fruit we have back home. The fruit from islands is always better than what we buy in the supermarkets."

Without warning, Rasoa; one of the oldest sellers in the area, and yet possessing the most energy of them all, pushed her way in between the two women and in perfect French said, "You don't want to buy from this woman, she lives in the poorest part of town where rodents and roaches roam freely. Here, take one of my apples as a gift and see if they aren't one of the best you have ever tasted!"

She was wearing her black and gray peppered hair in tiny braids that were traditional in that area. On top of her head was a lamba wrapped about so that her basket of apples could fit comfortably on top while she walked. Around her waist was a lamba that matched that of the one on top of her head. In her ears were a set of gold earrings that matched the gold rings on her fingers. From what Meva could tell, this woman had no need of selling apples any more than the president did of selling cheese. She just did it for sport. And she was very good at her hobby.

Meva glared at Rasoa and said, "You know me to be a clean person, why would you say such lies in front of strangers?"

The old woman shrugged and turned to the tourists and added, "We are both from the same generation, you and me. These young children just don't respect their elders like we did ours. Isn't that true? Please forgive the child's outburst; she wasn't raised with the same manners as we were."

Meva was about to say something much worse, when both women were interrupted by one of the tour guides. He was a Malagasy man probably from the big city who spoke French fluently. He warned the two, "Ladies, you don't know if these apples are clean or not or where they have been or where both of these women have been for that matter. Why don't you wait until we reach a gasoline station that has some things for sale and maybe you can buy some local items there?"

The two older women, with their money in hand, slowly put it back in their pockets. The excitement of buying had been squelched. They looked at each other and put their apples back in Meva's basket. Then they looked at Meva empathetically and said, "Merci". Meva smiled and watched them walk back onto the bus. The tour guide used the local dialect of the town to tell all the sellers to go away and that was the end of her attempts to make a sale.

All three tour guides began to huddle their people back onto the bus like cows returning to the barn. Meva began to walk home with her head held low when she heard a voice behind her say, "One moment Madame!"

It was one of the bus drivers from one of the other busses. "I need to buy a basket full of apples for my family as a gift when I return home."

He pulled out a 10,000 note and said, "'Fruit of the road,' you know."

This was the expression used for a souvenir when someone took a trip away from home. Often people would buy the produce that grew in the area they were visiting as most likely that couldn't be found where they were from, or if it was found, it was costly.

Meva held her head up high, while watching Rasoa stare from a distance as she handed over her entire basket to the man. With a quantity of that amount sold, the basket was normally given for free.

"Thank you very much!" the man replied as he packed his apples on the back of his tourist bus. Meva next tried to think of how best to put this money to good use for the rest of her month. She calculated how much it would cost to pay for her fruit stand rent for the week, then how much it would cost to go up to market and buy another basket of apples the next day, and lastly, how much she might need for a new hat for Ferdinand. She was too late to shop for anything in the market but decided to try her best to save some of the money so she could look for something nice to spend with the rest of it.

When she got back to the fruit stand, Eddie and Ferdinand were playing some sort of game with Eddie sitting on the ground, pretending to throw something and then jumping up and pretending to be the person who was getting hit by that something. Then he would do a little dance and chant, 'Go Ferdinand'. She watched the two of them for a moment and thought to herself how much she missed the meaningless play that one does as a child. Looking over her table she could see that everything was as she left it.

"Well, Monsieur Eddie," she asked with a professional tone, "How many apples did we sell?"

Eddie stood straight as an arrow and pulled out of a cardboard box the empty floor polish can that was used as a storage place for the money.

"More money than I've ever seen!" Eddie said cheerfully.

Meva looked inside the tin can and trying her best not to laugh as they hadn't even made enough to pay the rent for the day, Meva said, "Well done boys! You both are obviously very good salesmen, and I would like to avail myself of your services in the future."

Both boys' eyes beamed with pride.

A low rolling thunder could be heard over the mountain top. The black clouds that were looming served to warn all the street vendors that they had better pack up and go home. Eddie ran under the cardboard shelter his family had built outside the store front. Recently, the owner of the store gave them a piece of plastic to use so that their cardboard wouldn't get ruined from the rain. Ferdinand and his mother went home as fast as they could up the hill to where they lived. That night his mother began talking about what had happened that day at the town hall when she left him and Eddie to watch the stand.

"Eddie was right Nando," said Meva, which was her nickname for Ferdinand.

"There were three busloads of tourists just waiting there. And when I came with my apples, so many of them wanted a bite. They were all asking me the price until the man leading them all had to ruin it. I can tell from the look in your eye that you know what type of man this was, an 'Upper' as Eddie would have called him, if he had been there."

"He stopped some of them and said to them, 'you can't be sure where those apples came from or how clean this woman is, you had better wait until we reach one of the gasoline stations and just buy there.'"

"He didn't know I would be able to understand his French but I did and then he spoke to me in Betsileo and told me to go away. And to think he is one of our own people too!"

Meva never mentioned the lie Rasoa had told, as she didn't feel it was respectful to speak ill of one's elders.

"Can you believe that Nando? He would rather take them to those dirty gasoline stations as opposed to buying one of my apples that came straight from the countryside? Well, I walked away with no sales, but I wasn't bitter, I felt sorry for those poor people, yes I did. He was going to have them eating dirty gasoline station food instead of good produce like what we have here with us. Then you'll never guess what happened?"

She turned to Ferdinand with her hands up in their air as if she was being held up at gun point so as to give him a heightened sense of the dramatic. Ferdinand's eyes grew wide with anticipation.

"The driver from one of the other busses came and bought my entire basket of apples! It was a miracle. I can't remember the last time I sold that much in one day!"

Meva's laugh caused Ferdinand to laugh too.

"You see my boy, sometimes all we have to do is be patient and the right thing will come our way just at the right time, it makes no sense to feel sorry for ourselves."

She picked up a shiny green apple and took a bite, then gave Ferdinand a bite. In all the commotion, and in order to beat the rain, she didn't have time to stop and buy supper. Her daughter was taking night classes and ate near the school. So it was apples for dinner again. But they often just ate apples for supper.

On days like this, Ferdinand's mother would say things like, "It's good for our stomachs not to eat too much rice. Nando, so many of these town folks don't get the good vitamins they need from things like fruit because they would rather spend their every last dime on another cup full of rice."

Just the thought of rice made Ferdinand hungry. The apples only seemed to make him go to bed hungrier, but he would never dare say a word to his mother about it, she worked so hard to put any food on the table. It never entered his mind to complain about it. And besides, she seemed so happy over the day. If only Ferdinand could concentrate on his blessings like his mother did. All he could think of was how he was going to get back his hat.

The next day there were an unusual amount of people in the market. Ferdinand's mother came up close to him and asked, "Are you going to be okay while Mama goes up to the large market and buys a few more things for the stand? I thought by now Eddie would come but he isn't here yet and I'm running late to get the good apples. It worked out so well yesterday leaving the two of you here; I think I could do it again. Do you mind my dear?"

Ferdinand nodded his head. Meva went off with one of her friends who sold down the road. Normally, she bought fruit off her friend who went up every morning but this way the price of the apples would be cheaper and she could make more of a profit.

Ferdinand never minded being alone, as he was rarely ever alone. But after a while the freedom of being on his own made way for the longing for some companionship. He was thrilled when his second best friend in the world came up and rubbed up against his leg. 'Bow Wow' as Ferdinand, Eddie, and Meva called him, was their favorite neighborhood dog.

There really was no other word for a dog like Bow Wow as he had no home, no owners that anyone knew of, and he was loyal and protective of all the town's residents. Other stray dogs were just that, strays looking for any scraps of food they could possibly find along the side of the road. But Bow Wow was different. When Bow Wow came for a visit, he was more like a trusted friend seeing if there was anything he could do. And you rarely ever saw him sweeping the streets for scraps because everyone liked him so much they would often throw their left over bones and rice to him as he walked by. Bow Wow was particularly fond of apples.

Bow Wow sat up tall as close to Ferdinand as he could possibly be. His golden hair blew softly in the wind that breezed past. The two of them spent the better part of the morning watching the people walking by. On certain days, more so than others, everyone seemed to be in a rush and today was one of those days. No one was stopping to ask about the prices of anything. Everyone seemed to have an agenda. Except of course Lioka. His agenda it seemed could not be swayed by what others were doing. Ferdinand knew he must be approaching because he heard a low growl coming from Bow Wow's mouth.

"So, I see you're all alone today."

He snarled staring at Ferdinand in the eyes and holding his hands on his hips. Ferdinand could see that his backpack was opened slightly and a small piece of red which could have only been his hat was peering from the inside of it.

"You know, it's only a matter of time before I figure out a way to take every last thing you own off of your hands. It's not like it's any good to you anyways."

Lioka whispered this near Ferdinand's ears in case anyone might be listening.

Ferdinand had to think fast on his feet. Lioka's hand was reaching across his shoulder to grab his keychain. Ferdinand slapped Bow Wow as hard as he could and this sent the dog in a rage towards Lioka's leg. With one swift bite, Bow Wow had not only Lioka's pant leg but also a piece of skin nestled firmly in the grip of his bite. Lioka began to squirm and scream sending his back pack flying. Falling to the ground was not only Lioka's school books but also Ferdinand's red hat. Bow Wow grabbed the hat and went running down the street with it.

"Hey, come back here with my hat!" Lioka called out. He looked at

Ferdinand to see if he was going to say anything and when Ferdinand didn't reply, he ran down the street after the dog leaving his back pack there in front of him. After a few minutes Lioka came back breathing heavily as he wasn't accustomed to running like that.

"That dumb dog of yours ran off with my hat. Who would want it anyways now that it's been in that flea bags mouth."

With that, he picked up his backpack, his books that had fallen all over the sidewalk, and zipped it up securely. Ferdinand wondered how many other peoples things might be hiding in that back pack. Lioka walked off and Ferdinand was sure he wouldn't come back again. Between the tin cup the day before, and Bow Wow attacking him, Ferdinand's fruit stand was becoming an increasingly dangerous place for a bully.

Not long after Bow Wow came running up with the hat securely in between his teeth. He sat next to Ferdinand holding it like a store window model for perfect hats. Meva came not long after and seeing Bow Wow exclaimed, "Ferdinand look! Bow Wow has managed to find your red hat! Isn't that wonderful? It would seem it was here with us all along."

Ferdinand didn't say a word to his mother but looked down to Bow Wow and gave a smile to thank him for his hard work in retrieving his perfect red hat.

Meva dusted off the hat by taking it and rapidly beating it on her skirt. She then placed it securely on top of Ferdinand's head, making sure to smooth his hair out of his eyes when she did it. She bent down close to his face and smiled, "I told you son, if we are just patient, the right thing will come our way. We must have misplaced your hat in the zavona. And now, look its back. Everything is right with the world!"

Ferdinand was glad that he never had to worry his mother about his hat and Lioka. She already had so much to worry about and he was relieved that he was able to take care of this situation on his own.

Meva went back to work, organizing her apples and a couple pineapples she had bought while she was up there. Ferdinand felt whole again. His red hat had become a part of his daily uniform. Much like the school children wore the same blue smock every day on their way to school Ferdinand felt that with his red hat back, everyone would recognize who he was and he had his place in the world again.

Ferdinand began listening to some music a man nearby was playing on a radio he was holding in his hand. Distracted by the music he barely noticed his mother speaking to the neighbor lady who had recently moved in town from one of the bigger cities in the north. The woman was short and stocky, wearing a skirt that must have fit her much better several years prior. She held a handbag over her one arm and the other hand was up on her chest ready to hear the worst. Meva's words were unclear to Ferdinand but it sounded something like 'see you tomorrow'. What they actually said went something like this:

The neighbor lady asked Meva, "How old is your son?"

"Five years and ten," replied Meva.

"And how long has he been like that?" asked the nosey neighbor lady with her mouth gaping open in shock and her swollen feet standing like a duck in order to keep her balance.

"He has had weak muscles from the time he was born, but it's gotten progressively worse as he's gotten older, and he has been in that chair ever since he was old enough to walk. He has movement in his right hand and doesn't speak clearly but I can understand what he wants."

This was the usual reply Meva gave people who asked of Ferdinand's condition.

She never had the money to pay for an actual examination of his condition and so that was the best she could come up with in explaining it to others. Most never asked but just looked on sadly at the sight of Ferdinand sitting there in his wheel chair. It was an old chair that someone had given them when a family member died some years ago. But being broken, Meva had to devise a way for Ferdinand to sit on it. She tied on to the area of the seat, a plastic garden chair that she bought with a months' worth of wages. This way Ferdinand had a place to rest his arms when he sat and the seat was easier to clean and dry off than the original cloth one.

The neighbor lady continued, "Oh I feel so bad for you and your loss, to have to care for him must be very difficult for you."

The woman put her hand over her mouth to show her sadness.

Meva raised her hand to stop what she felt was only unnecessary empathy and said, "Oh no, he is a gentle boy. I don't know what I would do without him every day. Most boys his age have all sorts of worries. But my boy sits and smiles and is my constant companion. With him I am never alone. We are just on our way home now. I had better get a head start as it's a long push up that hill until we get to our home. May the evening finish well for you."

And with that Ferdinand's mother grabbed his wheel chair and began pushing him up the road that led to the tiny house where they lived. As usual, he carried the large fruit basket on his lap. The sky was still bright blue but the clouds had turned orange from the last few sunbeams that were setting behind the mountaintop.

The mountain was turning from a shade of deep green to that of black as nightfall was descending. A slight breeze blew past them giving them a chill and warning them that the zavona would be strong the next morning. Meva slid Ferdinand's red hat sideways on his head making him look more like his age and said, "You see my boy, there's always a bright side waiting for us around every corner.

You are looking very grown up in your red hat. Look! Bow Wow is following us home! What do you say; we cook up a big plate of rice tonight? I even had some extra money and thought we could celebrate by having popcorn while we listen to the radio!" Ferdinand let out a cry of joy. Maybe his mother was right, all really was right with the world, if only one was patient enough to wait for the right thing to come their way.

The End

IN THE LIGHT OF DAY

Caleb Rellie and his wife Nancy who he fondly called, 'Kick' went out for a date night as they attempted to do every Friday night. Although a priority, as of late, they had not really found the time or money to make it happen. Usually Nancy would peruse the local newspapers for discounts. On this particular night, they found no coupons or discounts. Caleb decided they should eat at a restaurant they had never eaten at before, "DiMaggio's". It was a newer Italian restaurant that had just been built. Caleb was on the brink of good news and so wanted to 'live it up' by ordering one of their better wines.

Normally, Caleb would not drink and drive. However, he felt one glass wouldn't hurt him espescially if they made sure to linger before they left. His day had been filled with efforts to merge another company with his employers'. One paper was left to be signed and the deal was done. All he needed to do was make sure the paper was signed in time for next Monday's business meeting.

This was a cause for celebration. The bottle of Shiraz, from South Africa, which he found ironic considering it was an Italian restaurant, seemed to suit the occasion nicely. He knew that with every sip, the stress of the day would melt away and he could concentrate on speaking with his lovely wife.

“It’s a bit dry in its aftertaste,” lamented Nancy.

“But it will do the trick,” grumbled Caleb as he tipped the last of the bottle over trickling it into his glass in order to finish it. He waved his hand to call over the waiter, “Check please.”

He never even hesitated as he signed the overpriced bill for the meal that he soon wouldn’t even remember he had eaten.

There was hardly a car on the road when they left the restaurant to head for home. It had been dark and the pavement was wet from the rainfall that took place while they had been dining. When the semi truck lost control its breaks locked and it swerved around the corner, Caleb felt his senses spring to alertness as he attempted to avoid it. He heard the tires squeal as he pushed on the breaks. And he felt the glass from the windshield shatter as they hit the concrete. But his senses weren’t sharp enough to control what happened next. Caleb passed out cold. It was three hours before the ambulance came to take him away.

The next thing he knew they were in the general hospital room awaiting the doctor’s examination. His head was aching but he had not been badly injured. As he sat on the edge of his hospital bed he could hear the doctor asking questions. There was a nurse giving answers after each question was asked.

“Time of arrival?”

“2:18 am Thursday.”

“Mark down room 404 as being occupied by one Mrs. Nancy Rellie.”

Caleb hadn’t really been sure what day it was but now the evenings activities were becoming clearer. He vaguely recalled last night in the restaurant. The sound of his car tires squealing began ringing in his ears, bringing back to him that they had been in an accident.

He looked up in his stupor and asked to anyone who might have heard him, "Please, where is my wife, Nancy Rellie?"

Still not being able to focus on who was in the room, he heard a voice reply to him, "She is right here Mr. Rellie, next to you. You have been in and out of consciousness. But we have checked all your vitals and they are stable. You are free to go as you please; however, your wife is going to have to stay for further observation. That bed that you are sitting on is not going to be used for the next couple of days by another patient that we know of. So you are free to sleep there with her here in the room if you prefer."

Caleb rubbed his eyes and could see clearly now that his wife was indeed lying in the bed next to him. It was a singular looking bed with iron rails and pale green sheets. Each bed had a side table with a telephone on it. With a faint awareness of others still being in the room he got up from his hospital bed and walked over to her.

"Nancy, it's me Cal. Can you hear me? Kick, please, honey, answer me."

He held her hand in his and waited, watching for any sign that she might reply but she did not so much as flinch.

"I'm sorry to inform you Mr. Rellie. But your wife Nancy is suffering from a comatose state. It seems the shock of your car wreck may have caused her to have minor cerebral damage. We are beginning now to check all of her vitals and will keep you informed as to any changes in her condition."

Caleb was in shock at what he was hearing. Still staring at Nancy with her limp hand held in his, he asked, "How long before she will wake up again?"

"It's difficult to say. Some patients with her same condition are more serious than others. There have been some patients known to wake up after only a few hours, others days, or, sometimes they remain in this state…" he paused slightly before continuing, "Maybe even indefinitely."

"When will you know for sure her actual condition?" asked Caleb looking at Nancy laying there.

"Thus far she has not spontaneously opened her eyes or given us any response to questions asked. Expansion of the pupils and respiratory pattern are also important, and her condition in these areas seems hopeful. Causes of coma are often diagnosed from blood work and analysis of her urine to evaluate blood chemistry, drug screen, and blood cell abnormalities that may indicate infection. We may also choose to diagnose from a CT or MRI scan. We are checking to see what is allowed by your insurance before carrying on with the larger tests that may be deemed necessary."

"Just do whatever you need to get her better, and I'll figure out a way to make the payments."

Caleb now fully aware that the situation was grave felt his heart sinking into the pit of his stomach. His wife looked very pale and quiet. Kick was rarely quiet. She always knew how to handle situations like this. Now it was up to Caleb to try and stay in control.

"We'll have the director of our payments department come in and speak with you about all that. Just try to focus on her care and the rest will fall into place. It will be important for her to have someone close to her here at all times in case she does wake up. Do you think you will have any family or friends who might join you here in watching over her?"

"I don't know. Her parents are older and they live out of town. My parents are no longer living. We both work full time and our close friends have jobs and families. I'm sure I'll be able to take the time off that I need to care for her. Don't worry, I'll make sure I'm here every step of the way."

"That's very good of you Mr. Rellie. We understand that at a time like this, it may be hard to stay focused. But if you feel you are up to the task, we will keep you as involved as we can. This no doubt will help greatly in her recovery."

The thought of Nancy being in a coma and needing to 'recover' as the doctor had put it, sent Caleb's head down on the bed next to her hand. Soft tears rolled down his cheeks and he couldn't utter another word.

The doctor lifted his chart and before walking out of the room said, "We'll give you some time alone. Your help with her will be very important. If you need anything just ring the nursing staff and they can assist you. You can use either this button connected to her hospital bed or you can dial the red button on this phone."

He picked up the receiver to show Caleb where the phone was located. With a professional looking smile he walked out of the room.

Caleb kept laying his head down on Nancy's arm for some time trying to wrap his head around the things leading up to the accident. When Caleb finally looked up again he squinted due to all the light in the room. The hospital room was a blinding stark white. White tile, white walls, and a white drop ceiling made the room very bright.

"No wonder people think they see a bright light before dying," he thought to himself. He got up and walked across the room to where a white cushioned metal chair sat near the window looking outside. He sat down firmly on it noticing that certain body parts were sore, probably from the accident. He had a strange tingling sensation underneath his right foot and began rubbing it while he gazed out the window.

Caleb wondered if the brightness in the room might cause his wife to awake from her coma. It had been some time since he had seen his wife sick. She was always the pillar of strength. Kick made sure to take care of herself despite their busy schedule. Her long chestnut hair was always flat ironed. Her makeup was never overdone, but highlighted the brightness in her eyes ever so slightly. As Caleb sat there starring at his wife of three years, he wondered if he would ever get to see those bright eyes again. Walking up to her bedside, he took out a comb from his pocket and began to comb her bangs to one side just the way he knew she always liked it.

As he was about to go into her purse which he noticed was sitting underneath the telephone table and look for her favorite lip gloss, the doctor appeared again. Caleb looked at the clock and was surprised that a couple hours had passed; it seemed as if it had only been minutes.

"Good afternoon, doctor thank you for coming," said Caleb warmly extending his hand. The doctor did not take his hand but went over to the bed and began doing an examination including eye checks, heart monitoring, and looking at Nancy's finger nails.

The doctor continued to examine Nancy in what Caleb assumed to be standard procedure. A tall nurse with red hair was standing behind him taking notes as he spoke, "The patient is now in an official comatose state. She has failed to respond to stimuli, sound, and light. The injury looks to have caused injury in the cerebral cortex."

"What does that mean?" interrupted Caleb. "Is she going to die? Is she going to wake up?"

"Further examination will be necessary in order to determine her condition." The doctor answered his question in an odd way in Caleb's opinion while continuing the examination; never looking up at Caleb directly. He was poking Nancy's left foot with a sharp device to see if she would respond.

"Coma is a medical emergency, and attention must first be directed to maintaining the patient's respiration and circulation, using ventilation, administration of intravenous fluids as needed, and other supportive care. It is extremely important for a physician to determine quickly the cause of a coma, so that potentially reversible conditions are treated immediately."

He then continued with more statements of diagnosis, speaking more to the nurse than to Caleb. Caleb felt at this time it would make sense to let the doctor know what led up to the accident.

"Doctor, my wife and I seem to have been in an accident. I had a few glasses of wine and before we left the restaurant that night and now here we are at the hospital. It might be helpful if we could look at the police report and compare what was written with your own findings."

Caleb thought this piece of information might be helpful but the doctor, looking very uninterested, and still not making any eye contact with Caleb continued to speak aloud as the nurse typed down everything he was saying in a computer that sat on a roll away cart.

"The patient does not appear to be in a permanent state of coma. Her body temperature is not at a dangerous level. There is no need to fear the worse."

With that, he poked his metal tool into her right foot.

Caleb began to pace the floor nervously feeling very uncomfortable. He decided to sit down and elevate his feet as the doctor carried on, hoping that the burning sensation that had taken over his body would end if he lifted his feet above his heart. He did not want to distract the doctor from caring for Nancy by bringing up any unusual symptoms he was experiencing.

The doctor paused and spoke to Caleb who was now looking quite silly with one foot raised on a fern pot and the other foot sitting too high on top of the window ceil next to him.

"Depending on the length of the coma, the patient may have a different recovery time. In some cases there is post-traumatic amnesia.

"So does that mean you think she will wake up?" asked Caleb with a voice filled with hope. He was still sitting in the metal chair awkwardly with his foot up on the fern.

The doctor again did not to respond to Caleb's question but continued his examination. Caleb could feel his blood pressure rising at the lack of communication he was experiencing from the doctor. As he was about to stand up and demand the doctor's attention, Nancy's right foot jutted up in the air hitting the doctor square in the jaw. The foot landed back down on the bed soundly, leaving the doctor to stand there and rub his jaw with the care of a mother who comforts her young child after an injury such as a scraped knee.

"Did you see that, did you see that?" Caleb said pointing to the leg in excited astonishment.

"The patient has shown spontaneous movement," said the doctor still examining Nancy rather apathetically.

"Nurse, please change the last statement to read, 'At 7:00 hours, Thursday May 21, 2012, the patient responded to painful stimuli and then returned to her state of coma.'"

Then looking at the nurse wearily he said, "We will return again for our rounds at the normal time."

The nurse nodded in the affirmative and hit the return button on the key board closing the report that she had been writing up on Nancy.

The doctor was about to leave the room without saying one word to Caleb about what had just happened. He signaled for the nurse to keep up the pace with him, handing her his clipboard he had been using to jot down notes. She quickly grabbed the clipboard dropping his pencil on the ground and hurried to catch up behind him. Caleb jumped up from his seat nearly knocking the fern pot over with his foot.

"Wait! That's it? Don't you want to try again?"

Caleb attempted to follow the two of them but hit his foot against the hospital bed leg which left him bouncing up and down in agony. Feeling slightly defeated, he sat down onto the bed opposite of where his wife was laying. The hospitals bedside manner did not impress him but seeing the doctor being kicked square in the jaw by his wife was enough to make his day turn into a positive direction more so than the fact that his comatose wife's leg had just twitched.

He looked over at her and began to speak.

"Thanks Kick. If only I had a camera, I really don't care for that guy, and apparently you didn't care for him poking around at you either," Caleb said musing as he continued thinking about the humor of what had just happened.

He let go of his foot and walked back over to her bed, sitting beside her on the edge of the mattress and staring at her beautiful face. She was tall and thin with a petite frame. Her face was always ivory gently sprinkled with nutmeg colored freckles. Caleb used to call her his favorite flavor ice cream. With a heavy sigh, he said to her, "I know you're still in there, Nancy. If you can just come back to me, we will be able to get through this. I'll make everything right. Please, forgive me for drinking that night, my darling. I had no idea it would affect me. I'm going to try to get to the bottom of what really happened, I promise. If you can just come out of this so that we can do it together, it would make me the happiest man in the whole wide world."

Being a middle-aged man who had been in the same job since the time he graduated high school, Caleb was not accustomed to having his routine shaken up. He had a stable job working as a manager for a real estate company. He prided himself in his managing skills and often would take courses held by the company like how to improve his business sense or how to act in a time of emergency. The real estate business was not doing very well in Caleb's area. Caleb hadn't had consistent daily work for some time. Recently, he was called back in to work on the merger of two real estate companies in the area that wanted to combine with the one he worked for. There was never a good time to have an accident. Yet, Caleb feared that this was an unusually bad time because without the completion of the merger, he might be out of a job.

However, Caleb was not worrying if this was a good time or not for his dear wife to be in the hospital. His mind was racing with the guilty thought that it must have been his drinking that caused him to swerve in the wrong direction and fly off the highway.

The car had rolled onto the street below the overpass but thankfully landed in a way that they were able to come out alive. Caleb had no time to inquire what exactly had happened and had only sporadic memories of that night. But he was sure there would be an investigation and he intended to be truthful about everything that had happened leading up to the accident.

It was four o'clock in the afternoon. Caleb turned to look again outside the hospital window at the ground below. The sky was blue with only a few wispy white clouds lacing the sky like curtains floating in the wind on a perfect spring day. The window seemed set in the ideal location for some people watching.

The emergency ward was on the bottom floor. They had first been taken to the ICU but then were transferred to one of the regular hospital rooms. They must have been high up on the third floor of the four-story hospital building. Caleb could see the cars parked below and where the property line ended. After a large concrete wall that bordered the parking lot, there was a large grassy park that was situated behind it where children were happily playing. He could hear them singing an indistinct sound and laughing as they skipped rope.

As he watched, the sun shone brightly in his eyes as if the beams of light went directly into his pupils. He tried to cover over his eyes with his forearm but it was of no use. The sun was making one last vain attempt to stay up before falling. One last shout out to the world that it would not be the last time it shone on mankind. It stood bright orange against the background of the blue sky. Blinded by its glare, Caleb closed the window shade for fear the temperature of the room was too warm for Nancy.

By the second day of Nancy's coma, Nancy's condition did not seem to be improving. Her color and statistics were good. Nothing had declined. Yet, she was still not waking up and had made no other spontaneous movements as she did that first day. Caleb began to speak to her normally as he would have every day. He started by talking in the way they would when they would go and sit in the coffee shops on Saturdays after their morning of doing household chores.

"Nancy, the grass is so green from the rain last night. It seems I'll have to cut it twice this week."

Then Caleb would pause as if waiting for her to respond.

"Mrs. Jensen next door will probably help water our flowers since we're spending so much time here at the hospital."

"The night nurse scares me. He looks just like your aunt Mildred only with a beard. Wait, Aunt Mildred did have a beard. Maybe that's why I think they look alike."

And so he kept the conversation going as it were. He would speak and she would not respond. Often as he spoke his attention would turn to her right foot hoping for another movement to give him hope that her sedentary state would soon end. In between little 'chats' he would tuck her in, or massage her legs to make sure she was getting good circulation.

By day three, visitors started to come. Often when they came and went Caleb had been out of the room. Nancy's mother and father had flown in. They both seemed very grave when they entered the room. Caleb could feel their eyes looking at him in cynical judgment. He didn't say much as one of the nurses had entered and was willing to update them on her situation. They said they could not stay but wanted to see how she was doing with their own eyes. Nancy's younger brother and his wife came while Caleb had been sleeping. Caleb's parents had died when he was a young boy due to a car accident. So there weren't many who would have come to see him personally. Most of the visitors were all from Nancy's acquaintances.

Caleb decided to make himself busy while he waited for more visitors to come. He began straightening up the hospital room, folding Nancy's clothes, wiping down the tables, and throwing out the left over cups people had left who may have brought in coffee when they came to visit.

The scent of citrus perfume filled the air and he knew who had entered.

"Well, what do we have here? Is my favorite student a little down in the dumps?"

It was Mrs. Bacon, Caleb's second grade teacher. She was tall with bleached blonde hair and too much makeup. Her face was stern as she spoke as if this new situation might be similar to a student who showed up tardy for class. He was grateful to have had someone who wanted to come and see him because the days in the hospital room had been very lonely.

"What a predicament you have found yourself in Caleb. Tell me, my dear, was it your fault?"

Mrs. Bacon seemed to be asking the most horrific of questions and yet Caleb was not shocked. He looked at Nancy and then Mrs. Bacon who was standing near Nancy's bed. He looked at his former teacher staring at him waiting for a response and said, "I don't know."

"I think you had better find out Caleb Rellie."

She was now holding her hands on her hips and pointing one index finger at him as she spoke.

"You know the police will be involved and if you don't have your story straight you might go to jail. And if you go to jail you may never see your wife again. If she wakes up, she won't know where you are or what they've done with you because there will be no one there to tell her. So think Caleb before you do anything else. More than you've ever thought before. What is it that happened that night?"

Without really finishing the conversation, Ms. Bacon had left. With her left the scent of citrus which had always left Caleb feeling calm despite the fact that she was always a little cynical. She had been his teacher the year his parents were killed in the car accident. Ever since, she would keep tabs on him, sometimes taking the bus just to see how he was doing. When he and Nancy were married, she attended the wedding. And each year around the time of the new school year, Caleb would make sure to take her the brightest shiniest apple he could find at the store in celebration. Mrs. Bacon came several times during the course of Nancy's hospitalization, always first thing in the morning.

Caleb got up and peered out of the hospital window to watch her walk off the property before saying to Nancy, "She's always a bit of an old bat isn't she?"

He could hear more footsteps coming down the hallway. When they neared their doorway they stopped, seeming to pause and then entered.

"Hello there Nancy, well what has happened to you?"

A strange looking fellow wearing loud shoes that made an echoing sound on the tile as he walked came into the room and approached Nancy's bed.

Caleb got up to shake his hand but the man went over to the bed and continued to speak to Nancy as if he wasn't even aware of Caleb's presence.

"We're going to have to do something about this situation aren't we?" he said putting his hand on top of hers.

"Don't you worry about a thing. I've got everything under control Nancy. We're going to take care of him."

"Take care of whom?" Caleb asked as he looked at the man in shock. He didn't recognize his face at all. Before he could ask for the man's name, he vanished.

Looking down at Nancy and scratching his head, he said in a low tone to her, "You never cease to amaze me Kick. You sure know a lot of people. But good 'ol Cal will be the one taking care of you and not that guy?"

With that, he laughed aloud not really understanding what had just happened but happy to have something new to say to her fragile form as it lay there.

The day nurse came in with an armful of books. She was a tiny, thin person of about age 25. Her wispy blonde hair was tied back in a pony tail and seemed to drop a strand of hair with each step she took. Although she had worked in several suburban clinics this was her first hospital job and she intended to be the best nurse she could be.

"I thought you might like to read these. Some family members even enjoy reading books out loud so that the patient can hear, although there has never been documented proof that the practice actually aids in the patients' recovery process."

"Gee, thanks. Do I need to pick out which one I want?" He asked this not knowing what kind of book he would like to read to Nancy as he wasn't really much of a reader but the idea sounded like a great way to pass the time.

"Oh no, you can have them all and when you are finished you can return them to the library located on the second floor. Do you know where that is?"

The nurse wasn't looking at Caleb as she spoke but checking the computer monitor for Nancy's latest statistics.

"I think I'll manage to find my way. Thank you for thinking of us," he said gratefully.

"You're very welcome. Reading helps ease the mind. And the mind can make us anxious in times like these. So just try to relax and I'm sure in no time everything will be alright."

The nurse walked out just as fast as she had walked in.

"Finally!" Caleb thought to himself, "a person with an ounce of bedside manner."

Caleb began to look through the pile of books. There was Wuthering Heights, which had been a favorite movie of his mother. Then there were some mystery suspense novels that he thought he might enjoy. Lastly, there were two romantic stories, which he thought Nancy might like, but he felt embarrassed to read them aloud if people were to walk in the room.

Having chosen one of the mystery novels he decided to sit down and begin reading it to her right away. The storyline was about a man who was a detective. Upon investigating a murder case, he discovers a conspiracy. Caleb began to read to Nancy around dinnertime and was surprised when he finished the third chapter and it had become dark outside.

Caleb put the books down and sat there. He began to try and think about his work schedule next week and wondered what he would do if Nancy still didn't wake up in time for that business merger he was organizing. There was another worker in the office named Larry who would gladly help him out. In fact, he would help him right out of a job since he was always trying to undermine everything Caleb did in the office in hopes of getting a higher position. But Caleb figured if all else failed, it would be in the company's best interests to have Larry do the merger. He decided he would wait a couple more days before making the dreaded call informing his boss that he wouldn't be able to handle it. Suddenly as he was thinking about work, Nancy made a groan and raised her right arm slightly.

"Nancy? Kick, I'm here, it's me Caleb!"

Caleb ran over to the bed, pushed the nurses' button and then held Nancy's hand stroking it in hopes that she would come to consciousness again. One of the night nurses soon entered the room.

"You called?" she asked with something in her hand as if she had been in the middle of doing something when he pushed the button.

"Yes! It's my wife I heard her make a noise, I think she's coming to. What should we do?"

Caleb said this all very excitedly. He began shaking Nancy's hand in hopes that it would help her come out of the coma. The nurse took her hand out of his and put her own hand on Caleb's shoulder in a patronizing manner.

"Maybe it would be better if you waited over there Mr. Rellie. I am going to ring for the doctor and I promise not to leave her side if she comes to consciousness. Things like this often happen and it doesn't necessarily mean that she'll wake up yet. But we will do all that we can to make it happen one day, even if she's not ready just now."

The nurse checked Nancy's eyes and pulse but saw no sign of further response.

"Thank you nurse," said Caleb in a whisper. He felt the pain of deflated hope. With his heart still racing over the excitement, he got up and walked over to the chair in the corner of the hospital room. Caleb sat down on the chair and must have fallen asleep because by the time he woke up it was morning again.

The room was filled with sunlight and there lay his precious wife with no look of her old self yet present. Being very disappointed in himself that he could sleep when something so exciting had happened as her making a sound, he decided to go get a cup of coffee to wake up.

The usual coffee machine that was near her hospital room was broken. He could tell something wasn't right as the smell burnt coffee permeated the room. He shook the coffee pot to see if there was any left but the coffee left on the bottom was now dry and crusty.

"There is another machine near the nurses' station," he heard a voice call out to him. He turned but they must have already left the room because there weren't any people standing near enough for Caleb to be the one that spoke to him.

He walked down the hallway, asked someone where the machine was located and then went in the direction pointed. As he turned the corner expecting to come upon the coffee machine, he heard the familiar sound of noisy shoes. Then, there was another voice that began speaking to the man with the noisy shoes causing Caleb to stop around the corner and listen.

"The condition is just as we expected it to be. The accident must be investigated further but it will be impossible to get the man to talk and tell us what we want to know. I think we should continue administering the medicines so that he can stay calm and we can try to get the wife to cooperate. It's still possible we can protect the interests of all parties involved, at least the ones that truly matter, anyway."

"Yes, doctor, of course. But how do you think we can go about doing this, they are not likely to comply with our wishes."

"Try to get the body out of the room and then we can handle the situation to our liking."

"What room number is it again, doctor?"

"Room number 404."

Caleb had a lump in the middle of his throat. That was Nancy's room! What did they mean they were going to try and move her from the room? The voices continued to speak.

"He's got the paper in his brief case. If we can obtain the information we need, then we'll be able to destroy the company's plans. Just leave it to me I'll take care of him."

Caleb tried to lean over as far as he could without being seen. All he could see was a man holding a sharp looking operating knife in his left hand. He was wearing a white office coat and in the pocket looked to be a syringe. He raised his thick hand to the needle and tapped it while smiling silently at the one he was speaking to. Caleb couldn't lean over far enough to see which one of these was the man with the noisy shoes or to make out either of their faces. He leaned just one inch more and knocked over a paper that had been taped to the wall where he had been leaning. The sound of the paper caused him to run off in the opposite direction, turning sharply down a stairway corridor so that if they had heard him moving they wouldn't see him as he ran down the hallway.

Caleb had forgotten about his much needed coffee. All he could think of was how to get back to his wife. He ran past the nurses' station on the floor below to the opposite end of the hallway. As was the case on any of the days before that he had set off to explore the building, there was hardly any staff on hand to help him. He saw another stairwell at the opposite end of the building and ran up that. When he got to room 404 his could feel that the shirt on his back he was still wearing since he had first arrived was soaked with sweat from running. But he was relieved to see that Nancy was in her bed still in a coma. No one had entered the room since he had left that he could tell.

Tired from the morning's activities, he decided to sit on the hospital bed next to Nancy and think about what he should do about the conversation he had just overheard.

"Surely I must have misunderstood," he thought to himself while at the same time wondering what exactly it was that the two strange voices had been talking about in the coffee room. As Caleb, sat chewing on his nails thinking, his friend Larry from work appeared.

"Hey buddy, how's it going?"

Larry, was a middle aged man much like Caleb only instead of being clean shaven he sported a goat-tee on his chin that made him look like he was trying to be a rock star. In reality, Larry was an account broker and the most exciting roadside venture he ever took was his trip to Vegas to do one of the casinos' accounting records.

"It's not going so good Larry. I don't trust this hospital. There are some strange people I have overheard speaking recently and I don't know what to do about it."

Caleb then went on to relate the details of the conversation he had heard and awaited Larry's response on what he should do.

Larry had a soft drink in his hand and would intermittently slurp on it as Caleb spoke. Caleb always had found Larry's lack of etiquette in listening to be annoying but he decided not to criticize the only ally he had under the current conditions. Larry's eyes were straying around the room. He looked down at the novel Caleb had been reading.

"Are you finding time to read amidst all of this trouble you've found yourself in?"

Larry asked as if amused.

"The nurse brought it in and said it might calm my mind."

"What's it about?" Larry asked picking up the book and thumbing through it.

"It's about a guy with a scruffy looking co-worker friend who is a lousy listener!"

Caleb grabbed the book from Larry's hand and flung it on the floor.

Larry got up trying to remain calm.

"Look buddy, I know this is a hard time for you. And I'm here for you. All I'm saying is, maybe your imagination is getting the best of you. You know, you are over tired, you're reading these mystery novels, and now you're coming up with conspiracy theories. It's a hospital for crying out loud, not the CIA headquarters. Just calm down and try to relax. Do you want me to speak with the doctor about getting you some sort of tranquilizers or something to help you stay calm?"

"No! I don't want anything. I'll be fine. Thanks for coming."

Not really buying into the fact that he was being paranoid Caleb began subtle attempts to put his friends mind at ease in order to get him out of the room.

"Thanks again for coming in to see me, Larry. You're right; I think I am over tired. Ever since Kick went under, I just can't stop thinking about that night and everything that happened. Did you know the police haven't come to make a report yet? I was thinking by now they would. I had some wine that night and I'm worried that maybe it could have affected my driving."

Larry picked up the book from the floor and put it by the nightstand that stood in between Nancy and Caleb's bed.

"Look pal, I wouldn't go dragging the police into this if you don't have to. Just concentrate on getting better and then the rest will take care of itself later."

"I'm not the one that needs to get better. Nancy does."

He looked over at her longingly realizing now more than ever before that she was always his sole confidant and that no one else could compare to her way of calming him down.

"Well, you know what I meant," Larry replied. He had a grim look on his face as he realized there was really no word of comfort he was going to be able to offer.

"Cal, I want you to call me if you would like me to stay overnight here with you, okay? Do you still have your cell phone after the accident?"

"I haven't found it, and keep forgetting to ask the nurses about it. It's probably still in the car."

Larry took his leather wallet out of his back pocket, opened it and pulled out a business card. He looked down on the hospital floor and noticed a pencil that someone had dropped. Larry picked it up and wrote a number on the back of the card. He handed it to Caleb who then held it in his hand reading over the number.

"There is my cell phone number Cal. Keep it on you at all times and don't hesitate to call me Buddy. You shouldn't be alone in a time of need like this."

"Thanks buddy, I'll be just fine. Don't you worry about me. Sorry if I scared you with all of that crazy talk."

"No problem. That's what friends are for right?"

Larry gave Caleb a solid pat on the shoulder and stuck the pencil behind his ear.

"You'll be back to work in no time. Nothing's going to change while you're away."

He then walked out of the room. Caleb hadn't realized how tired the day's activities must have made him and he began to doze off.

The hospital lights were dim when Caleb awoke from his sleep. There was no sound of footsteps in the hallway as there had been when he was last conscious. He could only hear the sound of a whirling machine in the background. He woke up with a thick headache sitting squarely in the middle of his forehead. His neck must have been out of alignment because it felt pinched and stiff as if he had been in the same position for days.

Putting his fingers through his now thick oily hair, he decided it might be best to take a shower. Not having a change of clothes, and it now being too late to run out and buy some, Caleb found the hospital robe that he must have worn upon arriving and used that. The shower made him feel fresh and renewed. When he got out the tile floor was cold against his sockless feet. He tip toed past the hospital beds and decided to put on his old socks until he could get some new ones from home in the morning.

He looked over at Nancy for any sign of life. Only her chest gently moved up and down. She looked so peaceful he thought to himself as he picked up a towel and a hospital robe. The tile floor was cold underneath his feet but in his sleepy stupor, he decided not to disturb

Nancy by wearing his flip-flops.

Only afterwards when he walked past her the second time did he realize just how silly it was to try not to disturb a comatose person. In fact, he wondered if he just shouldn't disturb her. Looking to either side of the room just in case someone was entering, Caleb gently gave Nancy's left leg a pinch. When this didn't work, he gave it a harder pinch. He was just about to pinch one more time when the phone rang and he picked it up.

"Hello?" there was no answer on the other end. The sudden click of the receiver being banged down on the other end, made Caleb jump. All the thoughts of what had happened the night before and what he had heard came flooding back into his mind. Now swimming with paranoia, he put the receiver down slowly, glanced over at Nancy, and let out a heavy sigh.

Caleb decided to go to the nurses' station and see if it had been someone attempting to call him.

He turned the corner at the end of the ward and thought he might call Larry for advice or explain to him in more detail of what he had heard the day before. Really, he just wanted someone to talk to. But, when he arrived at the waiting room and went to make a call, there was no reception. He took the elevator down to the second floor and attempted to make another phone call but to no avail. Not wanting to leave Nancy for too long in case the nursing staff came in to move her, he decided to go back up stairs and check on how Nancy was doing. He figured if he checked on her first, then he could go outside the hospital and make his phone call from the parking lot.

Upon entering the room, Nancy was gone! Caleb could feel the rush of panic wash over him causing his heart to race. Where could they have taken her? Why would they take her without having consulted with him first? Who took her? Was it the man with the noisy shoes? He ran out of the room to find some nurses but no one was at their stations.

The perspiration was now beginning to form on his forehead. The doors whizzing by him as he ran began to make him feel dizzy. He took a right at the first exit sign that he saw and ran down the staircase flying around the corners in one leap. He pushed the door open with both hands and went right again remembering this was the closest exit near to where he had parked his car. When he finally reached the door, he slammed into it as if he didn't know he had to open it first. Having fallen on his back flatly, a nurse came running up to help him.

"Sir, do you need help? Are you sick?" she asked leaning over him checking his eyes.

"No, I am fine."

He groaned still in pain from the fall.

"I just tried to exit the building and the door must have been locked.

"I don't think you actually got to the opening the door part, Sir. Here, let me have your hand. I'll help you back to your room. Which room number are you in?"

"404 is my wife's room number. I entered the room only to find that she was missing. I need help, someone has taken her and I don't know what to do."

Caleb realized that all of this sounded very desperate and unrealistic but he couldn't stop himself from uttering the words. The nurse walked with him to the elevator and they both entered in. He felt himself becoming increasingly paranoid about being alone with her there. As the elevator lights counted up the floor numbers.

They slowly entered the room together. There lay Nancy in her bed.

"I don't understand! She was gone and now she's here!"

Caleb looked around and the nurse was gone. Kick lay there so still, so unassuming, as always, like an angel. Caleb didn't know what he should do. If he left, they might come and move her again. On the other hand, had she really been moved at all?

Was he losing his mind? What was happening? Either Nancy really was in some sort of danger, or he was going insane. Caleb checked every bone of her body to make sure she was all right. It seemed as if not even so much as a sheet had been moved. He finally decided that maybe he was overtired and had imagined the entire thing.

All he could do was stand over her like a guardian watching every movement of her chest as it gently rose up and down. There was a rhythm to it, never did she gasp for air, and never did it pause as if not able to take a deeper breadth. If only she could open her eyes and speak to him, telling him that it was going to be okay. Then maybe he could find it in himself to fall asleep. But what if he was right and someone really was trying to move Nancy? Such disquieting thoughts kept creeping back into his mind the minute he attempted to calm himself down.

Fearing that he was starting to lose his mind, Caleb decided it might be best to call the nurses' station and ask about a sleep aid. When he picked up the receiving end of the telephone a man was on the other end.

"Caleb. Are you listening?"

The man's voice sounded to be muted, distorting it to make it unrecognizable.

"Listen to what we tell you to do and you won't get hurt. You have a paper in your brief case and we need that paper, Caleb. We have shown you what can happen if you don't listen. It will be very easy to alter your life in a way that is much more drastic that what you have experienced over the last couple of days. All you need to do is what we tell you and your wife will not get hurt."

"I don't understand what it is you want me to do!"

Caleb was speaking very loudly hoping that someone would hear him. He also grabbed the button attached to the hospital bed Nancy had been in and began to press it for help.

"Take the paper in your brief case and take it to the first floor of the hospital building. When you reach the basement stairs, go down them. At the bottom of the stairs, you will see a metal box. Open it Caleb, and put the merger paper inside. Leave the box, and leave the hospital. If you do as you are instructed, I promise you, your wife will be left alive."

Caleb's heart began to beat like the sound of a drum before the battle. He scanned the room for his briefcase which he had not taken notice of since they had been in the Italian restaurant the night of the accident. After looking under Nancy's table, bed and the metal chair by the window, Caleb saw it. It must have been sitting there underneath his hospital bed the entire time. Caleb ran over to the bed, kneeled down on the tile floor, and grabbed the bag. He got up and left the hospital room turning to the right, accessing the closest stairwell to the room.

Caleb, with his hospital robe still on and the briefcase in hand leapt down the stairwell taking the stair in twos and threes. Upon reaching the bottom step, he did not see the metal box that the strange man spoke of.

"It must be at the other end of the hallway where I was earlier," Caleb thought to himself. He went back up one flight of stairs so he could go back down the opposite hallway that would take him to the other basement stairs, since there was no tunnel that led to both ends. The only thing between the two stairwells was the hospital morgue and the access doors were securely locked.

The hallway lights were dark and dim; the florescent bulbs flickered as if ready to burn out. He was about to pass a visitors room on his right when he heard voices and decided to stop and listen to be sure it wasn't someone who would try and stop him from delivering the paper.

There was a corner mirror opposite the room and he could see a thin looking man with a larger mustache was standing at the corner of the visitors room entrance. He had something in his hand that looked like a paper bag. Caleb couldn't know that the syringes inside were filled with a sedative intended to keep him asleep for a very long time. However, his intuition, or possibly his paranoia screamed that these men meant him no good.

Despite thinking he had a good hiding spot, the man turned in time to see Caleb's reflection in the mirror opposite the room. Caleb gasped in horror as he saw the reflection of the man in the mirror moving slowly against the wall and towards the visitor room entrance way. The man was reaching into his paper bag for one of the needles as he slowly crept to meet Caleb at the door.

Caleb decided to back up and go the other way slowly while still watching the reflection in the mirror, hoping that the man would assume he was a hospital patient. As Caleb continued walking backwards the strange looking man slowly stepped forward, he noticed the man's eyes watching him in the mirror with every step he took. It made him nervous to the point that his brow began to bead with sweat. He reached into his jacket pocket to search for Larry's phone number but since he was still wearing his hospital robe, he had no pocket and therefore no phone number.

Not having time to go back to the hospital room he took off as fast as he could down the hallway.

"Run Caleb, run they are after you!" he thought to himself as he turned and whizzed past the nurses' station not seeing anyone there that might be of assistance to him.

The man in the mirror began to run quickly behind him and yell, "Stop! 'Don't get hysterical!"

The man running towards him called this out while extending his arm to Caleb as if trying to stop him from running any further.

Caleb opened the door to the stairwell and shouted out behind him as he began to leap down the stairs, "Hysterical is for people who don't have a plan. I've got one and you're not going to get it!"

In reality, Caleb had no plan. His plan was to run out of the hospital and find help as fast as he possibly could. When he reached the end of the hallway on the floor above where he had just been, he realized the hospital doors were locked tight.

"The nurse's station is my only hope," he thought as he ran in the opposite direction of the hallway he had just been down and towards the nurse's station that would have a telephone where he could call the police for help.

Caleb ran to the next nurse's station nearest the exits of the hospital. He saw the telephone sitting there and picked up the receiver to call for help. Before he could finish dialing, a man's hand grabbed onto his wrist in a deathly tight grip and banged it several times on the desk causing the phone to loosen from the grip of his hand. Caleb let out a cry for help but the man tried to muffle him with his free hand, still holding onto Caleb's wrist.

Caleb picked up the stapler that was sitting on top of the nurses' station and forcefully bashed the man over the head with it. The man dropped to the ground and lay there in a heap. Caleb kneeled down in his robe and bare feet and began to search through the man's pockets for anything that might give him a clue as to who the man was but found nothing but a key sitting on a chain that was on the man's neck.

The man groaned, moving his arm and in a jerk reaction, Caleb took the pencil that was still sitting behind his ear and plunged it into the skin between his thumb and forefinger leaving the pencil there. The man screamed in shock and pain, and then attempted to jump up but lost his footing and instead fell backwards hitting his head on the tile floor knocking himself unconscious.

When Caleb saw that he was making no further attempts to move, he dragged the man to the nurses' station desk. Caleb grunted and panted as he dragged the heavy weight as fast as he could. Grabbing some masking tape, Caleb began tying up the man's wrists and ankles. Finding no other place that seemed stable enough to hold him, Caleb taped the man up to the nurse's desk until he could call for help. He carefully unhooked the chain holding the key from the man's neck and placed it around his own. He picked up the phone receiver again only to find the line had been cut.

Feeling that he had no time to waste, he had to get Nancy out of the hospital and then maybe someone could help them both. He ran up the flight of stairs to her room. Nancy's bed was there, but she was not in it. It sat there empty. The phone rang again on the table next to her bed. Caleb slowly picked up the receiver and before it could reach his ear he heard the familiar voice that he had heard speaking before say, "We have her. You did not do as we instructed you to do. If you want to see your wife alive, we suggest you cut out the funny business and do what we have asked of you."

Click. The call had ended.

Caleb did everything he could not to break down and cry right there. He stared at the crumpled up piece of paper in his hand. He had never even gotten close enough to the metal box to put the merger paper inside. He then looked down at his chest at the key that was on the chain hanging around his neck.

"A key to where?" he wondered.

"Could it be the key to the room where they had Nancy?"

The only other place that he could think of was the storage rooms in the basement where the morgue was located. If he could make it in time, he could place the merger paper in the box and then go try to find Nancy there and get her out of the hospital to find help.

Filled with the energy of a man on the run, Caleb ran down the hospital corridor and down the steps to the first floor to reach the basement stairwell. He passed the same area where he had hit the man with a stapler, only the body was gone. He kept running and entered the stairwell of the hospital located at the far end of the hallway. Caleb leaped down the stairs barely making contact with the steps.

When he reached the bottom, the metal box was sitting at the end of the stairwell as promised. Next to it was the doorway leading to the storage room where he thought they may have hidden Nancy. Caleb opened the doorknob with both hands, swinging it open hard and causing it to hit the wall behind it with a loud bang. As he entered, he could hear the sound of the man with noisy shoes coming rapidly behind him down the stairs.

Caleb looked for something that he might use to be able to block the doorway.

"Maybe the man would only want the paper and then would release Kick. But what if he wants the paper and then just wants to kill us both because we know too much?"

Not knowing what to do next, Caleb tried to focus on finding Nancy but the sound of the man's footsteps was ringing in his ears. Caleb saw a tall metal filing cabinet and began pushing it towards the door. As he gave a final push, blocking the door. The man with the noisy shoes began to try to open it but couldn't. Caleb ran in the other direction to the sound of the man banging and pushing on the door trying to get in. He knew the simple blockade would only hold for a matter of minutes at best.

As Caleb ran down the dark corridor in search for Nancy, he tried to drown out the sound of the man hitting the file cabinet with the door. The sound in his ears changed from that of the banging of metal, to that of a sloshing noise. Caleb looked down and the floor was filled with water as if a pipe had broken. The water was rushing down towards a set of double doors that must have led to the morgue. The doors were locked. Anxious to get inside as he was sure that's where they were hiding Nancy, Caleb began searching for something to break the double doors glass windows with.

There were old computer monitors sitting on a table nearby. Caleb ran over to the table splashing water with every step and picked up the heaviest monitor he could find. With one huge throw he sent the computer monitor crashing into the glass. It fell apart into pieces onto the watery floor below. The glass looked unharmed. Caleb grabbed a second monitor, this time running up to the glass, trying to use his body weight to force the monitor through. His body crashed into the window with full force causing some glass shards from the monitor to imbed themselves into his chest. Looking down at his chest he saw the key sitting around his neck on a chain.

"That was it!"

Caleb ripped the key off of his neck and began trying to wiggle it in the key hole.

The door opened but the force of his body trying to enter caused him to slip and fall to the floor on the other side of the doorway. His body landed flat on the ground, and his clothes were instantly soaked. He stood himself up but the force of the water was now stronger than before. Using the floor to hold him, he shifted his body weight from one foot to the other as he stood upright. The water was rushing over his calves now and it was becoming hard to stand up straight.

This part of the basement had no sign of windows but only other doors that led to other hallways of the hospital. There were panels in the walls around him and he assumed that he was in the morgue where the bodies were stored. Caleb ran to the opposite end where another locked door was. His key wasn't working on that door and he feared that he had reached a dead end to his search.

Turning to the right, he ran towards a storeroom. Several rolling cots were in the way and he pushed them over knocking them into a metal examination table nearby. Grabbing the key once again, he began to jiggle it into the keyhole. After two attempts the key broke off. Caleb beat his fists against the door and screamed, "Nooooo!"

The water in the on this floor was rising. Faintly, he heard a voice inside.

"Caleb! Caleb! Is that you?"

It was Nancy's voice. He could hear her crying but it was as if she were miles away from him, locked away in the storage room in which he was attempting to open.

"Kick…..hang on! I'm coming for you…hang on!"

Caleb kept screaming as he attempted to open the door but it was of no use. The water had now risen to his thighs, making it very difficult to stand upright.

"Caleb! I'm here! I'm here!"

Nancy yelled from inside the storeroom.

"I'm coming Nancy, please don't be afraid, I'm coming for you!" Caleb cried as he kept hitting the door with his fists hoping that somehow it would miraculously open. He began to bang his head against the door when he thought of an idea. If he could use one of the carts he had pushed over to the side with all his body weight, maybe it could work.

Caleb went over to where the carts were. The force of the water made it difficult for him to move as quickly as he wanted. If he were to gain enough force between he and the water he might just be able to knock the door down. He backed up feeling the pressure of the water against his calves. But the pressure turned into something much stronger. As if hitting a wall behind him he stopped as he backed up into something. It was the man who he had hit over the head. The man grabbed him by the arm, clasping a pair of hand cuffs on him and began dragging him towards the door that led to where Nancy was being held. Caleb tried to fight but the weight of the water sent him sinking down below. He was now being dragged by the man with his one good hand. The water was rushing over Caleb's shoulders and he was taking it in with huge gulps causing him to begin to choke.

"Now you'll drown right alongside her," screamed the man over the sound of the rushing water. We have the papers. We have everything we need. And we won't be needing you or that wife of yours any longer."

"But I gave you what you wanted! Why don't you just go and leave us alone!"

Caleb's cries were of no use. The man was holding an electric device; it looked like paddles only it wasn't hooked up to any machine. Caleb looked at the paddles in his hand, and then looked down at the water rushing underneath him. The man smiled as he immersed the paddles into the water below sending an electric current surging through the water and soon after surging through Caleb's body. He felt his body seize up in a fire that coursed through his veins. As he dropped into the water below he yelled, "NANCY!!!"

"Yes, dear, I'm here."

Caleb looked up to see his wife standing over him as he lay in a hospital bed. They were in room 404.

"Where am I?" he said groggily as if waking up from a Saturday morning sleep in.

"Caleb, you're in the hospital."

Nancy leaned into his face so that he could look into her eyes. She was rubbing the hair off his forehead in a calming fashion.

"Nancy, what happened? Are you alright? How did you get free?"

Nancy looked up at the doctor who was entering the room before she could reply. The doctor was the same one Caleb had seen before, caring for Nancy. Only this time she spoke to him and he seemed to be replying to her instead of ignoring her as he had done Caleb. The doctor had a throbbing red-purple bruise on his chin.

The doctor then turned his attention to Caleb.

"Mr. Rellie. I need you to answer some questions for me. I know you are an intelligent man but I am going to be asking you a string of questions and I need you to tell me the answer whether or not you think the answers to be obvious."

As he asked the questions, he poked and prodded at Caleb. He was wearing a large orange stethoscope that had a matching flashlight with which he was using to look into Caleb's eyes. The light was blindly bright and Caleb wondered if he would be able to see clearly after the doctor was finished. The doctor asked, "Are you up to answering a few questions, Mr. Rellie?"

"Alright, I can do that."

The doctor dropped Caleb's left eyelid and stood over him and began to ask a series of questions.

"What is your name?"

"Caleb Rellie."

"How old are you?"

"I am thirty-four years old."

"How many people do you see in this room, and can you give me their names?"

Caleb turned to look at Nancy and seeing that she was the only other person replied, "There are only two besides myself, you and my wife Nancy only I don't know your name."

"I'm sorry, my name is Dr. Ledbetter. I have been your doctor for the entire length of your stay here."

The doctor smiled at Caleb and began rubbing his bruised chin. "Let's just say, you've come out of this kicking and fighting. That's how we like to see it."

The doctor stopped rubbing his chin and continued speaking.

"You have been in a comatose state for several days. Yesterday your heart stopped beating unexpectedly and we had to shock your heart back into a regular rhythm. Your lungs were also filling with fluids, which we now seem to have under control. Treatment occurred within five minutes so there should be no risk of permanent brain damage."

At this statement, a gasp escaped Nancy's mouth. The doctor looked over at her reassuringly and said, "I realize this is a lot to take in, since he's just become fully conscious for the first time in days."

The doctor then said in the direction of a male nurse who entered soon after him The doctor went through several stats and then ended with, "All his vital signs seem to be normal. He has come out of the coma as well as can be expected but we'll still need to keep him for observation for a day or two."

The nurse typed for several minutes further and then hit the enter button and wheeled the cart away.

The doctor looked down at Caleb and smiled, "I think you have some catching up to do with your wife Mr. Rellie. If you have any questions after she's updated you on this week's events, just give me a call. I'm making my rounds now but I'll be returning in an hour to do a more detailed examination."

With that, the doctor walked out of the hospital room leaving Caleb and Nancy alone. Nancy, who had stood up when the doctor entered, came closer to the bed, taking Caleb's hand into hers.

"Oh my darling, I'm so sorry for what you've been through!" Nancy continued. She sat at the side of the bed but now she had retired from brushing the hair of his brow and was now holding his left hand into hers rubbing it gently.

"It is good to see you again, Kick. But may I ask what exactly is it that I've been through?"

Caleb then put her left hand onto the top of her right to help her focus on giving him every detail.

"We had an accident darling. You went into a severe coma. We don't understand what was happening to you the past few days. You would come in and out of it in the strangest ways. At times, when we had visitors you would respond. Yesterday evening your lungs filled with fluid, you went into cardiac arrest and they had to use the crash cart, they attached pads to your chest and shocked you. You whispered my name as you went out again. However, the doctor said you were breathing normally and we had only to wait for you to wake up. It was the most terrifying experiences of my life, Caleb. We really thought we were going to lose you."

"I know what you mean," Was all Caleb could think of to say as the events he thought had actually happened came back in his mind in vivid pictures.

Nancy stopped speaking for fear she would begin to cry. She wanted very badly to be strong for Caleb as he learned what had really happened to him. Nancy and Caleb sat that night talking about everything.

While they spoke the janitor came in. He was wearing a very noisy pair of shoes. He looked at Nancy and then Caleb and gave them both thumbs up. Then he took a coffee cup from the table next to the bed opposite the one Caleb was in and placed it in the garbage bag he was holding. Nancy got up and shook his hand and said, "Thank you for keeping up with all of my empty coffee cups. It seems I have single handedly caused the hospital to run out several times due to all my drinking.

"I'm just happy to be of help."

The janitor gave her his wrist instead of hand as he was wearing gloves and thought it might not be clean for her to touch him. He nodded his head again and smiled at both of them leaving the room with his bag which sounded like it was filled with hospital papers. This reminded Caleb he himself had some paper work he needed to tend too. Nancy turned to look at him once again.

"My report for work...The papers for the merger...I remember, they were due on Monday. I've been here in the hospital, so it couldn't have made it on time."

Caleb asked questions as he began to remember some of the things that had happened before the accident.

"Actually, honey, at one point you came out of your coma. You began ranting and raving and the doctors had to restrain you to the hospital bed. But I knew you were not hallucinating. You kept saying,

"I've got to get them the paper. Nancy, we are finished if I don't give them that paper."

The hospital had metal safe boxes in each room to keep important papers. We kept your briefcase in it just in case there was something we needed. When you kept saying this about the paperwork, I looked through the brief case and found the merger paper. I called your boss at work and he sent Larry, the accountant with the funny beard in to pick it up for you. Larry said he would make sure you got credit for all the work and that you shouldn't worry that you would have some sort of inner office conspiracy on your hands."

She laughed at the thought. Now Caleb knew that his conversation with Larry had not been completely based on fantasy.

"That was nice of him to leave work to do that for me."

"Well, he said he used it as an excuse to take a soda pop break so I don't think he minded at all. I was happy you had some visitors here for you. My family came but you were mostly out of consciousness the entire time. I think Larry might have helped remind you that you still had business on this earth to attend to."

She gave Caleb a wink and he winked back at her acknowledging that part of that must have been true.

Caleb looked at his wife with all the admiration he could muster. Thinking of how even throughout all her worries, she still managed to care for him in the little ways that he would have needed after he awoke made him love her all the more.

Nancy looked at him very concerned and said, 'Tell me Caleb, are you hungry?"

Caleb thought for a moment and realized that the entire time he had been 'out' and 'dreaming' or whatever it was that he had been doing, he never once ate and so should therefore have been very hungry.

But he didn't feel hungry at all.

"No, honey, I'm not hungry. It must be the I.V.'s they've had me on, I feel just fine."

Nancy giggled and said, "Well, you kept saying something about bacon and then you would carrying on talking. So I assumed that you were hungry. There were certain moments when you came in and out of your coma. When this happened, you would say the strangest things. At times when the doctor would come in, it was as if you were attempting to respond to him, but your words were never really clear. Every morning the nursing staff would bring me your tray of food to eat, which of course you could not. It was usually something simple like orange juice or slice grapefruit. I remember thinking how you would have hated it and preferred something like bacon instead. Maybe it was the I.V.'s although you didn't seem too happy about those either."

"What do you mean?" asked Caleb not understanding her statement.

"At one point as the doctor was administering an I.V. you had a spontaneous reaction and grabbed at him in a stabbing motion. He said that if you had actually had something in your hands he thinks you could have done some damage. In fact, in a reaction to your swinging he had to take your arm and restrain you to the bed. You can still see a little bit of a bruise from where you fought."

She pointed at his wrist. He looked down at it and recalled the incident with the pencil that apparently had been no incident at all but his sub-conscious struggling to return.

Caleb now understanding the length and breadth of what had actually happened took her hand that was placed very close to his and said, "I need to ask you something about the accident."

She looked at him with soft eyes that were filling with tears.

"What is it that you want to know Cal?"

"Was it my fault? I had been drinking wine that night and I hate the thought that anything I did could have put you in grave danger."

"Actually, you refused to drink that night my dear, don't you remember? I said that the wine was dry and you called over the waiter to return it. In fact, you grumbled that you couldn't believe you were leaving with an empty glass when you should be celebrating. But you didn't want to risk it since you were driving home. She smiled and patted Caleb's hand as she got up to walk over to the chair next to the window. Caleb felt an instant sigh of relief over come him.

"Well, it's enough to make one never take risks again." Caleb said looking at her as she sat down. Her eyes looked tired as if she had been up for days. She still had some scratches from the accident and he wondered if she was in any pain or if she was feeling sore.

The day nurse came in as if wandering.

"Hello there! It's so good to see you up and about Mr. Rellie!"

She looked at Caleb and smiled as she took some books off his nightstand table.

"Well, I haven't really gotten up yet, but I'm thinking that will be my next move since I've been told that I've overstayed my welcome." Caleb responded cheerfully.

"You can never over stay your welcome Mr. Rellie, but we find that when left with a choice, most people would rather be able to leave the hospital walls rather than stay here forever."

Nancy chimed in, "Thank you for allowing us to read those books."

The nurse went over to Nancy and took the one from her hand that she was extending. "Oh that's no problem at all. Did it help pass the time?"

"Oh yes, I chose one I thought my husband would like. I'm not sure what he got out of it but I really enjoyed it. Thanks again for all your help."

"No problem Mr. and Mrs. Rellie. If there's anything else you need just let us know."

With her arms full of books, she promptly left the room.

Nancy was sitting on the ledge of the window much as Caleb had remembered doing when he thought she had been lying in the hospital bed. Caleb asked, "What do you see outside the window, describe it to me."

"It's funny you should ask that. I sat here every afternoon and told you what I saw as I looked out the window. I figured maybe you could hear me and it would help you come back to me. Beyond the hospital gate there is a park and…"

"Children are playing." Caleb said with a smile.

"Yes! How did you know?" Nancy asked her eyes brimming with tears.

"I have a feeling there's a lot of things that went on these last few days that I might have been aware of."

"Were you aware that I was here?" Nancy asked Caleb searching his eyes for an answer in the affirmative.

"Let's just say, finding you again was what brought me back. And I'm happy to see the light of day again."

Nancy smiled and walked over to the bed, leaning over and kissing Caleb softly on the mouth.

Caleb dozed off in a peaceful slumber he hadn't felt for days.

The End

ABOUT THE AUTHOR

H. C. Heartland is a native of Michigan and a devoted wife, who, with her husband, travels throughout many developing countries doing volunteer work. This lifestyle and the myriad environments and cultures she has encountered provide the inspiration for most of her short works of fiction. She is always looking for the next opportunity to develop a fantastic tale to be shared for the enjoyment of others.

28715939R00167

Made in the USA
Lexington, KY
29 December 2013